He should ~~be thrown~~ **off course by how sweet and softly rounded Dana looked by candlelight. He was entitled to ask questions and have them answered**

"Dana," Conn said. Something in his tone must have caught her attention. She shot him a startled look.

"Conn, before you say anything, please understand that I'm sorry for biting your head off earlier. I wanted to make amends and this—" she gestured at the dinner on the table "—this was the only way I knew how to do it." Her gaze was beseeching.

He didn't know how to deal with this. With her. His relationship skills were rusty, to say the least. "Don't you understand that I care that something might happen to you? I've known you several days, and you don't seem to have anyone who checks on you regularly."

"But I do," Dana said softly. "I have you."

Dear Reader,

Happy New Year! Harlequin American Romance is starting the year off with an irresistible lineup of four great books, beginning with the latest installment in the MAITLAND MATERNITY: TRIPLETS, QUADS & QUINTS series. In *Quadruplets on the Doorstep* by Tina Leonard, a handsome bachelor proposes a marriage of convenience to a lovely nurse for the sake of four abandoned babies.

In Mindy Neff's *Preacher's In-Name-Only Wife*, another wonderful book in her BACHELORS OF SHOTGUN RIDGE series, a woman must marry to secure her inheritance, but she hadn't counted on being an instant wife *and* mother when her new husband unexpectedly receives custody of an orphaned baby. Next, a brooding loner captivates a pregnant single mom in *Pregnant and Incognito* by Pamela Browning. These opposites have nothing in common—except an intense attraction that neither is strong enough to deny. Finally, Krista Thoren makes her Harlequin American Romance debut with *High-Society Bachelor*, in which a successful businessman and a pretty party planner decide to outsmart their small town's matchmakers by pretending to date.

Enjoy them all—and don't forget to come back again next month when a special three-in-one volume, *The McCallum Quintuplets*, featuring *New York Times* bestselling author Kasey Michaels, Mindy Neff and Mary Anne Wilson is waiting for you.

Wishing you happy reading,

Melissa Jeglinski
Associate Senior Editor
Harlequin American Romance

PREGNANT AND INCOGNITO
Pamela Browning

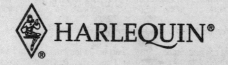

TORONTO • NEW YORK • LONDON
AMSTERDAM • PARIS • SYDNEY • HAMBURG
STOCKHOLM • ATHENS • TOKYO • MILAN • MADRID
PRAGUE • WARSAW • BUDAPEST • AUCKLAND

For newlyweds Neill and Melanie:
May you live happily ever after.

ISBN 0-373-16907-8

PREGNANT AND INCOGNITO

ABOUT THE AUTHOR

Pamela Browning once captured a wounded baby falcon in her backyard—which wasn't easy, since it was hopping around in terror and she was eight months pregnant. Three weeks later, her son was born, and he is half of the newlywed couple to whom this book is dedicated.

The falcon was rehabilitated and released to the wild: another happy ending!

Books by Pamela Browning

HARLEQUIN AMERICAN ROMANCE

Don't miss any of our special offers. Write to us at the following address for information on our newest releases.

Harlequin Reader Service
U.S.: 3010 Walden Ave., P.O. Box 1325, Buffalo, NY 14269
Canadian: P.O. Box 609, Fort Erie, Ont. L2A 5X3

TALK-SHOW HOSTESS A NO-SHOW!

Beautiful Day Quinlan fled the scene of her popular talk show, and the rumor mill has been working around the clock over the cause of her disappearance. Could it be a serious illness (note: she has been looking a little green around the gills lately)? Did extraterrestrials swoop down to use her for experiments? Or has she gone on safari? If you have any information on the whereabouts of Day Quinlan, contact us immediately!

Prologue

The studio lamps were bright, too bright. Worse, the tears in Day's eyes fractured the light into piercing shards, sharp enough to stab her through the heart.

Day feared that she was losing it. And she knew she mustn't lose it. Not here, not now. She could cry later.

The theme music came up, and Camille peered myopically into her face. "You all right, Miss Quinlan?" her assistant asked on a note of anxiety.

"I'm fine," Day said. Her voice quavered, then steadied. She wondered if Camille noticed.

No time to care. She had to get on with this. *Day Time* was live today, which was why she planned to make her announcement on the air. If this had been a taped show, as it sometimes was, the show wouldn't air for two weeks, and her fans would have read her remarks first in the tabloid newspapers. Day thought she owed them better than that.

A fanfare, highlighted by a drumroll, and then the sonorous voice of Patrick Rourke, the show's announcer. "And now, here's the star of *Day Time,* Da-a-y Quinlan!"

It was the same introduction Day heard at the beginning of five shows a week, forty weeks a year, and it prepared her for action. Camille shoved a hand mike at her, and she clutched at it as if it were a lifeline. She tensed briefly, blinked the tears from her eyes, and curved her lips into her trademark Day Quinlan smile, the same smile that had been dazzling talk show audiences for eight years.

And then she was bounding across the floor, high-fiving her stage manager on the way up the stairs, acknowledging the audience's applause with a graceful incline of her head as she always did.

But this time she didn't proceed to the dais with its two comfortable chairs, which were awaiting her and her scheduled guest. Instead she lowered herself to the edge of the stage, something she did occasionally to increase rapport and a feeling of intimacy with the audience.

This sitting-on-the-stage bit wasn't in the script. Off to one side, her stage manager narrowed his eyes, then appeared nonplussed. Day ignored him. She shook a gleam of pale-blond hair back from her face, drew a deep breath and plunged ahead.

"Today," she said, but she felt her throat catch. She stopped, swallowed hard, tried to smile and began again. "Today I have something important to tell all of you. It will come as a surprise, I know, but I hope you will all wish me well. Certainly, I wish the best for all of you." She paused, gauged the reaction, saw a mixture of puzzlement and confusion on audience faces. She drew another deep breath. "What I have to tell you is, it's time for me to decide whether or not to renew my contract with the General Broadcasting Network. I've made up my mind in the past few days. I'm quitting my show."

There. She'd said it. After a horrendous climb up the tortuous ratings heap, after surmounting all sorts of obstacles and taking on Oprah and Sally Jessy and Leeza, after all of it, she was through.

A stout woman in the front row gasped and clapped her hand over her mouth. A shocked silence gave way to a buzzing in the audience, or was it in Day's ears?

Day felt foggy, and dots swam before her eyes. She thought she might faint. But all she did was reach for the glass of water that was always placed within arm's reach outside camera range. When her trembling hand lowered the glass, she saw her stage manager climbing over a welter of cables and frantically waving his clipboard. Camille was staring stunned and openmouthed from the sidelines.

Day regarded all of this as if from a great distance. Miraculously, inside her, she thought she felt the baby move for the first time. Or was it only wishful thinking? At least it reminded her why she'd made her little speech.

She slid her hand inside her jacket and rounded it protectively over her abdomen.

I won't let anyone hurt you, she told the baby. *Not now, not ever.*

And then she lurched to her feet and, without speaking to anyone, whisked herself offstage and directly into a waiting limo that sped her to the airport.

As she had planned, she dropped out of sight. She became Dana Cantrell, which was her real given name. The tabloids could speculate about why she had not renewed her contract, her so-called friends could give interviews, Philip could rant. But Day Quinlan would be impossible to locate because she had ceased to exist.

None of the people who thought they knew Day Quinlan would have been familiar with the name Cougar Creek, Arizona. Nor, she was sure, would the tabloids know or care about that small speck on the map. Philip, certainly, wouldn't have a clue. The cabin at Cougar Creek was the one place that Day, like her father before her, held sacrosanct. It was there that she would go to lick her wounds in private.

At Cougar Creek, she would settle in, look after herself and take care of the new little life growing inside her. She would wrap herself in a protective veil of self-pity.

And then she would decide what to do with herself, now that she wasn't anybody anymore.

Chapter One

Cougar Creek, Arizona,
October, Three Months Later

Dana came upon the kestrel as she rounded a red sand-stone boulder near Libya Mesa, stirring up a cloud of dust that almost obscured it. The kestrel, which she recognized instantly because she had once written a school paper about birds of prey, was in trouble, no doubt about that. It didn't take flight when it saw her clambering awkwardly over the rocks but merely hunkered down into the landscape. When she drew closer, it blinked once.

She couldn't tell if it had a broken wing or was perhaps more seriously injured. She'd been in a hurry to get home because the sky was covered over with billowy gray clouds that heralded, she was sure, a rainstorm. But she stopped anyway and studied the situation.

The bird didn't move. It looked as if it were in shock. It was a pretty little thing, the top of its head slate blue with a reddish spot on the crown. Black patches were on the sides of its head and the nape, while its back was a rusty brown. It had a white-tipped reddish tail and a bit of ashy blue on its wings.

There was something wrong, she knew it. The bird should have been fleeing from her, but instead it stared at her, a terrified gleam in its eye. And was it keeling over to the left, or was that her imagination?

She acted out of instinct, though perhaps not wisely. She bent and tried to pick it up, receiving a sharp nip on the tender, fleshy part of her hand between thumb and forefinger for her trouble.

"Ouch!" she exclaimed as she leaped backward, which was no easy feat now that she was six months pregnant. The kestrel glowered at her, and she glowered back. She'd only been trying to help.

"Stay away from that hawk!"

The harsh command startled her, and she swiveled around. Out from behind a thicket strode a tall, broad-shouldered man wearing a leather jerkin and boots that laced halfway up his calves. At the exact moment that he appeared, the clouds parted and admitted a beam of light that caught the blue highlights in his unruly black hair, a lock of which fell engagingly across his forehead. The forehead was wrinkled into a fierce scowl.

"I was only trying to help it, and it pecked me." She pulled a tissue from her pocket and wrapped it around her hand. The pressure stanched the blood but didn't do anything to stop the pain.

"Demelza is a trained bird of prey. What do you expect her to do when you're threatening her?" He bent to look at the bird, crooning to it in a surprisingly soft voice. Belatedly Dana saw the leather thongs attached to the bird's legs.

"I had no idea it was a trained bird. How was I to know?" Dana returned hotly.

The man spared her an exasperated eye roll and pulled something from his pocket. It was a small leather hood embossed with a design of some sort, and he slid it gently over the kestrel's head before picking up the bird. His hands were large—big powerful hands, sinewy and with long fingers. While Dana watched, the kestrel sidled along his arm to the heavy glove he wore. It perched there on his wrist, calm and quiet, while he slid the leather strap on his glove through a metal ring joining the thongs on the bird's legs. He didn't smooth the bird's feathers or touch it again.

"Is it hurt?"

"She seems all right. Probably tangled with a feisty sparrow instead of chasing grasshoppers like she's supposed to do."

"You shouldn't—"

"I don't need advice. I'm a master falconer, experienced at this sort of thing. I take care of my hawks. My name's Connor McTavish. And who are you?" She'd heard of the falconer; a loner, they said in town.

For the first time he looked directly at her. His eyes were umber, varnished with gold, and they pierced into her, through her. For a moment she had the impression that the two of them might have been the only two people on earth.

She broke the spell by stepping away slightly. As always, she was wary about introducing herself. She never forgot that someone, despite the changes in her shape and hair color, might recognize her.

"I'm Dana Cantrell," she said. "I live on the other side of the mesa." She held her breath, but he showed no flash of recognition.

"You must be talking about Homer Cantrell's cabin."

"He was my father."

"You've wandered a little far from home, haven't you?"

She didn't like his challenging manner. "I like to take walks," she retorted.

His gaze traveled down, paused at the bloom of her belly under her shirt front, continued downward. She felt an urge to turn and flee, which was ridiculous. She had every right to be here.

"Isn't rambling around the countryside a little dangerous in your condition?" he asked bluntly.

"Walking is a completely natural form of exercise. My doctor recommends it."

"I didn't mean the walking itself. I meant the things you're likely to encounter out here. Snakes, critters—" he cast an eye overhead to the clouds, which were now building again "—and thunderstorms. Come on, you'd better go home with me."

"I have plenty of time to get back to the cabin." She turned away, but he grabbed her arm with his free hand. The kestrel still sat quietly on his left wrist.

"Wait just a minute," he said. He threw his head back and pointed his chin toward the west. "Look over that way."

She did. Lightning zigged across the sky, followed by a muffled snarl of thunder. The storm was thrashing its way closer by the minute.

"If you're living in that tumbledown old place by the stream, you won't make it back before the storm hits. Could be some hail in this one, too. Look at the height of those clouds."

It was alarming to see them rolling in this direction. She stood indecisively, the freshening wind whipping at the hem of her shirt, not wanting to go with this man but not sure she had much of a choice. If she'd had only herself to consider, she wouldn't have minded sheltering under an overhang of rock somewhere along the path, but she couldn't take chances with the baby.

"My hawk wagon's right around the bend. I'll take you back to my place, doctor that hand of yours. I feel responsible, I admit."

Dana wrapped the tissue more tightly around her hand. She wondered if this man had any idea who she was. Probably not; she had let her hair revert to its natural reddish gold, and she'd had it cut into a short sleek bob. She'd also gained more weight than she liked to think about.

She sighed, wavering.

He pursed his lips—nice lips, full and expressive. "If it will set your mind at ease, I was an Eagle Scout and a member of my church choir when I was growing up."

What else could she do? "Okay," she said, still not sure she should trust him.

Nevertheless, she fell in beside him. For a moment she thought he might take her arm to help her over the rough spots in the path, so she remained a fair distance from him as they walked. A glance at the hooded kestrel—Demelza—reassured her that the bird wasn't in pain, or at least it wasn't obvious if she was. She, Dana, was in more pain, probably. Surreptitiously she refolded the tissue, clamped it tightly with her thumb and stuck her hand deep down into her pocket.

"Don't worry, I'll take care of that when we get to my place." He didn't miss much, this man.

Ahead of them was parked a dusty white pickup truck with a camper shell over the truck bed. Connor moved ahead of her and wrenched the back open. Two pipes covered with artificial plastic turf ran lengthwise in the vehicle's interior, and he set Demelza on one of them. The kestrel settled down on the perch with a brief flurry of feathers.

"And now you," he said to Dana, moving around to the cab's passenger side, opening it and all but boosting her in. He went around and got in the driver's side, boots striking on solid rock, while she self-consciously adjusted the seat belt to accommodate her girth. After an anxious look back at Demelza through the window of the cab, Dana spared a glance out of the corners of her eyes as her companion threw the vehicle into gear and backed and maneuvered on the narrow road until they were bumping their way around the mesa.

The falconer was movie-star handsome, but then, she was accustomed to thinking in show-business terms. She tried to appraise him with a little more restraint, but the thing was, there wasn't anything ordinary about the way he looked. There was something dangerous about him and something held in reserve, as if he didn't like to reveal too much of himself. He was spectacularly built, intensely masculine and gave the impression of powerful strength. Yet there was a grace about him, a way of movement so lithe and fluid that she could well imagine how he would move in bed.

In bed! Shaken, she forced herself to look out the window at the clouds scudding in the distance. Roiling and dark they were, tumultuous to their depths, just like her reeling emotions. What was wrong with her? What was it about this man that engendered a wildness in her, a pounding of her heart, a rush of the wind in her ears? She'd better stop it right this minute. She couldn't afford to let her imagination run away with her.

He steered the truck up a winding, bumpy road into the hills, wending his way around small boulders and branches that had been blown out of the underbrush by the wind. After turning right at a fork in the road, he pulled up in front of a small house built of weathered stone and turned off the engine.

He jerked his head toward the front door. "Here we are. You might as well go inside while I take care of Demelza."

"But where—"

"I'll put her in the mews behind the house. That's where I keep my hawks."

"That's terrible. Keeping them cooped up like that, I mean."

"You don't know what you're talking about. Go in and wash off that wound with water from the sink. I'll be there in a few minutes."

She slid out of the car as he went around back and

removed the bird. She watched for a moment, wondering why he thought it was okay for a wild bird to be kept captive.

"Go on in," he said again, sounding as if he were losing patience, so Dana went to the door of the house and pushed at it until it opened.

The hinge was rusty and gave out a long groan. Inside, she found herself in one big room overhung by a loft. At first she thought the place was sparsely furnished, but as her eyes adjusted to the dim light within, she realized that the house wasn't lacking in comforts at all. The impression of sparseness came from the fact that everything was very simple—wood furniture with clean lines, and not a lot of it; a massive stone fireplace with a mantel that appeared hand hewn; a patterned Navajo rug covering only part of the polished wood floor; windows hung with panels of natural linen slung over whitewashed poles; a fur robe draped over the couch. And books, lots of them, ranged on low shelves around the room.

A small low-ceilinged kitchen was tucked under the loft, and Dana went and turned on the water. There was a window above the sink, and through it she could see large wooden enclosures connected by a screened passageway. That's where Conn kept the birds, then. He must be inside one of the cages because she couldn't see him.

She ran water over her hand, wincing at the pain. A jagged bolt of lightning rent the sky outside, followed by a crash of thunder that rattled the windows in their panes, and, frightened, she jumped back from the faucet. Without any warning, Connor McTavish blasted in through the back door. A swift wind blew in with him, but he slammed the door on it. Then he took two long strides until he was standing in front of her.

"Let's see," he said. It was a command, not a suggestion. Dana held out her hand.

His fingers probed carefully. "You'll live," he said. "I never—"

He brushed away her words as if they were so many pesky gnats. "I've been bitten before. I know it hurts like hell." He reached into a cabinet behind her, his shoulder brushing hers. She scrunched herself against the counter.

"This will sting," he said. He sprayed something cold and antiseptic on her cut, and unbidden tears welled in her eyes. "Sorry," he said, more gently now.

She blinked the tears away, but one slid down her cheek. She swiped at it with her other hand.

He reached for a paper towel. "Use this," he said. Dana dabbed at her cheek, feeling stupid. But the truth was that ever since she'd been pregnant, her emotions had gone haywire. It didn't help that this man smelled of pine, clean and woodsy and muskily male. It also didn't help that he radiated sex: it was in his every gesture, it permeated the air when he was in the room.

She was pregnant. She wasn't supposed to notice such things.

But she did.

While she was thinking this over, he broke open a large Band-Aid and yanked off the protective strips. Then he applied it to her hand, smoothing it carefully.

Another rumble of thunder followed a slash of lightning from the direction of the creek, and as the clouds settled in, the light from the windows faded perceptibly.

"Guess I'd better turn on some lights in here," he said. He went into the living area and switched on a lamp, which lent a mellow glow to the stone walls and smooth pine floor.

He gestured at the couch. "Won't you sit down?"

Overly conscious of her bulk, she moved out of the kitchen area and went to a window. "Mr. McTavish, maybe you could take me home before it rains."

"Call me Conn. And it's raining already."

He was right; large round drops were spattering against the ground outside, scattering wet pockmarks in the dust.

"I—um, I feel as if I'm in the way."

"Don't. We're neighbors. Ever since I heard around town that someone had moved in, I've been meaning to come over and see who's living in the old Cantrell place. I didn't expect it would be a woman, and a pregnant one at that."

She ignored most of this. She loved being pregnant, but at the moment she wished he'd stop reminding her of the fact.

"Did you know my father?" she asked, in order to make conversation about something else. Dana sat on the edge of the couch, watching Conn as he knelt by the fireplace and held a match to the dry grass that served as tinder.

"No, I wasn't in residence when he came here on fishing vacations. But Cougar Creek is a small town. I gather that Homer Cantrell was generally well liked."

"He was. The cabin has been vacant since he died."

The tinder caught, and the fire spread to the kindling. A glow illuminated Connor McTavish's face, softening the cragginess of his features. "How long has that been?"

"Ten years now."

"No one mentioned that old Homer had a daughter."

"I never came here with him. This was Dad's retreat. No women allowed." She smiled at the memory. In fact, though she and her father had been close, she had seldom set eyes on the property, and when she'd arrived a couple of months ago she'd been aghast at the condition of the place. It had taken almost all this time to make the place livable.

The burning logs filled the room with the pungent odor of woodsmoke. The crackle of the flames seemed to make it unnecessary to talk, which was fine with

Dana. She didn't know what to say to this man who seemed so self-assured, and she was sure she was being a nuisance.

He stood in front of the fireplace, facing away from her. After a few minutes, he turned and went to a stereo system in one corner, where he inserted a CD of Native American flute music. Then he sat down in a huge easy chair. He pulled a wooden bowl of nuts across the small table beside it and cracked one open. He offered it to her, but she shook her head.

Again lightning flashed across the sky outside, thunder following almost immediately. The flute music took on an eerie sound, like a wolf howl heard from a long distance away. Dana wondered why he had chosen such music; it seemed to bespeak a lonely heart.

"That lightning was close," he said.

Dana unclenched her fists and tried to relax. She wasn't afraid of lightning, but she didn't like it much, either.

"Tell you what—I'll get you a glass of iced tea. Or a beer, if you'd like."

"Tea will be fine."

"Oh—that's right. I suppose you're not drinking alcoholic beverages." He gazed pointedly at her rounded stomach.

Dana extended her flattened hands protectively over the baby. "Not for the duration," she said.

He spared her a sharp nod, then went into the kitchen and came back with a glass of cold tea. A second trip to the refrigerator produced a tall bottle of dark beer, which he tilted upward to drink. Dana watched the muscles of his throat working as he swallowed and discovered that her hands were damp. She wiped them surreptitiously on her jeans and thought about what a fool she was; she had not reacted this way to any male member of the species in years, if ever. She ought to be immune to men by this time and in her condition.

"So," he said. "You're here for a couple of weeks?"

"More than that," she said reluctantly. She was so accustomed to secrecy that it made her uncomfortable to reveal anything about herself, even though she was sure that this man had no idea who she was.

"And living alone?"

She bit her lip. "Yes."

He cocked a dark eyebrow. "I suppose you know that the nearest hospital is eighty miles away as the eagle flies."

"I'm aware of that, yes." Her eyes met his with resolve, letting him know, she hoped, that she wasn't stupid. She had everything planned: she'd stay at her father's fishing cabin until a week or so before the baby was due, then drive to Flagstaff, the nearest large city, where she would stay in a small apartment hotel and give birth to the baby in a hospital there. Then—but there was time to decide about the future when the future was here. And that wasn't now.

"You've made provisions for emergency care if the need arises?"

"Well," she said, not sure how to answer that. Her pregnancy had proceeded normally so far. She had no indication that it was going to be otherwise.

"You need to think about it," he said sharply and, she thought, with disapproval.

She stood abruptly, then walked to a window. Outside the cottonwood trees were thrashing in the wind, and it was darker than ever.

"I've thought about it," she said. She didn't want to have this conversation. She hated it when anyone implied she was incompetent. She didn't need anyone, least of all Connor McTavish, telling her what to do. She knew what was best for her and the baby. They would be fine, just fine.

Conn stood, too, and came up close behind her. Too

close. His male scent disturbed her, made her feel edgy. She whirled and stalked to the middle of the room.

He stood regarding her, and she wrapped her arms around herself as she felt a sudden chill despite the warmth from the fire.

"Look, I don't want to be too inquisitive, but women who are about to bear children usually don't take up solitary residence in the wilderness."

"I'm here to have a vacation. And to think about some things. This seemed like a good place to do it, that's all." She knew she sounded defensive, but this man was altogether too incisive and annoying. It was disorienting to be on the receiving end of an interview; in her profession she was usually the one asking questions.

"Hmm," he said. He took another sip of beer. "I take it there's no man in the picture?"

She drew her dignity around her, although it was quickly fraying. "If you will forgive me for not answering that question, I'll forgive you for asking," she said.

Conn ran an impatient hand through his hair. "I see."

"I doubt it. Guys usually don't."

He set his beer down on the table and walked to where she stood. He folded his arms across his chest and glared at her. "I don't know who put that chip on your shoulder, but I'll tell you this—I am not trying to knock it off."

She lifted her chin and stared up at him defiantly. "I didn't ask you for your help or advice."

"No-o-o, you didn't. You merely hiked out of nowhere and were foolhardy enough to pick up an injured bird of prey. Which is why I'm not likely to trust your judgment in any other matter."

If there were anywhere she could possibly have gone, Dana would have marched out of the cabin and into the storm. If she could have been swallowed up by the folds of the blue-shaded mountains in the distance, she would have. But none of that would have done anything to convince this man of her good judgment. So she only glared at him.

He stared back. And then, incredibly, he started to laugh. He laughed long and loud, huge peals of mirth that rang against the beamed ceiling. She felt her ears growing hot with embarrassment—or was it some other emotion? She wasn't sure.

"What exactly is so funny?" she said through gritted teeth.

"I think I've ruffled your feathers. You look exactly like an irascible prairie falcon that I used to have. When she got mad at me, she'd fluff herself all up and try to stare me down. Like you're doing."

"I didn't come here to get insulted," she said stiffly.

"And that's not why I brought you here," he said, sobering.

Something happened in that moment—perhaps it was a retreat, but then again, maybe it was a stand-off. Dana sat down on the couch again, catching her breath sharply as she felt the baby settle against her spine.

He noticed, of course. "Is anything wrong? Are you okay?"

She shook her head. "I felt the baby, that's all."

"Oh." He seemed perplexed and at a loss for words. She wondered if most men felt that way when confronted with a pregnant woman who talked about the way it felt to be in that condition.

Not that she ever had much of a chance to discuss her pregnancy with anyone. She'd talked earnestly with her doctor about what she was going through, and she'd chatted informally with his nurse, but she didn't have any friends who even knew about her pregnancy. Regret stabbed through her, and for a moment she missed the people she'd left behind—gossipy Raymond and Tricia and Noelle, her best friend, especially.

"I suppose this isn't any of my business, but do you feel the baby move often?"

She tilted her head to one side. The unexpectedness of the question had set her off guard, but she wanted to answer it. She wanted to talk about this to someone, to anyone. Even to Connor McTavish.

"The baby has regular waking and sleeping cycles," she said. "I think it's just like a regular baby. I mean, one that's already born."

Connor looked startled. "I didn't know they did that. I've never known a pregnant woman, at least not one that I talked to about it."

Dana's spine was hurting, and without thinking, she stuffed one of the couch pillows behind her back.

"Why'd you do that?" Connor asked sharply.

She looked at him. The answer seemed so obvious. "My back hurts," she said.

"It's not because of the kestrel, is it? Bending over or something, to pick her up? Because if it is—"

"No, no, nothing like that," she hastened to reassure him, and then, because she couldn't help it, she smiled.

He subsided, then tossed her another one of those sharp looks. "You'd tell the truth, wouldn't you?"

Had he already marked her as someone with a secret? The thought agitated her. "Of course I'd tell the truth," she said stoutly and, she hoped, convincingly.

Again, a sharp look. She wasn't sure he believed her, but he gave her one of those curt little nods. At that point she chided herself for being paranoid. There was absolutely no reason to believe that anyone she met in the Arizona boondocks could figure out who she was, and as far as the press was concerned, they'd never find her. Not here. Not for a while, anyway, and if things worked out as she had planned, she would not be discovered before the baby was born.

It was time for a change in subject.

"You said you're a master falconer. What does that mean?"

"I took a course. I have a license. That's it in a nutshell."

"Falconers need a license?"

"The government says so if you want to own a hawk."

She hadn't known that. "And this course—what kind of course?"

"In falconry. It's the only one in the United States. My friend who used to own this house was the teacher."

"Where is he now?"

"Steve's in a hospital in San Diego where his daughter lives. He won't be coming back here." For a moment, he looked sad.

"I'm sorry," Dana said.

"So am I."

Dana wanted to know more about the birds, but she didn't think Conn would welcome any more questions. It struck her that maybe he was a lot like her—hiding.

"I still don't like the looks of this storm," he said, going to the window and pulling aside the drapery. "I think you'd better stay a while longer."

"I can't. I mean, I don't want to impose."

"Of course you can." He went to the refrigerator and opened it. "I have the remains of a meat loaf, and I can throw together a salad."

"I don't—"

"Well, I do. I'm not taking you home in this weather. If you want to be useful, you could get plates out of the cupboard over there and silverware out of the drawer."

Figuring that it would be useless to object, she did as she was told, seething all the while. Meanwhile, Conn heated the meat loaf and gravy in the microwave and dug in the back of the refrigerator until he found a bowl of mashed potatoes. "These will heat up just fine," he said.

"Are you always so bossy?" she blurted.

He spared her a mild look. "When I know best," he said.

"Which is all the time?"

He grinned, and those marvelous eyes, so golden in their depths, twinkled. "Give me a break. Do I really come across as a know-it-all?" He dug croutons out of the back of the refrigerator and set them on the counter.

"Yes," Dana said. "It's not becoming." She pulled the head of lettuce toward her and began to cut it into the salad bowl.

"I'm so glad you told me. I would hate to turn people off without knowing it. Not that I see many people, however. You're the only close neighbor I have."

"And why are *you* living way out here?" She didn't mind going on the offensive with this man; it would keep him from doing the same to her.

"Maybe," he said with a maddening grin, "it's for the same reason that you're living where you are."

She let the knife drop into the sink. "So you can think things over?"

"Sure. Is that so strange?"

"Well, no," she said reluctantly.

"All right, then. Maybe," he said, leaning even closer so that he was looking directly into her eyes, "we can accept that we each have our reasons for living out here. And even accept help when we need it."

"If you're saying that I owe you for giving me refuge from the storm, I hasten to remind you that I was willing to walk home."

"But I wasn't willing to have you caught in a flash flood in the arroyo or falling down and hurting yourself. With a storm like this one in the offing, no less."

"Is there salad dressing? Or should I make some?"

"Oh, make some. By all means," he said. He set the meat loaf and the mashed potatoes on the table.

She didn't have to measure; she never did. She

dumped approximately one-third portion each of olive oil, cider vinegar and water into a custard cup and drizzled it over the salad. Then she seasoned the whole liberally with salt, garlic salt, and pepper before tossing it around in the bowl. Noelle had shown her how to do this years ago, and it made a light dressing, tart but flavorful.

There were only two chairs at the table, so presumably Conn McTavish didn't have more than one visitor at a time. He held one chair for her, adroitly sliding it beneath her as she lowered herself to its seat. Conn had manners, then. Most guys didn't know how to seat a woman properly, and she wasn't accustomed to having the chair hit the back of her knees at precisely the right time.

"So," he said from across the table. "Help yourself." He dealt himself a large portion of meat loaf and shoved the platter toward her.

She filled her plate, and he said, "The salad is good. You'll have to teach me how to make the dressing."

"I'll tell you now," she said, and did. It gave them something to talk about as the trees outside swept back and forth in a fearsome dance; wind and faraway thunder kept the windows and doors of the cabin rattling. At least it was warm in here, with the fire hissing and spitting in the fireplace, and at least Conn seemed to have made up his mind to be pleasant company.

Or had he? This man had a way of retreating every so often, withdrawing into himself in a way that almost challenged her to say something. Perhaps she was being touchy about this, and maybe she was expecting too much from a man who, judging from the way he lived, was not accustomed to being with people. And yet she didn't think he had always been that way. His attention to the social graces told her that he had been no hermit.

She glanced around the cabin. There was no telephone here, but then, she didn't have one, either. There was no computer, no fax machine, no copier. Did he work at all? Or did he make his living with his birds somehow? It seemed impossible that falconry, as he had described it, could produce enough income to live on, but there was probably a lot she didn't know.

"Something wrong?" he asked.

"I—um, well, no. I was only wondering what it is that you do for a living."

"Ah. The inquisitive mind wants to know."

This was much too close to the slogan of a well-known tabloid newspaper, and she bit her lip. She hated the tabloids, and her well-being and her baby's depended on not attracting their attention. But he couldn't know that.

"Yes, I suppose it does," she said, hardly skipping a beat.

"As it happens, falconry is my hobby. So, if you were wondering, the birds do not support me."

"I see."

She was trying to think of some other conversational avenue when the lights flickered and died. It was a relief not to have to school her expression to look blank, and she closed her eyes, thanking the powers that be for this providential loss of electricity. Sometimes things really did go her way, she reminded herself. Everything couldn't be awful all the time. It only seemed that way now and then.

"I've got candles," Conn said, and he dug around in a drawer before finding a box of matches. He struck one, and a wick flared. He brought the candle to the table and set it between them.

"How romantic," Dana said, and then cursed herself for a fool. Why hadn't she kept her mouth shut? There was nothing romantic about this, nothing at all. She had been given shelter by a man who probably wished he hadn't come across her out there on the trail, and he couldn't possibly have any romantic feelings at all about a woman whose stomach was way out to here and who seemed to annoy him, anyway.

But he only smiled at her, and somehow she could have melted. She couldn't remember the last time she'd sat across a table from a virile, handsome man and had his full attention. Oh, sure, she'd gone out with Philip often enough, but he was a busy network executive who considered her a trophy, and usually when they did go out it was with groups of people that he wanted to impress. Most times they'd been followed by reporters and photographers who had hollered at her to "turn this way, please," and at Philip to put his arm around her for a picture.

She had hated going out in public with Philip, and she had hated being treated as nothing more than a piece of arm jewelry. But she hadn't realized it then. It was all part of the life that she had left behind.

The baby did a flip-flop, and she took heart from the fact that it was such an active baby. It was the only thing from her former life that she wanted to keep, and keep it she would. She never wanted to be as alone as she'd felt in the early days of her pregnancy when she'd had to decide what to do, knowing that Philip and his overbearing mother would want her baby to bear his name and would likely fight for custody.

"I asked you if you'd like some dessert," Conn said, and Dana realized that she'd tuned him out completely. Embarrassed, she shook her head.

He didn't talk and neither did she as they cleared the table. Afterward, Dana excused herself and went into the bathroom, which was in a lean-to off the kitchen. She stared at herself in the cloudy mirror over the sink. She looked tired, she thought, and her face seemed puffy. Maybe it was only because the mirror distorted her image. Whatever it was, she had eaten off most of her lipstick, and she hadn't brought any with her. Feeling dispirited, she wiped off the rest of the lipstick and went back out into the main room, where Conn was reading by the light of the candle.

The storm hadn't abated in the least. The little house was snugly built, though, and although the wind scoured the outer face of it, its fury could not penetrate the stalwart stone. Sighing, Dana took up her seat on the couch and repositioned the pillows behind her. This drew a look from Conn, but he didn't comment. She leaned her head against the back of the couch and closed her eyes.

When she opened them, Conn was puffing air at the fire with an old leather bellows, sending up a swirl of sparks. She stirred and straightened, and he turned around.

"I was wondering if you would wake up," he said.

"Was I asleep?" she asked. Her mouth felt dry and cottony, and her legs were stiff.

"Yes," he said. "I didn't want to wake you, because I figured you needed your sleep."

"I have to get home. What's the storm doing?"

"Hail and the whole works. You won't be going anywhere."

Alarmed, she set her feet wide apart and struggled up. She knew she looked ridiculous as she did it, but this was what pregnancy did to a person. For a moment she was embarrassed, but if Conn noticed her awkwardness, he gave no sign.

She went to the window and pulled aside the drapery. Hailstones were shredding the leaves of the trees and bouncing off the ground. She turned around and gazed at Conn bleakly.

"You're staying here tonight. I'll give you my bed, and I'll take the couch." He reached around her to pull the drapery closed again.

"Bed?" There was no bed here. Unless the couch pulled out and made into one.

"Oh," Conn said, looking abashed. "It's up in the

loft. On second thought, I guess I'd better take the bed. You can sleep on the couch."

"I can't—"

"Why can't you?" he demanded.

At a loss for words, she shrugged. She didn't have a toothbrush. She didn't have her makeup. She didn't have a way to get out of here, and that was the worst knowledge of all.

Conn went to a closet and dragged out a puffy comforter and a pillow in an embroidered case. He tossed them on the couch and rubbed the back of his neck.

"You know where the bathroom is if you want to wash up," he said. "Other than that, all I can say is, sweet dreams."

"Thank you," she murmured. "I'm grateful for your hospitality."

"No need for that. I'll see you in the morning." He spared her a nod and pulled a ladder down from the loft. Then he climbed it rapidly. She heard him up there, presumably taking off clothes that he then tossed on the floor in a series of muffled thumps. Soon the sounds ceased, and she heard the rustle of bedclothes.

She wondered if he slept in a single bed, or if it was a double. Maybe it was even king-size, though she wasn't sure the loft was big enough for that. She wondered if the bed was plump with a quilt and pillows or stark and austere, the sheets as rough as a monk's.

She wished she had thought to ask him if he had an extra toothbrush. She could still taste the garlic from the salad.

She spread the comforter out on the couch before lying down. The pillow was soft goosedown, and she shoved the couch pillows around her stomach and between her legs so she would be comfortable lying on her side. After she had blown out the candle, she listened for sounds from the loft as her eyes adjusted to the darkness.

For a while she remained wide awake. The baby aimed a few rabbit punches at her kidneys, shifted slightly, then was still.

She had almost dozed off when she heard the soft sound of Conn's deep breathing above her. It was oddly reassuring to know that he was there, and she snuggled deeper into her warm nest before falling asleep to the soothing rhythm of rain on the roof.

Chapter Two

Conn dreamed that night, a long convoluted nightmare about climbing to a hidden city of caves honeycombing the mountainside. He was looking for a nest of hawks that he somehow knew was there, but he kept sliding backward. And he was terrified of falling, of losing his step on the loose scree of the path up the mountain. He scrabbled for purchase in the crevices until his fingers bled and his shoulders ached, but he never found the nest. Which was a shame, because if he'd found it, he could have removed one or two of the nestlings and raised them to be fine hunting birds.

The dream ended abruptly when he lost his grip on a ledge and fell backward. He heard himself cry out, and then he woke up.

His heart pounded wildly in his chest. He'd had this dream before, many times. It always ended the same way—with a fall from which he could not save himself.

He felt safe and relieved when he realized that it had only been the same old nightmare. What would happen if he didn't wake up? he wondered. Would he keep falling until he met an ignominious end? Would he dream his own death?

Today was different. He had a guest who might have been awakened by his cry. He stretched and listened for sounds from below, and when he didn't hear any, he stood up and looked over the loft railing.

Outside the morning was a clean wash of blue and green with an overlay of golden sunshine. He didn't see much of Dana except a blanketed mound on the couch and a silky spill of short reddish-gold hair on the pillow. He wondered if she had slept well; he wondered why she really had chosen to move into that tumbledown little cabin over near the creek. He didn't believe her story, not for a minute. It sounded fishy. But he would respect her right to privacy.

That was a laugh, and the corners of his mouth curved upward in a rueful smile. He'd been fired over a privacy issue, which was why he wasn't working at present. He'd been here for five months now, trying to make sense of a life that had gone seriously awry at the age of thirty-five.

He pulled on clean clothes and made his way quietly down the ladder. The old boards of the cabin's floor creaked slightly under his weight as he tiptoed out the back door. Dana didn't wake up, though, or if she did, she didn't stir.

He traversed the short distance to the mews and checked his hawks. Demelza seemed none the worse for wear; still, he wouldn't work her today. The others, he would.

When he went back into the cabin, he was surprised to see Dana up and about. She was standing at the kitchen counter mixing orange juice concentrate with cold water.

She looked around with a shy smile. "I hope you don't mind," she said.

"Mind? Of course not." But he had to admit that it seemed strange to find a pregnant woman in her stocking feet making herself comfortable in his kitchen.

"The electricity came back on during the night," she observed. She nodded toward the windows in the living area. "And there's a rainbow."

The rainbow arched upward out of a swirling mist into a clear blue sky, one of the prettiest ones he had ever seen.

"Nice, isn't it? It even looks as if it ends over at my cabin."

He didn't reply to that; his stomach was rumbling. He realized that he couldn't eat without feeding her too.

"How about breakfast? Eggs? Bacon?" he asked.

"I could skip the bacon. Since I've been pregnant, I can't stand the smell of it cooking."

"Sausage then."

"That sounds good."

He bent over and removed a frying pan from the cabinet. "How do you like your eggs?"

"Any old way will do."

"Scrambled?"

"Fine."

He flicked his eyes toward the bathroom. "You can take a shower if you like."

"I don't want to be a nuisance."

"Don't be silly. You're not. I insisted on bringing you here."

"A quick shower would feel good," she said.

He showed her where the towels and soap were, and she disappeared into the bathroom and closed the door. He soon heard the shower running, and he thought, *What have I gotten myself into?*

He liked living here by himself. He stayed away from the townspeople because he had little in common with them. And now he'd opened his door to someone who might want to visit back and forth, who might want to be friendlier than he did. A woman. Women could be talkative. They had a need for socializing. He had an idea that it wouldn't be long before this woman would be walking over to borrow a cup of sugar or asking him to dinner or suggesting that they take intimate walks together.

He didn't want that. He wanted nothing more than to work with his birds and ignore the world until such time as he deemed it possible to return to normal life.

And that wasn't yet. Not by a long shot.

Dana emerged from the shower as he scraped the scrambled eggs onto two plates.

"Mmm. Looks and smells wonderful," she said.

So do you, he thought. It was an involuntary reaction to the way she looked, so pink and damp around the edges, and the way she smelled, which was clean and fresh.

Good thing he had only thought those words, not said them. Rather than let her know that he found her attractive, he merely grunted.

"You can sit over there," he said, more or less ungraciously. He didn't pull the chair out for her as he had last night. He didn't want her to get the idea that he liked her company.

She may have picked up on this because she ate quickly, and she didn't speak.

When he had finished eating what was on his plate, he cleared his throat. "I'll be flying my hawks today. I'll drop you off at your place."

"I can walk."

"There's no need. I'm going to Shale Flats, and your cabin is only a short detour."

"Before I go, may I see the birds?"

He hadn't expected this, and it threw him off balance. "You'll see them in the truck."

"I meant in their cages. Where they live."

Her tone made it sound as if she wanted to make sure he wasn't mistreating them. Well, he wasn't. He knew a lot about birds, had let them take on more importance in his life than a mere hobby. So, even though he didn't share the hawks with most people, he'd show her that he kept them clean and comfortable.

She helped him stack the dishes in the sink and offered to wash them, but he told her he was in a hurry to get out in the field. He led her outside and back to the mews. Inside it was cool and damp from the rain last night. The birds were quiet on their perches.

"What are their names?" Dana wanted to know. She

was eyeing the hawks with an interest that he hadn't foreseen, and he pegged her attitude as—well, polite. Not belligerent, as she had been yesterday. The fact that she wasn't baiting him allowed him to warm to the topic.

"You know Demelza, the kestrel. She's what used to be called a sparrow hawk. Roderic is my red-tail hawk, and Fairleigh is a gyrfalcon. This merlin is Nickel. The ones on the other side are Suli, Rosalie, and Muscatel." He pointed to a compact bird with deep blue plumage. "That's Aliah, my female peregrine, top of the heap. She's called a falcon, but if she were a male, she'd be called a tiercel, from the Latin word for *third,* because the males are one-third the size of the females."

"She's beautiful." Dana stood beside Roderic, a magnificent bird with cinnamon-colored tail feathers and a noble profile. "He's gorgeous, too," she said.

"Not 'he.' She."

"I thought Roderic would be a male's name."

He couldn't help grinning at her in amusement. "Roderic is indeed a male, but hawks are always referred to as 'she.'"

"Like ships," Dana said.

"Exactly."

He began to transfer the birds to the truck while Dana watched. She was full of questions, wanting to know in rapid-fire order how he fed them, when he flew them, if they flew every day.

Conn answered her questions patiently. He'd thought her interest would fall away once she'd seen the birds, but apparently it had only stirred her desire for more knowledge. When he had loaded the birds into the truck, she climbed into the cab before he could open the door for her.

The rainbow had faded, and the sky was clear above the mesa. Dana didn't comment on the loss of the rainbow; she seemed quiet, remote.

Which was fine. Hadn't he been thinking that he didn't want to get too friendly? That he'd rather not encourage her? Yet when he glanced over at her profile, he felt regretful that he couldn't make more of an effort. He thought that she might have depths that he would never fathom, and for some reason this disturbed him.

She turned to him when he eased the truck down the rutted road leading to the Cantrell place. "You can stop here," she said. "I'd like to walk the rest of the way for exercise."

He braked to a stop. Better that she walk here than around the mesa, which was so far from her cabin.

She opened the door, then hesitated. "The hawks," she said suddenly. "It's sad in a way. That they are captive, I mean, instead of flying free."

"We are all captive in some way," he said. He kept his face impassive.

She stared at him across the space between them. "I suppose so," she said thoughtfully. She slid out and slammed the door. "Thanks," she said through the open window. "You've been most hospitable."

From where he sat, he couldn't see her shape. He could only see her from the shoulders up, and he realized that she had a lovely face. A perfect oval, the nose straight, nostrils slightly flared, a creamy porcelain complexion. A pretty woman.

"You're welcome," he said, and she smiled a little self-consciously before turning and walking away. He waited until she rounded a curve in the road before he backed the truck around and headed for the highway into town.

He didn't think a woman in Dana's condition should be living out here in the wilderness. But he'd told her that, and it had only made her angry.

Oh, well, what did it matter? It wasn't as if he ever intended to see her again.

AFTER CONN DROPPED HER OFF, Dana went inside the cabin and planned what she would do to fill up her day. She'd always thought that she would enjoy having nothing to do for weeks on end, but she was learning that it wasn't easy to keep from being bored.

It was hard to remember, sometimes, that she was no longer the person she had once been. For years she'd been known as Day Quinlan, not Dana. Dana was the name she had shed when she started making her mark as a television newswoman, then an anchor. She'd chosen the name Day because it reminded her that her career was a new day in her life, and the name reminded her of the name her parents had given her at birth.

Day Quinlan had been on top of the world at age thirty-two. She had served as honorary chairman of Chicago's Heart Ball two years in a row. As the host of *Day Time,* she'd spoken knowledgeably about the television business to a stellar gathering of TV commentators in Dallas; traveled to the health-and-fitness spa, Maine Chance, twice a year to shed pounds for the camera so that her figure would retain its svelte allure; flown on the network's company jet on a regular basis. She had headed up a personal staff of twenty-four, not counting security, and lived in a luxury penthouse overlooking Lake Michigan.

That was when she was Day Quinlan. She was Dana now. She was still thirty-two, but almost everything else in her life had changed. And she was bored out of her mind living out here in the boondocks.

The library in town helped, though it wasn't much more than a hole-in-the-wall storefront place run by Esther Timms, an overly plump woman who sat at the lone table and drank coffee most of the day while reading one book after another. Dana had occasionally joined her for a cup of coffee, and it was at Esther's suggestion that Dana had recently taken up counted cross-stitch. If she didn't go blind doing it, Dana would eventually complete a set of two samplers to hang in the baby's room. And of course there was always cleaning. Today, she decided, she would scrub down the tile around the tub in the bathroom. The tile was thick with lime deposits from the water here, which was abundant with minerals.

The physical labor had a cathartic effect, and she threw herself gladly into the task. But what Conn had said kept playing through her mind: that we are all captives. It was so true.

Once she had been a captive of her own fame. She had thought she was escaping by running away. But now she was as surely a prisoner as she had been before—a captive of her unusual circumstance.

It was something she had in common with Conn's hawks, and because of it she had a special empathy for them. One thing for sure, though—Conn was much more interested in those birds than he was in her.

WHEN CONN RETURNED to his house from Shale Flats, he felt at loose ends. For the first time since he'd lived here, he actually wished that he had some company.

That woman, Dana. Had she spoiled this for him? Coming into his house, flashing bright looks at him, making him realize that he missed the companionship of other human beings? He had been fine, just he and the hawks, doing what he loved to do, accountable to no one. And now—as of this morning—he felt melancholy. Empty. Alone.

He threw himself down on the couch and tried to read the magazine he'd picked up at the drugstore yesterday. He knew one of the writers, and critiquing his friend's article was a good mental exercise. He had brought his laptop computer to this place, but he'd never gotten around to unpacking it. He'd left every other apparatus of his profession in his apartment in Los Angeles. Maybe what was wrong was that he missed his work, his writing.

He tossed the magazine on the table, and as he stood up, a glint of gold caught his eye. He bent over and picked up a bracelet, a heavy and elaborate solid gold chain with a charm in the shape of a heart dangling from it. The charm was initialed *D. Q.*, and underneath were engraved the words, *Thanks for caring*.

D. Q.? Her name was Dana Cantrell. Or so she'd said. Well, it was none of his business. Anyway, the initials may not have stood for her name. They could represent a motto, like Don't Quit, or a place, like Docker's Quay. Or Dingbat Quotient, for all he knew.

Conn pocketed the bracelet. He'd have to take it to her. He hadn't planned to ride into Cougar Creek this afternoon, but if he craved company, why not sample lunch at the diner and hang with the locals for a while? He could stop by the Cantrell place on his way back from town.

It wasn't that he wanted to see Dana, he told himself, especially not so soon. But she might miss the bracelet, and he wouldn't want her to think she'd lost it out on the trail. He was only doing what needed to be done. He was saving her the trouble of searching for the bracelet on the trail when he didn't think she should be out walking at all.

THAT AFTERNOON Conn pulled up in front of the Cantrell cabin and stopped the truck. When he'd dropped Dana off this morning, they hadn't been in view of the place, sheltered as it was behind a clump of cottonwoods, and now that he saw it, he was shocked. This was where Dana lived? The cabin looked even worse than it had the last time he'd been here, which had been some years ago when he and Steve had gone fishing in the creek.

The weathered wooden structure seemed to lean sideways toward a gully that was normally dry, but today, after last night's storm, it churned with muddy water that spilled into the nearby creek. Several shingles were missing from the cabin's roof, and one of the porch steps lacked a board. The windows were shining, however, and the porch was swept clear of leaves and debris from the storm.

Dana materialized at the screen door. He wouldn't have recognized her through the sagging mesh if it hadn't been for her shape.

He slid out of the truck and hailed her. "I found something at my place that belongs to you," he said. He scooped a bag of jelly doughnuts off the seat; he'd almost forgotten that he'd picked them up at Susie's Powwow Diner in town.

She came outside, and he held up the bracelet. "It was on the floor in front of the couch."

"It was good of you to bring it over," she said. As he moved closer, he noticed that Dana's eyes were the darkest blue he'd ever seen, and they shone with the brilliance of star sapphires. In that moment he thought she reminded him of someone, but he couldn't think who it was. He stepped up onto the porch, skipping the broken stair.

"You really should get that fixed," he said, referring to the step. He dropped the bracelet into her hand.

She tried to fasten it around her wrist, but her injured hand made it difficult. He watched her struggle for a few moments.

"Here, let me help," he said. He gave her the bag of doughnuts, and she wordlessly handed him the bracelet and held out her wrist, avoiding his eyes.

This seemed utterly personal, too much so, indulging in the little intimacy of helping a woman with her jewelry. Her skin beneath his fingertips felt warm, and as he fastened the bracelet's clasp, he couldn't help but feel her pulse racing. It jittered beneath his fingertips like the fragile heart of a bird. He shot her a surprised glance, unsure what this meant.

When he had finished with the bracelet, he dropped her hand and saw with bemusement that a blush had started in the hollow of her throat and was working its way upward. He had the thought that her fast pulse could be due to her pregnancy, but he just as quickly realized that it couldn't be. Pregnant women didn't develop racing pulses for no reason at all. He would have had to be a total numbskull not to recognize this for what it was—sexual attraction.

Had he been giving off vibes in that direction? He didn't think so. But he did find her attractive, not to mention disconcerting with those big blue eyes of hers, the depths of which seemed boundless.

She opened the bag and inhaled the aroma. "Mmm, fresh doughnuts. This is a treat."

"Susie at the diner claims they're a new batch, hot off the truck."

Dana shot a glance up at him out of the corners of her eyes. "Won't you come in for a cup of tea?" she said, but she offered as though she didn't expect him to take her up on it.

Tea. He didn't drink tea. He considered it a drink for wusses. He almost suggested coffee, but he thought such a request might embarrass her if she didn't have any. Still, surprisingly enough, he wanted to stay.

She was looking at him expectantly, the blush having receded to two dusky spots of color high on her cheekbones.

"Sure," he said as easily as if he drank tea all the time. It had taken him less than the space of a heartbeat to decide.

He followed Dana inside, expecting the interior of the cabin to be dim. But the space was filled with sunlight due to large windows in the back overlooking the creek. The ceiling was high, giving a further impression of light and space. There was a separate kitchen and a sleeping alcove that could be curtained off from the main room by use of a sprightly patterned curtain.

She said "Come on in here," and Conn trailed her into the kitchen. It was small but neat with surprisingly modern conveniences, such as a dishwasher and a microwave oven. There was a newly painted kitchen table with four chairs, and it didn't escape his attention that the windows were freshly scrubbed and that the place mats on the table looked new.

"Looks like you've been working around here," he said as she turned on the burner under the teakettle.

"The place needed sprucing up," she said. She put a hand to the small of her back in that poignant gesture that pregnant women have, and he wondered how far along she was. Five months? Six months? He had no idea.

"Are you sure you should be working around here?" he asked, eyeing the canisters on top of the wall-hung cabinet. At five-four or so, he knew she wasn't tall enough to reach them without standing on a ladder or a chair. He didn't see a step stool around.

"You mean because I'm pregnant?" she said.

"Exactly."

She poured hot water over tea bags in a teapot, her hands moving dexterously. "There isn't anyone else to do it."

He warned himself not to get impatient with her. "Don't take chances. If you need someone to climb on a ladder for you, I'll be glad to."

She lifted her eyebrows. He hadn't noticed before, but they were pale and arched as delicately as a sparrow's wing. "I won't. Need anyone, I mean."

He sat down at the kitchen table and watched as she assembled sugar and lemon, two cups and spoons. She moved gracefully despite her bulk, and he allowed himself to imagine how she'd look in a nonpregnant state. She was delicately boned, and he had an idea that her pregnancy had allowed her to put on weight. Not that she was fat— far from it. Nicely rounded was how he would put it.

And although the curve of her hips was hidden beneath the folds of the man's flannel shirt she wore, the line of her breasts was revealed by the softly clinging fabric. He knew that the size of pregnant women's breasts increased soon after conception, and he found himself wondering if her breasts had been anywhere nearly that big before her pregnancy. His mind produced a vision of large, dark, slightly pouty areolae. He was glad when she slid the cup of tea across the table at him so that he could concentrate on putting in sugar and stirring. He didn't want to speculate about this woman's breasts. He was on a self-imposed hiatus from women.

She sat down across the table from him and offered him

a doughnut from the bag. He took one, although he almost never ate sweets. He liked the way she bit into hers with gusto, but daintily. She licked the sugar from her lips, completely unaware that there was anything arousing about the pink tip of her tongue.

"Back to this nonsense about not needing anyone," he said, hoping she wouldn't mind if he backtracked to their previous conversation. "Why is that?"

She looked disconcerted. "I don't, that's all."

"Your family must be concerned about your living out here all by yourself." He was intrigued by her insistence that she didn't need anyone during a time in her life when most women reached out to others—mothers, sisters, girlfriends.

"I don't have a family, no relatives at all." She clamped her lips together after she said it.

He could identify. "Neither do I. Well, I have an aunt somewhere from my father's side of the family, but she never stayed in touch after my dad left, and since she married and changed her name, I've never tried to find her. But you, being pregnant," and he stopped to clear his throat. "You must have friends. Siblings. Someone."

"No one." She had withdrawn behind a curtain of privacy, and she seemed determined not to let him see behind it.

Possible scenarios chased through his mind. A husband who left her? One that she'd left? Why?

"So what do you do on holidays?"

She shrugged and didn't answer. "And other than your aunt, you have no family, either, you say." She was looking at him across the table, clear-eyed and straightforward.

"Well, there's my mother, but for all practical purposes, she's lost to me. She has Alzheimer's disease and lives in a nursing home in California." Maybe by opening up to her he could convince her to open up to him.

"Oh, I'm sorry," Dana said, and he sensed that this

wasn't just something she said, that she really meant it. This touched him, although he couldn't have said why.

"I've had a long time to get used to it." He didn't add that he hadn't, not really. His mother had sacrificed for him when he was growing up, and they'd been very close. He couldn't accept that she'd never be well again, would never be able to give him her approval, would never understand that it was her principles and her scruples that he had chosen to live by when asked to do the unthinkable by his boss.

"I suppose that when that happens to a parent, it doesn't get any easier no matter how much time has passed."

"True. Anyway, I go to visit her now and then, but it doesn't matter if I do or not. She doesn't know me."

"It sounds like you don't like going there."

He shifted uneasily in his seat. "I've put my mom on a waiting list for a premier care facility nearby, and I'll feel a lot better about her situation when I've moved her there."

Dana curved her hands around her cup. Behind her the window opened on a clump of willow trees, and from somewhere he heard the chatter of a blue jay. For the first time he noticed the skimpy bouquet of wildflowers she'd stuck in a jelly glass on the table. Her wish to beautify her surroundings was something that he found oddly touching.

She spoke carefully, giving him the impression that she didn't often talk about personal things. "My mother and I had our differences, but my life would have been better if she hadn't died when I was so young. She was griefstricken after we lost my father, and I've always thought that the stress of adjusting to life without Daddy hastened her death. She died less than a year after he did. A massive coronary from out of the blue."

"That must have been hard on you," he replied.

"It was awful. I sold the family farm, since I knew I couldn't run the place alone, and moved to Chicago," she said.

"Why Chicago?"

"A job offer. Advertising," she said quickly.

He narrowed his eyes. He knew immediately that this wasn't a true statement.

When Conn had been a working journalist, he had learned of a way to find out if the subject of an interview was telling the truth. The key was to note the subject's eye movements. Everyone had a pattern—when they were telling the truth, they might look upward to the left or the right. Conn learned to establish a pattern with an interviewee by asking him casual questions about things that Conn already knew to be true—where the subject was born, his position in his company, things like that. He noted the interviewee's eye movements when answering such questions, and if, during the interview, the subject gave himself away by flicking his eyes in a different direction from the established pattern, Conn would know the person was lying.

He already knew that Dana glanced upward and to the left when telling the truth, as when she'd said that her mother had died within a year of her father. But she had flicked her eyelids briefly down and to the right when she'd told him that she'd worked in advertising. This set off an alarm in his head.

Why would Dana lie about her profession? What difference would it make if he were to know what she really did for a living in Chicago? What was going on here?

Dana seemed completely unaware that she had betrayed herself. She had changed the subject and was talking about the hawks.

It took him a moment to regain his equilibrium, and by the time he had, she was asking where he got his birds.

"My friend Steve Karos—the one whose house I bought here—owned most of them. Aliah is mine, though. I bought her from a Saudi businessman."

"I thought maybe you had to catch the birds in the wild."

"You can. I've been wanting to capture some eyases—"

"Some what?"

"Eyases. Birds taken from the nest and raised by hand. I'd like to train a bird of my own."

"Where would you get one?"

"Around here. They nest in the rocks. If I know there's a nest, I'll go looking."

"Is that fair? To take them?"

"I care for my hawks very well."

She helped herself to another doughnut. "I see that." She paused, took a bite. "I've been thinking about what you said this morning."

"About?"

"Captivity."

"Ah. You agree with me."

"Mostly."

"That must mean that you consider yourself a captive—along with everyone else, of course."

She looked at him, an unfathomable look. "I think about your birds, how they must want to fly free."

"They do fly free. They aren't tied to me by a chain or a line when they're up there in the air."

"What makes them come back?"

"Depends on the bird. With an eyas, you've hand raised her, and a falconer likes to think that she has true affection for him. That's why she comes back. On the other hand, a hawk trapped in adulthood is trained to come back for food. Some of them don't, you know. I've lost a bird now and then."

"Then there is a possibility that they could be free if they chose."

"You could look at it that way."

"That makes me feel better. Perhaps they are more able to choose than we are."

Privately he wondered what she meant by that. He was framing his next remark in his mind when she stood up, went and got the teapot, brought it to the table. From the back, he almost couldn't tell she was pregnant.

She noticed that he hadn't drunk much of his tea.

"Doesn't it taste all right?" she asked anxiously.

"It tastes fine." He took another doughnut so that he wouldn't have to make an excuse to leave.

"Do you mind talking about the birds?" she asked curiously.

"Why would you think that?" he said.

"Every time I think we're on the subject, somehow we get off of it." She dabbed at her mouth with a napkin, and he noted that it was made of cloth. He knew hardly anyone who used cloth napkins anymore.

"Do you want to know more?" He doubted that she would answer in the affirmative.

She tilted her head to one side, considering. "I do. Yes," she said, surprising him.

"And why is that?"

She drew a deep breath, measured his mood with a glance.

"I think I want to fly a hawk. Will you let me?"

Conn sat back in his chair, more surprised than he let on. No one had ever put this question to him before, and he had no stock answer. He considered his hawks a private indulgence, a place he could go, a thing he could do alone. And now this woman, this Dana Cantrell, wanted to intrude upon his privacy. He had been right; she would shatter his solitude, infringe upon his life.

Yet, when he spoke, he heard himself saying, "Of course you can fly one. Tomorrow you'll come with me to Shale Flats."

Chapter Three

Dana, bundled up in a warm, fleecy sweatshirt against a light morning frost, was waiting for Conn on the front porch when his hawk wagon came bumping through the pale-gray half-light of dawn the next morning. Her stomach kept performing nervous little flips that had nothing to do with morning sickness. Ever since he'd agreed to take her along, she'd been having serious second thoughts about going.

Maybe it hadn't been such a good idea to ask Conn to take her to Shale Flats, and if she'd thought about it at all, she probably could have made a good case against asking in the first place. In retrospect, it seemed like such a cheeky thing to do. These second thoughts had cost her a good night's sleep the night before, and she'd spent the night tossing and turning.

Conn got out of the truck, leaving the engine running and the driver's side door open. He hailed her with a grin, which was a more good-natured greeting than she had expected. She stumbled on the broken step on her way down to meet him, and somehow he managed to catch her. She felt a rush of confusion, of excitement at the strength of him as his arms balanced her.

"I'll fix that step for you," he said close to her right ear, and she pulled away before she could feel any more. That was the thing about this man that was so confounding; he made her *feel*. She had managed to hold off feeling anything about anything but the baby since she left Chicago, and now she was beset with inappropriate thoughts and emotions whenever this man was around.

As she collected herself, she saw him studying the faulty board, measuring it with his eyes. She wanted to say, *I can fix that step myself,* but she knew she couldn't. She didn't have the tools, she didn't have the skill, and the best she could do would be to hire someone to see to it.

"I'll get someone out here. Esther at the library has this nephew—"

Conn interrupted. "I'll do it today." There seemed to be no point in further discussion, so she climbed into the front seat of the truck while Conn came around and got in his side. Something about being so near to him made her feel as if she couldn't breathe, or maybe it was the baby pushing up against her lungs. She shifted in the seat, trying to get more comfortable, and when that didn't work, she rolled down the window and inhaled deeply of the breeze winding in from the hills. Conn kept his eyes on the road, not talking, and she didn't want to fill the air of this quiet morning with meaningless chatter, so she kept her silence. By the time they had started up the hills, their gentle slopes a patchwork of autumn colors, she was feeling almost normal.

Dana had never been to Shale Flats before, and she leaned forward in her seat, eagerly taking in the scenery. The pickup jounced past an old mine, the Piccolo, its abandoned buildings ghostly in the purple haze. By the time the glow of the rising sun had become visible behind the mesa, they had reached a wide flat meadow bordered by a tall stand of cottonwoods, their leaves shivering in a chill breeze.

While Dana watched, shifting from one foot to the other and wrapping her arms around herself to keep warm, Conn unloaded perches for the hawks, bowed metal stands that he set on the ground. He fastened a leather gauntlet on his wrist and reached into the back of the hawk wagon where Dana could see the vague shapes of the birds arrayed along its length. They were quiet, but when he reached in, one of them jumped onto his wrist. He quickly slipped a hood over the hawk's head before bringing her out into the light. She was slate-blue above, her breast streaked and barred, her face marked like a mustache. The peregrine, Dana thought.

"The hood makes her easier to handle," Conn said, but Dana had already figured that.

"That's Aliah, right?" she said, watching closely as he threaded a leather thong on the gauntlet through a metal ring joining the two leather straps attached to the peregrine's ankles.

He shot her a sharp look. "Very good that you remembered," he said. He finished tying a knot. "You may have noticed that my hawks all wear a pair of these leather straps. They're called jesses." He carried Aliah to a scale. "I weigh them before they fly. She has to make flying weight before I let her go."

"Flying weight?"

"If she's even an ounce or two overweight, I can't count on her being hungry enough to come back when she flies. This morning I know she'll want food, so it's okay." The weighing done, he nudged Aliah's legs with his gauntleted wrist so that she either had to step forward or fall backward. She stepped forward onto the gauntlet.

Conn strode out to the middle of the flat, tall and silhouetted against the golden sky. The sunrise was behind him, and in that moment, with the light behind, he seemed to hold the sun within him. He dazzled her so that Dana lifted her hand and shaded her eyes against his brilliance. Legs splayed wide for balance, he untied the jesses and lifted the bird up high. Dana might have mistaken the gesture as a kind of salute to the morning until Aliah unexpectedly raised up and unglamourously expelled a dropping.

"They all do that," he said over his shoulder, explaining. "It's called muting, and it lowers their flying weight even more."

Illusion had become reality once again. Dana moved closer, watching intently as Conn flung the bird into the air. Aliah began to flap her wings, caught the air, glided. Dana felt her heart rise in her chest, almost as if borne along with the falcon. It must be lovely to fly like that, she thought, to leave the heaviness of the earth below, to breathe in great drafts of clean, fresh air, to ride on the crest of an air current toward the warmth of the sun.

She felt herself grinning at the sight of the bird rising free; she couldn't help it. Conn was busy untangling a line with two gray-feathered wings at one end.

"How long will she fly like that?" Dana asked.

"In good weather like this, she'll fly for hours if I let her." He glanced up at the falcon. "She's feeling her strength, almost ready to get serious," he said as Aliah cruised and dipped above them. It was hard to tell, but Dana thought that the falcon had reached an altitude of forty-five feet or so, never going far, always circling and returning to where they stood below watching.

Conn went to the middle of the clearing and let out a long whistle. "I'll show her the lure now," he said. Then he began to swing the line with the wings around and around over his head, his movements swift and fluid.

Aliah banked sharply, homed in on the lure, picked up speed, zoomed toward it with wings tucked back in a vee. Suddenly she angled her feet forward, talons outstretched, and Conn yanked the lure away only a moment before she would have captured it. The falcon wheeled around and soared so high that for one heart-stopping moment, Dana feared that she was lost.

But no. Aliah circled above them, spiraling down and down. In a few moments Conn whirled the lure again, and again Aliah seemed poised to attack, foiled only when Conn jerked the lure away at the last second.

"It seems cruel," Dana said. "Not letting her have it, I mean."

"This is play," he said. "It's what Aliah was born to do. Don't worry, she'll have her reward."

Again and again he swung the lure, and time after time Aliah bore down upon it, the morning sunlight glinting on her pale feathers. She was a picture of beauty and grace, and Dana was thoroughly captivated.

"Want to try it?" Conn said when Dana thought he had forgotten she was there.

She cranked up her nerve and stepped forward to accept the lure from him. He showed her how to hold it, then stepped back. She wished Conn would stay closer in case she did something wrong, but then she decided that it was good that he trusted her to do this on her own.

She began to swing the lure, low at first, then higher as her confidence grew. The string hummed, the lure caught the rays of the rising sun, and Aliah began her dive. The lure skimmed through the air, and the falcon came straight toward Dana.

"What she's doing now is called stooping," Conn said from behind her. "She'll drop low, then come up to take the lure."

It didn't happen that way. When Aliah was almost upon the lure, she suddenly lofted upward and soon was only a speck in the sky. For one heartstopping moment, Dana thought the falcon might keep flying and never come back. But Aliah caught an air current and glided back around, hardly moving her wings at all.

"Try again," said Conn. "You want her to increase her pitch—the height at which she circles—so that she can stoop effectively."

Dana did as he said. Aliah flew lazily above, seemingly uninterested.

"She sees the lure," Conn said close behind her. "Now swing it higher."

Dana swung the lure up and up. Aliah executed a delicate

turn and started down, and Dana almost held her breath as the falcon aimed her body earthward in a dive. She seemed to intensify her speed as she grew closer, her feet tucked back under her tail, her eyes intent upon the winged lure.

She swooped down so close to the ground that Dana thought she might land, but then the falcon lifted higher, and Dana jerked the lure away from her outstretched talons. The falcon soared up over their heads, the rush of wind from her wings ruffling Dana's hair. Dana bubbled with delighted laughter, and behind her she heard Conn laughing, too.

"Can I do it again?" she asked, almost too eager, and Conn nodded yes. She threw the lure another time and then another, totally aware of every muscle in her body moving in harmony as she worked to bring the falcon in. It was as if she experienced all her outer senses in a new way, and that made her aware of her inner ones as she never had been before. She was part of the moment, totally engaged in what she was doing.

She was so much a part of the moment, so enthralled by the interaction with Aliah, that it came as a surprise when, close behind her, Conn spoke. "Now it's time for Aliah's breakfast," he said. He removed something from a cooler on the ground, and to Dana's questioning look he replied, "Skinned quail." She handed the line to him and stepped back.

Holding the quail in his fist, he threw the lure, and this time he didn't yank it away when Aliah stooped. She struck the lure with the long talons on her back toes and dropped with it to the ground.

Conn reeled in the lure and showed the falcon the quail in his hand. Aliah lost interest in the lure and jumped to his wrist, and Conn quickly fastened her jesses to the gauntlet before letting the falcon have the quail. She pulled it apart with her beak, and he let her eat.

"Falcons are raptors, and so are hawks, owls, eagles,

ospreys and vultures. That means they specialize in hunting and killing prey,'' Conn said.

''I guess that means they're at the top of the food chain,'' Dana observed.

He nodded. ''Few animals threaten them in the wild. Humans are the biggest danger. Some species have nearly been wiped out because of pesticides. Encroaching civilization eliminates their habitats. A lot of them have run-ins with cars, and sometimes people shoot them.''

''That's sad,'' Dana said, unhappy to think of these beautiful birds in danger.

In only a minute or so, the quail was gone, and then, while Dana watched, Conn flew the other birds. She sat on the ground, protected from the dew by a ground cloth that Conn spread for her. He was solicitous, and that surprised her. Pleased her, actually. She was so accustomed to going it alone that these little kindnesses, like spreading the ground cloth and making sure she was comfortable before he took the other hawks out of the wagon, touched her immensely.

A fresh breeze riffled Conn's hair where it lay upon his neck. Dana longed to touch the strip of tanned skin beneath, to run her fingers across the hard edge of each vertebra. The thought made her cheeks warm, warmer than the first flush of golden sunshine would render them, and so she clenched her fists at her sides and made herself concentrate on the birds. She tried to remember their names—Demelza, the kestrel, she knew, of course. Roderic was the red-tail hawk, and Fairleigh, large and all black except for white streaking on her belly, the gyrfalcon. The merlin, she recalled, dove-sized and looking like a miniature Aliah, was Nickel, and then there were Rosalie, a prairie falcon, and Muscatel.

Muscatel was the last one to fly. A young red-tail hawk, she soared so high that Dana had to strain her eyes to see her.

''Don't worry,'' Conn said when he saw Dana shading

her eyes with her hand and scanning the sky for some sight of Muscatel. "She's hungry. She'll be back."

And he was right. Muscatel glided in as soon as Conn began to swing the lure. Dana watched mesmerized, feeling giddy and slightly drunk with the heady fragrance of pine and sunshine on warm stone, a scent she knew that she would forever associate with Conn.

After he had flown all the hawks, Conn started to pack up. He noticed Dana as she struggled to get up from her place on the ground, and he came over to give her a hand up. "I should have brought a folding chair where you could sit," he said.

"I could have sat in the cab of the truck," she pointed out. "But in there I couldn't have had such a good view of what you were doing." He didn't comment. He only went to retrieve the birds from their perches.

When Conn had returned the birds to the hawk wagon, Dana trudged back and forth helping him load the equipment—perches, leashes, hoods—back into the truck.

"You don't have to," he said, but she demurred.

"I'm stronger than you think. Stronger than I look," she told him.

He thought about that and decided it was probably true. The windows in her little cabin, for instance—she had washed them by herself. He didn't like to think of her doing hard work, wondered if pregnant women were supposed to do all the bending and stretching that she'd obviously been doing.

She was full of questions as they bounced their way down the rutty road down the hill. How long had birds been trained for hunting? How were they trained? Had *he* ever trained one?

"Falconry probably began in Asia before 2000 B.C. It flourished in Europe in the Middle Ages, and a man's social status determined what kind of hawk he was allowed to own."

"I thought falconry was a sport. Now I see it as both an art and a science with its own vocabulary," she said.

"It's not only art and science, but there's a lot of ritual involved," Conn said.

"It's different from keeping a bird as a pet, isn't it?'

"You may have noticed that although I'm gentle with them, I don't talk to them—or about them—as if they were pets. I believe that these birds are as close to the way they would live in the wild as possible. For one thing, they hunt much as they would if they were free. Hunting is their natural behavior. I don't teach them, I only assist them to do what comes naturally."

"How did you first get involved with hawks?" She focused wide blue eyes on him, rendered even darker by the navy of her sweatshirt. A crisp white collar overlapped the sweatshirt's neckline, and it looked like the collar of a man's shirt. One of her father's, perhaps.

He pulled his eyes away, thinking that it was easy to forget that she was pregnant. "When I was in my early twenties and living on the West Coast, my friend Steve showed me what falconry was all about."

"Did you—" she began but stopped talking.

He cast a sidelong glance at her. She was biting her lower lip, a sure sign that she was thinking over what she'd been about to say.

"Go ahead," he told her.

"I was curious about whether you felt the same way I do the first time you saw them fly."

He was amused. "I hardly know how you felt," he pointed out, grinning at her.

She flushed slightly. "Exhilarated. Amazed. And completely unable to recall anything so thrilling."

He laughed. "That's *exactly* how I felt."

Dana didn't ask any more questions after that but appeared thoughtful and contemplative. Her silence gave him a chance to recall what he meant to do for her. When he headed toward his house instead of down the road to hers, she looked over at him blankly.

"I'm going to drop the hawks off, pick up my tool kit. No reason not to repair that step right away."

"But—"

"No buts."

She settled back into the seat and stared out the window. He told her not to get out of the truck when they reached his place, but she did, anyway. She helped him by moving the equipment out of the truck while he saw to the hawks, putting them in their cages and closing the cage doors securely.

When he was ready to leave, she hung back, peering through the mesh of the cages at the hawks. "Come on," he said, trying not to let impatience seep into his tone.

"I was thinking that they are freer than they seem," she said. Her eyes searched his, and the strange thing was that he knew exactly what she meant. But he wasn't used to sharing his feelings, not even about the birds.

He tossed a scrap piece of board into the back of the hawk wagon. "If we hurry, I can finish up that step before lunchtime," he said. She got into the truck and watched his hand as he reached for the ignition key and turned it. The truck roared to life, and he slammed it into gear.

"Thanks for taking me this morning," she ventured. "I mean, you didn't have to. I loved it, I really did."

This would have been the time to ask her to go with him tomorrow morning, but something stopped him. He mumbled something more or less gracious and discovered to his surprise that his palms were damp. Why? She was making him nervous. He asked himself why he should be unhinged by her presence, but again he didn't know.

Surreptitiously he wiped his damp hands on his pants legs, hoping she wouldn't notice. A glance at her profile told him that she wasn't looking, and in that moment he thought he knew who it was in his past that Dana Cantrell resembled. Francesca Sorisi, that's who it was, a girl he'd been crazy about in the fourth grade. Francesca had ignored him completely, and then the next year, when they were eleven and had become friends, she'd moved away. He hadn't thought about Francesca in years, but Dana had the same sweet curve to her lips and the same determined chin.

They drew up in front of Dana's house, and she went inside while he repaired the stair. It didn't take much. All he had to do was tear off the old board and put on the new one, a simple task. When she came to the door, she handed him a glass of water.

He hammered in the final nail and stood up. She had brushed her hair back behind her ears, and she was smiling. He took the water and drained the glass, not realizing until the glass was empty that he'd halfway been hoping she'd ask him to come in. But she didn't.

"Thanks," he said.

"I'm the one who should be thanking you. For taking me to Shale Flats and for fixing my step."

"No thanks necessary." He stood with one foot on the new board, looking up at her.

Perhaps it was just as well that she hadn't invited him inside. If he stayed, he might get more involved than was appropriate. And anyway, with a pregnant woman, even one with no man in evidence, what was appropriate?

She was still standing on the porch when he drove away, and he thought, but couldn't be sure, that she waved before he disappeared around the curve in the road.

DANA INSPECTED THE NEW step before she went back in the house. She'd wanted to invite Conn to stay for lunch, but all she had to eat was a couple of cartons of low-fat yogurt. She sat down at the kitchen table and thumbed through a catalog of baby items while she ate. But for the first time since she'd found out she was pregnant, she couldn't summon any interest in cribs and blankets, baby monitors or little playsuits. All she could think about was going back to Shale Flats.

Conn hadn't mentioned that she could go with him again, but she'd been hoping he'd offer. Now that he'd left, perhaps she wouldn't have another chance to ask him if she would be welcome on another morning.

She'd loved watching him fly the hawks, his confidence as he tossed them into the air, his athletic grace as he swung the lure. And the birds—Dana was sure she'd never get enough of watching them as they circled and dipped, as they winged upward on streams of air, as they so precisely homed in on the lure and dived for it. When Aliah had come swooping toward her, she'd caught a glimpse of those luminous golden eyes, had felt caught up in the drama of the attack. It was something for which she had not been prepared, that sense of participation.

Perhaps that was why she was drawn to experience falconry in more depth than she had today. She felt cut loose from everything about her former life, and in a sense she was. Her career had been all-encompassing, and her work had dictated what she did in her off hours, whether it was attending network soirees with Philip or meeting his society-maven mother, Myrtis, and her friends for lunch. It was important to be with the right people, to do the right things to advance her career.

Not that she missed all of that. She'd been weary of it for a long time. But here there was nothing to take its place unless you could count reading dog-eared books from the Cougar Creek library and working on counted cross-stitch.

The yogurt wasn't enough to satisfy her appetite, but it really didn't matter. All she could think of was that she wanted to fly Aliah again. And maybe Roderic and Fairleigh, Nickel and Muscatel. What were the others' names? Oh yes, Rosalie and Suli.

Roderic and Aliah, Fairleigh and Nickel, Muscatel, Rosalie and Suli.

The birds' names became a kind of litany, and she recited it out loud as she rinsed off her spoon and glass in the sink.

Somehow she'd convince Conn that he should take her along with him to Shale Flats again.

It gave her something to look forward to, and she needed that. She needed it a lot.

CONN DROVE INTO TOWN that afternoon for what had become his weekly mail pickup. Cougar Creek, with its row of shabby buildings hunkered along one dusty main thoroughfare, would never show up on *Lifestyles of the Rich and Famous.* He passed LaVaughn's Shear Delite, a hair salon, and Finnegan's Hardware, where you could buy anything from a butter churn to a cricket bit, and the Cougar Creek Dry Goods, established in 1897 and still, Conn wagered, carrying some of the same dusty merchandise stocked on opening day.

The post office was a tiny building on Main Street with mailboxes built right into the outside wall. Waiting for him were several bills, a circular from the local hardware store and two letters, one from the administrator of a nursing home in California and the other from Martin Storrs, his former managing editor.

He chucked the circular, stuck the bills in his back pocket and tossed the letters through the open window of his truck. He read the one from the nursing home as soon as he got home.

It informed him that his mother was now fifth on the waiting list for Catalina-Pacific House, the elite nursing facility that he'd been hoping would accept her ever since she'd been diagnosed with Alzheimer's. The administrator wanted to know if he still wanted the space.

Conn threw the letter down on the kitchen table and went to stare out the window at the sun setting on the other side of the hills.

Hell, yes! He wanted to take his mother out of the mediocre home where she'd been for the past several years and install her at Catalina-Pacific where she would have outstanding care. Gladys McTavish deserved the best of everything after raising him alone. She'd been abandoned at a young age by a husband whose whereabouts no one knew. She had worked hard in a textile mill all her life, and Conn owed her everything. He started to pick up the phone to call and tell them that his mother would be there as soon as the space became available, but then he remembered that he didn't have a phone.

The reason he didn't have one was that he didn't want people like Martin calling him, needling him, wheedling him to do things he didn't want to do.

Which reminded him that he hadn't read Martin's letter yet.

He picked it up and slit the envelope, reluctantly removing the *National Probe* letterhead and walking back to the window where the light was better for reading. The postmark was over a week old, and the letter was handwritten, which was a nice personal touch.

Conn,
Hey, buddy! I hope all is well in your Arizona retreat.
  Actually, Conn, I've been thinking about you a lot lately. You're the best reporter I ever had on my team, and I want you back at the *Probe*.
  Why not let bygones be bygones? I'll be waiting to hear from you. You'd better call me—if you don't, I might take it into my old gray head to trek out there to talk to you in person!

                                    Best regards,
                                    Martin

Conn wasn't surprised at the conciliatory tone of the letter. After all, he and Martin had been friends for a long time, even predating Conn's hiring at the *National Probe*. But he was amazed that Martin would be audacious enough to suggest that he return after the big brouhaha that had precipitated his firing, an episode that even now embarrassed him. He'd been so hot under the collar that he'd upended a trash can on Martin's desk to make his point. He hadn't realized that the remains of thirty-six hot wings could get that moldy in only a week, which was how often they emptied the office garbage at the *Probe* offices.

Conn had no intention of returning to the *Probe*. It would be a cold day in hell before that happened. A very cold day indeed.

DANA WAS ON HER WAY down the produce aisle at the Cougar Market when she spotted Conn out of the corner of her eye. He was hefting a six-pack of beer and studying a row of packaged chicken in the poultry section. It was unfortunate that he was so good-looking, so heartstoppingly handsome, the kind of man she would notice no matter where she saw him. Not that she was all that aware of men at this point in her life—far from it. The episode with Philip had been enough to make her wary of men, and she had been guarded around Conn at first. Now she felt at ease with him, though.

She found what she wanted at the near end of the meat cooler, a package of Italian sausage, and walked quietly up behind Conn. He seemed preoccupied.

"Finding what you want?" she asked.

"Well, no, I—" He turned, his face relaxing into an easy grin as he recognized her. "For a moment I thought you were the woman who works behind the meat counter."

"You look slightly lost."

"I heard they had quail on sale, but I guess they're all gone. If I could buy them locally, I wouldn't have to drive to Flagstaff when it's time to replenish my stock."

"I suppose the hawks can eat their way through quite a few quail in a week," she said.

"Yeah." He cast a last look at the chicken lined up in neat shiny cellophane-wrapped packages of thighs and breasts, leg quarters and wings. He shook his head. "Looks like I was too late."

Dana tried to think of something to say that would naturally lead the conversation toward what she wanted most—to go with him back to Shale Flats. But Conn seemed distant, distracted, his demeanor aloof. They started walking toward the checkout, where there was only one girl checking groceries.

Conn secured the six-pack under one arm and reached for one of the tabloid newspapers on the rack. It was the *National Probe,* the one Dana hated most. The reporters and photographers of that particular publication had made her life miserable for many years, and she supposed if she really thought about it, the *Probe* was one of the main reasons that she'd ended up living alone in Cougar Creek, cut off from everyone and everything in her former life.

"Are you thinking of buying that newspaper?" she asked, surprised. From the looks of the bookshelves in his cabin, she had thought Conn's reading tastes ran to nonfiction and the classics.

"Not really." Conn leafed through the *Probe* casually, pausing to study the table of contents, stopping to peruse a picture of a well-known rock group. "It's something to look at when I'm standing in the checkout line." After a minute or two, he stuck the paper back in its slot and drew his wallet out of his back pocket.

"I'd never buy a tabloid," she said firmly. She couldn't believe he would, either, but then, Conn McTavish had probably never been trashed by the media. She had, plenty.

He gave her a funny look. "Would you mind telling me why you feel that way?"

"Shoddy reporting. Bad reputation. Terrible writing. They pay sources for information, so how can any of it be accurate?" She clipped off the words sharply, hiding her distaste.

"Aw, come on," he said. "Why so uptight? What would life be without interesting little tidbits about Hillary and Chelsea? Gwyneth and whoever?"

"Give me a break, Conn. You don't read that stuff."

She hadn't either at one time, but she could have given him an earful if she'd been inclined. There was the time that *Tattletales Weekly* had published a front-page photo of her kissing a well-known baseball star who liked to dress in women's clothes; the trouble was that it was a picture of someone else's body with her head pasted on it. Another time, the *Probe* had reported that she was an alcoholic, which was completely untrue. And then there was the article in *Wild World Times* that claimed that she had been abducted by an alien spacecraft and her brain embedded with a microchip that would enable her to overthrow the government of Canada. That one had been such a howler that she'd had the story framed and hung in her office at GBN.

The man in front of her picked up his groceries and moved away, and she stepped forward to the cash register. It was then that she caught the expression on Conn's face. He looked flushed and queasy and generally upset, which was certainly not in keeping with his earlier joshing. The checker said, "Will plastic bags be okay?" and whatever she might have said to Conn about tabloid newspapers or anything else was lost in the ensuing shuffle.

Dana waited while Conn paid for the beer, then walked with him out of the store. Time to change the subject, she thought.

"Conn, I was wondering," she began.

He seemed to pull himself back from thoughts that had taken him far away, and he looked down at her blankly as if he'd forgotten she was there. That made it doubly difficult to extend her invitation.

"I bought all the makings for stuffed manicotti, and I thought you might like to come over for dinner tonight." She held her breath, unsure how this would sit with him. He didn't seem to be in a great mood; on the contrary, he looked moody and depressed.

"If you don't want to come, that's okay," she added hastily when he didn't pick up on her invitation right away.

"I felt like doing something for you because you fixed my step."

"Well, you don't have to do anything, but I'd like to come," he said, staring down at her in that unfathomable way of his. "What time?"

"Oh," she said, thinking. "Six-thirtyish?"

"That's good. And, well, I know you're not drinking, but would you mind if I brought a bottle of wine?"

She smiled warmly. "Of course not. See you then?"

"I'll be there." He managed a thin grin as she waved goodbye.

What was wrong with Conn? She'd thought they were getting along well up there at Shale Flats, and he seemed to have warmed to her interest in the hawks.

Maybe she shouldn't have asked him to dinner. Like it or not, however, she was committed.

CONN THOUGHT ABOUT DANA all the way back home.

He didn't want to think about her, but he couldn't help it.

First there was her dislike of tabloids, which hit him where it hurt. Dana was not the only person he'd known who distrusted the tabloid press. And for good reason some of the time, though Conn knew better than most that some of the tabloids were trying to clean up their act. The problem, he knew, was not so much with the tabloids themselves. If people wouldn't buy tabloid newspapers, they would cease to exist. As it was, they fed the lowest-common-denominator segment of the public, readers who liked to see the press tear people apart. The editors of the *National Probe* knew that the public not only wanted the dirt on famous people, they wanted blood.

There hadn't been a chance in the checkout line to defend the *Probe* and other publications like it. He wasn't even sure he'd wanted to. It would mean he would have to reveal too much about himself, and for now there was no point in doing that.

As for Dana and her invitation to dinner, was she making a play for him? That was the signal he was getting, but she was six months pregnant or thereabouts, so it was an incongruous thought.

Maybe it was the hawks. Maybe that was her focus.

He'd been trying ever since the morning they went to Shale Flats to shake the image of her that he held in his mind—Dana gracefully swinging the lure for Aliah with a rare exuberance, her laughter ringing clear as glass chimes in the burnished blue air as Aliah stooped and soared. Sunbeams had danced in Dana's hair, and the sweep of her gold-tipped lashes had cast shadows on her rosy cheeks. He had hardly been able to keep his eyes off her.

And that was crazy. He couldn't be attracted to a woman who was so obviously pregnant. He had sworn off women, hadn't he, after Lindsay? He didn't want to get close enough to another woman to be involved. He didn't want the pain of losing, that hurt, in his life ever again. So why was he letting this woman make inroads into his imagination? Maybe because she was pregnant, she wasn't a threat.

He dressed carefully for dinner in khakis and a real shirt, not his usual T-shirt or jerkin. He wore loafers, not boots. And even so, he didn't think he looked good enough. He even shaved anew, studying his reflection in the bathroom mirror. And cut himself because he wasn't paying attention.

Before leaving the house, he selected a bottle of cabernet from his stock, remembered that she wouldn't be drinking it and put it back. He decided on a bottle of Burgundy and put that back, too, finally settling on the cabernet after all. It troubled him that he was acting like an inexperienced kid, and he was anything but.

A thought struck him on the way to her place: he was like one of his hawks. He kept coming back to Dana because he was hungry. And not for food.

Chapter Four

Hungry or not, Conn thought the manicotti smelled wonderful; its hearty fragrance wafted all the way out to where he parked the truck. Conn bounded up the porch steps of the cabin, noting with satisfaction that the one he'd repaired didn't even wobble. Dana was at the door before he could knock.

She pushed the door open and stood aside so he could enter. "Hi," she said.

"Hi," he said. He saw through the door to the little kitchen that she had set the table with gleaming glassware and plates in bright colors, and that they sat on a flowered tablecloth. Suddenly he felt like a chump; he should have brought her fresh flowers. That would have meant another ride into town, or he could have picked them up after he left her at the grocery store, but he could have done it. As it was, he didn't have anything to offer her except the cabernet, which she couldn't even drink.

He handed the wine over to her, wondering if a light kiss on her cheek was called for, then decided that it wasn't. She looked lovely, wearing a pink silky-looking oversize blouse and dark leggings tucked into laced-up boots. Not the heavy boots that she'd wear for hiking, but something more elegant. They were expensive, a soft leather. He knew expensive when he saw it. He'd lived and worked in L.A. long enough to get an overdose of high-maintenance women, and these boots of Dana's were what he would have expected one of them to wear.

"Would you like to open the wine? I'm a real klutz with a corkscrew, or I'd do it myself."

"I'll be glad to," he said before following her into the kitchen. Dana bent over and opened the oven door, and he caught a glimpse of the manicotti bubbling and browning around the edges. When she straightened, her face was flushed from the heat.

"The corkscrew is in the drawer to your left," she said.

He found the corkscrew and inserted it into the wine cork. By the time he had the cork out, she had set a glass on the kitchen counter. "That's for you when you're ready to pour," she said.

While she sprinkled croutons over the salad, he went and looked out the back door. "The creek widens behind your house," he said. "I've been fishing here before."

"Before?" she asked, looking puzzled.

"I used to visit Steve, my friend who lived here. We liked to fish sometimes."

"Your friend—you said he's sick?"

"Yes. I've bought his place from him."

"So you don't plan on being a temporary resident," she said.

He shook his head. "Nope. I'm here for the long haul."

"Any thoughts about returning to civilization?"

"Hardly any."

"And where did you come from?"

"Los Angeles. Not my favorite place."

"You didn't grow up there, then." A timer dinged, the simple wind-up kind, and she bent to take the manicotti out of the oven.

"I grew up in South Carolina. A native son of the South."

She glanced over at him. "You don't sound Southern. No accent," she said.

He lifted a shoulder and let it fall. "I've lost it somewhere along the way." He spotted a gallon can of paint on one of the kitchen chairs. "Want me to move that?" he asked.

She glanced over her shoulder. "If you don't mind. It can go in there." She gestured with her eyes toward the open shelves at one end of the kitchen. He set the paint, a package of brushes and a roller next to a roller tray on the middle shelf.

"I wish you could have a glass of wine with me," he said as he poured it.

"I have a glass of water. Bottled water," she added. "I haven't learned to like the local H_2O. Too many minerals."

"That's understandable." He paused. "Well, anyway, *salud.*" He lifted his glass to her, and she lifted her glass of water, and they both drank. She felt a little embarrassed that she wasn't drinking wine. She must seem unsophisticated to him. In a way this disturbed her, but in another way, it didn't. She had led a life of glamour and excitement back in Chicago, had hung out with Philip and all his social-climbing friends, and in retrospect, she knew that she had never really been happy. There had always been the promise of happiness, the hope that after the February sweeps and resultant high ratings she'd feel good about herself, or that she'd be truly happy once she and Philip were engaged, or by the time she interviewed the sports star that no one else could snag, or even if she acquired a new gown from the latest trendy designer. But somehow once those things happened, she wasn't any happier. And she hadn't even noticed until recently that she'd been chasing rainbows down some murky road that always came to a dead end.

"Want me to put that on the table?" Conn asked, gesturing with his head toward the manicotti.

"Sure. I'll get the bread and the salad."

When they were seated on either side of the small table, Dana spread her napkin in her lap. She served both her salad bowl and his, and they each helped themselves to the manicotti. She noticed that Conn dug into his with gusto.

"This is delicious," he said. "Really."

She was pleased. Philip had hated what he called "peasant fare." He'd insisted that she hire a cook recommended by his mother who specialized in French cuisine, his favorite. The cook, whose name was Jean-Marc, had effectively banished her from her own kitchen. Dana had missed puttering around, concocting improvements on standard recipes the way she'd done ever since she was a kid. Cooking had always been a refuge for her, a way to forget the day's troubles. One of the best things about living alone and far away from Philip was being able to cook again.

"I like cooking," she said, and she started to tell him how she had learned to cook. It had happened when her mother was laid up with a broken foot the winter she was ten. "I began with the simplest recipes, and Mother told me what to do while she sat in a kitchen chair and supervised."

"Ten seems a little young."

"Oh, I didn't think so. By the end of that summer, I could cook a whole dinner, complete with apple cobbler for dessert, all by myself. My mother was lavish with her praise, even though I never cleaned up the messes to her satisfaction." She laughed a little at the memory, recalling how her father had proclaimed her mashed potatoes the best he'd ever eaten, in spite of the lumps.

"But I'm boring you," she said. She got up to refill her water glass.

Conn said, "No, you're not. I like to see someone who is enthusiastic. You sound like me when I first discovered falconry."

This conversational turn was more to Dana's liking. "I know you said your friend Steve introduced you to it," she replied. "How did it happen?"

"He took me out with his hawks one day, like I did with you," Conn told her.

Dana set her fork on the edge of her plate and leaned over the table. "I'd like to go again, Conn. To Shale Flats with you. If I wouldn't be in the way, that is."

He couldn't turn her down. At one time he might have been able to, or at least if she had been any other woman. But now, gazing across the table at her, feeling well fed and comfortable, noting the avid interest in her eyes, he didn't want to deny her the excitement of working with the hawks.

"You wouldn't be in the way," he said slowly, watching her carefully for her reaction.

"I could help you set up, whatever you'd like me to do."

"That isn't necessary," he heard himself saying. She was gazing at him happily, excitedly, as if he had just given her the best present in the world. Well, perhaps it was. He recalled how eager he'd been to have Steve show him the ropes after the first time he'd gone with him to fly hawks. Nothing, but nothing, would have made him happier.

"So will we go tomorrow morning?"

"Not tomorrow," he said before draining his wineglass. "I have to drive into town early." He had to call the Catalina-Pacific administrator and let her know that he still wanted his mother to be admitted, and he needed to call Martin before Martin made good on his threat to show up here.

Dana looked disconcerted. "I thought you flew them every day."

"I'll be flying them the day after. You can go with me then." He tore a bit of bread off the loaf and buttered it.

"I'm so glad you're going to let me," she said. In that moment she again reminded him of his lost love from fourth grade, Francesca Sorisi. Maybe the thing he had liked about Francesca wasn't the way she looked, which reminded him of Dana, but her unbridled enthusiasm in all things. Dana's enthusiasm was much like Francesca's, at least in the case of flying the hawks.

"Why are you looking at me like that?" she said, cocking her head sideways in a way that he was learning was characteristic of her.

"Was I?" he said.

She shrugged lightly. "I thought so. Perhaps I was mistaken."

"You remind me of somebody," he said. He popped the rest of the bread in his mouth.

Dana stood up abruptly. If he wasn't mistaken, the color had drained out of her face.

She fiddled with the timer on the kitchen counter. This didn't make a whole lot of sense, since nothing was cooking anymore, especially since Dana then opened a cabinet door and shoved the timer inside. It made even less sense when he saw that the cabinet held a supply of canned goods, not utensils or devices like timers.

She didn't ask him whom he thought she resembled. But seeing her confusion or embarrassment, or whatever it was, made him wonder what her reaction would be if he told her. It wasn't that he thought there was any chance that Dana was Francesca Sorisi. He'd heard from someone years later that Francesca had moved permanently to Italy with her father after her parents divorced, and by this time she was presumably married to a nice Italian man and had several children.

"You remind me of my grade-school sweetheart," he said, watching through narrowed eyes as Dana's shoulders sagged in what he interpreted as relief.

"Is that so," she murmured. When she turned back around, her face was composed, but two red spots of color had appeared above her cheekbones.

"Something about the mouth and chin," he said. While he helped himself to more manicotti, he waited for her reaction.

"I see." A pause while she let this sink in, and then she sat down across from him again.

"Aren't you going to eat any more?"

"I've had enough. I try not to eat too much. None of this eating-for-two business for me."

"Mmm," he said. He let a few beats go by before asking, "When is your baby due, Dana?"

She sighed. "In December."

"You plan to stay here until then?"

She looked away. "I'll most likely leave earlier."

Conn waited for her to elaborate, but she didn't. So was she planning to leave in early December? November? When his plate was empty, she urged him to have more salad, but he couldn't have eaten another bite if his life depended on it.

"This food was wonderful," Conn told her. "A real treat." It was true.

She refused to let him help her with the dishes. Instead she stacked them in the sink and said she would put them in the dishwasher in the morning.

"I think it's cool enough for a fire tonight," he said. "Want me to build one?"

"I haven't had a fire in this fireplace yet. I don't even know how to build a fire. It would be nice if you'd show me how to start one."

He went out and got some logs from the woodpile behind the house and took his time building the fire. Dana watched him from the big green sprung-out easy chair on the other side of the room.

"I'll know how to do it next time," she said as he settled with his back against the couch.

"How is it that living in the frozen wastelands of the Midwest you never learned to build a fire in a fireplace?"

"We always had gas logs. My mother never liked fireplaces. They were messy and dirty, she said. She was a clean freak, and that's probably why my dad loved this place so much. When he was here he could grub around and not shave for days and build fires in the fireplace to his heart's content."

"Sounds good to me," he said. He had learned that he

liked living alone, but now, in this unimpressive but comfortable room, there was a coziness that he hadn't found in his house. Or maybe it wasn't the room. Maybe it was feeling connected to another person. To Dana.

She was gazing into the crackling flames. "You know, my father never even had a telephone installed here. He didn't want anyone to be able to contact him."

He turned to look at her. Her face was gilded by firelight, her expression ruminative. "You should have a phone, Dana," Conn said gently.

"I never seem to get around to ordering it. I suppose there's a waiting list."

"I could see about it. I need one, too." He hadn't thought so until today, when he'd received the letter from the administrator of Catalina-Pacific. In order to call the nursing facility, he'd have to use the phone in front of the Cougar Creek drugstore, where it was impossible to hold a private conversation. Ditto the call he planned to make to Martin Storrs. The idea of anyone who happened along hearing what he needed to say to these people was unappealing. He didn't like the townspeople knowing his business.

"When I first came here, I thought my cellular phone would work fine," Dana said. "Well, time for a reality check—I'm too far out of range here between the mesa and the hills." Once she had been so attached to her cell phone that it had seemed like an extra appendage.

"How about if I drop by the local phone company's office tomorrow and ask when they can install phones out here? I could report back to you. And I think you should have a phone in your car."

"No car phone, please. It probably wouldn't work any better than my cell phone. As for a phone for the house, sure, if you wouldn't mind asking about it, that will be fine. I'll be here all day. Painting the kitchen, if all goes well."

He frowned at her. "Are you sure you should be doing that?"

"I think it's okay. It's latex paint, I'll keep the windows open so there won't be any noxious fumes, and if I get tired, I'll stop and pick up where I left off tomorrow."

He rose to his feet. "Maybe I could help you," he suggested. Her eyes were the darkest blue, all pupil and very little iris. He saw the fire's twin reflections in their depths, and something more. Gratitude?

"That's not necessary, Conn." She placed her feet wide and levered herself upward. At one time he would have found such an awkward transition ungainly, but with Dana the maneuver took on a grace and charm all its own.

"If I'm able to help, I will. I think you should be more careful."

"You worry too much," she said. "Pregnancy is a perfectly normal state. People have babies all the time, and they work at ordinary jobs throughout their pregnancies, and they cook and clean and do all the things I do. I'm by no means unique."

"You don't have anyone around to look after you," he pointed out. "If something goes wrong, there's no one to call. And no way to call them."

"Nothing will go wrong," she said, and he detected a stubborn edge to her tone that reminded him of the day he'd found her on the trail trying to capture Demelza.

He thanked her again for the dinner, put on his jacket and walked to the door. She followed, and when he looked around for the last time, he thought how pretty she looked. He was sure she was unaware that she was so lovely with those wide blue eyes and that soft, reddish hair, and before he let himself out into the cool night air, he had the sudden impulse to kiss her on the lips.

But he didn't know how she would react to such a gesture, which seemed too forward under the circumstances, and so he didn't.

On the way home, through the dark night studded by a thousand stars shining down out of a clear sky, he wished he'd gone ahead and kissed her anyway.

He might as well stop deluding himself about why he hadn't. It wasn't that he was worried about her reaction. He'd never kissed a woman yet who had complained about it. His real concern was that kissing her would lead to a relationship, and he didn't want her to find out the truth about him.

He already knew what she thought about the *National Probe* and its ilk. He could just imagine what she'd say if she ever found out that he had, until six months ago, been the *National Probe*'s star investigative reporter.

DANA WOKE UP LATE the next morning. She lay in bed behind the curtain in the sleeping alcove and listened to the birds singing outside in the trees. Funny, but she hadn't ever been aware of birds that much before she came here, perhaps because in the city there wasn't so much variety. Here by her little creek, birdsong blended with the purling of the water over the rocks and the sighing of the wind in the trees to create a kind of music that spoke to something deep in her soul.

She thought about last night and how Conn had scarfed down the manicotti. He'd seemed so appreciative of the home-cooked meal, and yet she knew he cooked and did it well if the meat loaf she'd eaten at his place was any indication.

At least he seemed to have warmed to her. Her interest in the hawks was probably what accounted for that. She couldn't have expected him to have any other interest in her.

And yet—before he'd left last night, when they were standing by the door, his eyes had lingered with what she had thought at the time was longing on her lips. Just on her lips, but that was enough to engender a tension and excitement deep in the pit of her stomach. She was experienced enough to be able to tag this as a sexual feeling, which was ridiculous. There was no way she could be having sexual feelings for a man she'd only recently met, and anyway, it wasn't as if she expected him to be attracted to her.

She padded into the bathroom and turned on the shower. She let her nightgown fall away from her body as she stared in the mirror above the sink. She couldn't see the rise of her belly in the mirror, but her breasts were large and the nipples swollen and dark. Her body was preparing itself for childbirth.

Not lovemaking.

And so she might as well stop thinking indecent thoughts about Conn McTavish and face the fact that no man would want to make love to her for a long time. If ever.

WHEN CONN WALKED UP to the customer service desk at the phone company, the clock on the wall said nine o'clock. When he walked out, it was five minutes later. This was a pleasant surprise; after living in Los Angeles where everyone had to wait in line everywhere for everything, Conn still expected things in Cougar Creek to be difficult in that respect.

"I'll schedule installation for next Friday," said the gum-cracking young woman behind the customer service counter. "Will that be soon enough?"

It was so much sooner than he'd hoped that it was all Conn could do not to cheer. Next door was a store where he could buy phones, and he bought one for himself and one for Dana. The one for himself was ordinary beige, but he recalled that the paint she'd bought was a color called whisper blue, so he bought her a blue one.

After leaving the phone company, he stopped by the only public phone in town, which was located in a kiosk outside the only drugstore. He called his former boss first.

Martin Storrs was out of the office, said the person who answered. She was apparently someone new, someone he didn't know. "I can put you through to Mr. Storrs's voice mail if you like."

"That's fine," Conn said, and he left a message telling

Martin in no uncertain terms that he wasn't interested in working for the *Probe*. "Not now, not next week, not ever," he said firmly. That should settle the matter for good, he thought to himself.

When he phoned Catalina-Pacific, a sweet-voiced female picked up the phone on the other end of the line. "Catalina-Pacific, how may I direct your call?" she answered liltingly.

Conn asked to speak to the administrator of the home, and after an interval during which he was serenaded by a Chopin nocturne, someone came on the line and said, "Beverly Rencken."

This was the administrator, so Conn identified himself and told her that he was indeed interested in having his mother admitted to the facility as soon as possible.

"It will most likely be a couple more months, Mr. McTavish, but I can assure you that we are eager to have your mother at Catalina-Pacific. I'll transfer you to our admitting department, and they'll take your financial data so that we can move forward. And, Mr. McTavish, we're so glad you have chosen Catalina-Pacific for someone as dear to you as your mother clearly is."

More Chopin, and he was transferred to a John Ayalla in admitting. "Of course we'll need a deposit from you," the man told him.

"Of course," Conn replied.

Ayalla named a figure that was higher than Conn had anticipated. "Excuse me?" Conn said. He thought that perhaps the family of four that was noisily erupting from the drugstore behind him had caused him to misunderstand the figure.

But when Ayalla repeated the amount he had quoted in the first place, Conn was nonplussed.

"And the monthly fee?" he inquired, multiplying numbers rapidly in his head.

The monthly fee was exorbitant. When Conn expressed surprise, Ayalla adopted an overly patient tone and explained that since Conn had first added his mother's name to the waiting list for Catalina-Pacific, operating costs had risen across the board. "In addition, we offer the very best in nursing care to all our patients," he told Conn. "In order to do that, we must pay our employees the highest salaries. I'm sure you understand."

When Conn hung up the phone, he stood for a moment at the telephone kiosk fighting shock and dismay. Underlying those emotions was the fact that he was determined that his mother would have the finest care available. Gladys McTavish should want for nothing as long as she lived.

But now that he knew how much it was going to cost to maintain his mother at the new facility, Conn doubted seriously that he could afford it.

DANA WAS WORKING on the front porch when Conn drove up in his truck, and she saw right away that he was in a bad mood. The slump of his shoulders, the way he planted his boots along the walkway as he trod his way up the path—these nonverbal clues told her a lot about his frame of mind even though she didn't know him all that well.

She stopped stirring the paint and waited with hands on her hips as he approached. Today he wore jeans and a red-and-black-checked wool shirt over a T-shirt. He was better looking than a man had a right to be—so handsome that he made her head spin.

"Good morning," she called, telling herself that she should be used to the way he looked by this time.

"Good morning," he replied, not smiling. He took the porch steps two at a time and stood in front of her on the layer of newspapers she'd spread under the folding table that she was using as Paint Central. She'd arranged the paint and the brushes and roller pans and rollers in neat lines preparatory to starting the job.

Conn carried a bag, and now he took a box out. "This is for you. Your new phone."

"I didn't expect—" she began, but Conn interrupted.

"I know you didn't, but accept it as a hostess gift. That was a great dinner last night."

The phone was pale blue, almost gray. "It will match my decor, such as it is," she said.

"The good news is that I've arranged for phone service for both of us. Someone will be out to install phone jacks next Friday and turn on the phones."

"That's good."

"I feel as if I'm opening a Pandora's box by getting a phone, but it only makes good sense. I can't go on using the one outside the drugstore every time I have to call someone."

Dana wondered who it was that Conn needed to call. His mother, perhaps, if she was able to talk. His friend Steve, who was in the hospital.

"Here, why don't you let me stir while you slide a roller cover on the roller?"

"I didn't really expect you to help," she objected as he reached for the paint stirrer.

"I'd feel pretty bad if you fell off a ladder or something while you were painting. I can do the high spots, you can do the low."

Whatever had been on his mind when he first drove up seemed to have receded to a place of less importance. Conn concentrated on his stirring. He still looked serious, though. Too serious to her way of thinking.

"Are we painting the kitchen today?" he asked.

"No, the living room. I chose this color because I thought it would blend with the gray of the rock fireplace."

Inside, she had set up a stepladder in one corner, and she had pushed the furniture to the middle of the living room before arraying drop cloths around the edges. "You should have let me help you with that," he said sternly when he saw what she'd done, but she said, "It's not heavy furniture. No big deal."

She thought she caught him rolling his eyes as he mounted the ladder, but she wasn't sure.

Conn painted around the trim while Dana wielded a roller on the other side of the room. At first they worked mostly in silence. Dana didn't want to chatter—considering his low spirits, she didn't want to make a nuisance of herself. She appreciated his help. If he hadn't shown up, she knew she'd be looking at two days' work, probably three, and it was important to her to get the room painted in a pleasant, restful color. Her father had, for some unfathomable reason, painted the room a deep, bilious green. Not hunter, not forest, but bilious.

"I like the color you've chosen," Conn said.

She smiled over at him and dipped her roller in the paint again, carefully rolling off the excess. "It reminds me of the color of my room when I was a kid. I hope the blue will bring the outdoors in. The sky, I mean."

"It'll do that, I think," he said, stepping down from the ladder and standing back to see what she'd accomplished.

She finished what she was doing and joined him to appraise their work. "It looks the way I hoped it would," she said in satisfaction.

Their shoulders brushed as they each returned to their own side of the room. Conn climbed the ladder, and Dana began to touch up a few spots where she'd rolled the paint on too lightly.

"You said this color reminds you of your room when you were a kid. Was that a happy time for you?"

"Mostly. I wished I'd had brothers and sisters so I wouldn't be so lonely, but my mom and dad both adored me and let me know it. I think I felt really secure as a child because of that."

"Letting a child know it's loved is the greatest gift a parent can give," Conn said thoughtfully.

"Sounds like you know something about that," Dana prompted. She left her comment right where it was, hoping he'd pick up on it.

"My mother was as close to a saint as you can get." Conn came down from the ladder and moved it over a couple of feet before climbing back up. "She worked at a job she hated so I could go to the best schools."

"What kind of work did she do?"

"She was a mill worker in one of the biggest textile mills in the South. It was dirty work, hard work, but she never complained. At least, not to me."

The catch in his voice, which she almost didn't detect, made Dana swivel her head to look at him. He was working along the ceiling, cutting in the paint between ceiling and wall, and he was concentrating on keeping his hand steady.

"How did you find out she had Alzheimer's, Conn?" she asked.

"She had moved out to L.A. to be near me, and she kept forgetting where things were. That went on for months, but it seemed normal to have lost track of things that might have been packed. It wasn't until I flew her dearest friend from our hometown out to see her that I realized the problem was more serious. When Ruth had confirmed she was coming, I asked Mom one night when I was there for dinner if she was looking forward to Ruth's visit. Mom said, 'Ruth who?' She clearly had no idea who I was talking about."

"That sounds awful," Dana said. It had been terrible when her own mother and father had died in such a short period of time, but she couldn't imagine the horror of losing a parent in the manner that Conn was describing.

"I got her the best medical help I could, but Mom deteriorated rapidly, and there was nothing anyone could do."

"I'm so sorry, Conn." It was all she could think of to say.

"So am I, but I've accepted it. I only wish I..." He stopped, seeming to think better of what he'd been about to say.

When he didn't seem inclined to pick up where he left off, Dana set her roller in the pan and stretched. "I don't know about you, but I could eat something. Maybe some of the manicotti from last night? Heated up?"

"Hey, that would be great," Conn said. He smiled at her

from the top of the ladder, and she went into the kitchen.
All the while she was reheating the manicotti, she thought
about Conn and his reluctance to say much about his personal life. She could relate. She certainly didn't want to
talk about her personal life, either. At the same time, it was
difficult not to discuss what normal people usually discussed.

At Conn's suggestion, since the sun was high in the sky
and it had turned into an unseasonably warm day, they took
their plates down by the creek and sat on a large stone on
the bank beneath a black walnut tree. Dana listened to the
hum of a bee on the opposite side of the creek, and they
watched as a large fish—Conn thought it was a crappie—
chased away some minnows in the shallows below them.
A couple of blue jays chattered in a nearby clump of pines.

It seemed like a bold thing to say, but the sunshine and
the purling water had lulled her into a sense of relaxation.
"Haven't you met some people around here since you arrived, Conn? You seem like such a loner." Like me, she
added mentally.

He didn't seem annoyed by her question. "I've met people, sure. No one with whom I have much in common."
His eyes met hers with dawning comprehension. "Do you
mean women?"

She ducked her head and chased a bit of pasta around
her plate with her fork. "No, that's not what I meant. Not
at all." At the same time she realized that maybe she had.

"There hasn't been a woman in my life for a long time.
The whole time I lived in L.A., I played the field. I had no
interest in settling down."

"Mmm," she said noncommittally. If he had come to
Cougar Creek to get over a lost love, he wasn't about to
admit it. But somehow she didn't think that was why he
was here.

"Well, I'd better get back to work," he said. "We might
as well finish up as fast as we can."

"Might as well," Dana agreed. It surprised her when he

gave her a hand up off the rock, but then again, it didn't. He was proving to be a thoughtful guy.

A thoughtful guy who didn't give too much away. But that was all right, because she didn't, either.

CONN COULDN'T HELP GRINNING to himself as he drove home late that afternoon. Dana and her questions, which were designed to find out if there was a woman in his life, were so transparent.

He turned the radio in the truck up loud, thinking about tomorrow morning when he and Dana would go to Shale Flats. He was looking forward to it more than he could have imagined. The physical activity of painting had done him a lot of good, bummed out as he'd been over what Catalina-Pacific was going to cost. He had some time to figure out how to scrape up the money, and Dana was proving to be a good diversion.

When he drove up to his house, his mind was on the hawks and which one he'd allow Dana to fly all by herself. So when he saw the draperies on the front window were open, he did a double take. He had closed them earlier as he always did before he left the house.

He had learned early in his days as an investigative reporter that he couldn't be too careful. He never knew when someone might take it into his head to get even for a story he had written. He stepped down from the truck cautiously, unsure whether to call out a warning or simply to enter.

Then his former boss, Martin Storrs, beer in hand and wearing an incongruous felt cowboy hat, sauntered out from behind the house and greeted him with a wide, expansive smile.

Chapter Five

"You really shouldn't leave your door open for anyone who happens along," Martin told him.

"In this part of the country, no one 'happens' along." He bounded forward, glad to see Martin despite all that had happened when he left the *Probe*. "How did you get all the way out here, anyway?" He saw no sign of a rental car.

"Kid by the name of Billy Wayne. Hair purple on one side, orange on the other. Nice kid, though, and he seemed interested in the birds. He says he's the librarian's nephew." They shook hands, and Martin clapped him on the back. "I warned you that I'd come scouting for you if I didn't hear from you," the older man said.

"I didn't receive your letter until yesterday," Conn told him.

"I mailed it over a week ago."

"Well," Conn said sheepishly, "I've only been picking my mail up at the post office once a week."

"You mean there's no home delivery here in Hicksville, Arizona?"

"The Cougar Creek natives would not appreciate your rechristening their town. And no, there's no home mail delivery in Cougar Creek and environs. Say, Martin, you look great." Except for the cowboy hat, which was entirely out of character for the man, but Conn didn't say that. His former boss had lost ten pounds or so and was dressed casually in a way he had never dressed for the office, where he had always maintained a certain formality.

"Yeah, well, I bought some new clothes after they insisted on changing the dress code. At the *Probe* these days, we don't have casual Fridays. We have free beer Fridays and casual Mondays, Tuesdays, Wednesdays and Thursdays. That's another reason I think you'll enjoy coming back to work. Say, do you like the hat?"

"Trust me, Martin, it's not you." Conn held the door open, and Martin preceded him into the house. He saw that Martin had deposited a brown canvas duffel in the middle of the living room floor. "You're planning on staying awhile?"

Martin tossed the hat over the elk antlers mounted on the wall. "I thought I'd get in some R and R. Maybe you could let me watch you do whatever it is that you do with those birds."

This statement caught Conn in the middle of removing a beer from the refrigerator. He thought about Dana and taking her with him to Shale Flats tomorrow. Did Martin's presence mean their date was scrubbed?

Before he could answer, Martin rocked back on his heels and studied the books in one of the tall bookcases on either side of the fireplace. "You've got some good reading matter to keep you company."

"You're welcome to read any of it. Much of it was Steve's, and he left it here. I brought some of it from my place in L.A."

"You still own the apartment in Marina Del Rey?"

"I kept it, sure." It was an expensive place to allow to sit vacant, and eventually he'd have to figure out what to do with it.

"Good. Glad to hear you kept it." There was no mistaking Martin's meaning, that since Conn still had a place to live on the coast, his return to the tabloid would be that much simpler.

"Apparently you haven't checked your telephone messages at work," Conn said.

Martin snorted. "In case you didn't notice, there's no phone in this house, so I could hardly call the office when I arrived. I refuse to carry one of those chirping wireless phones the size of a matchbox, it would drive me nuts. I suppose I should have stopped in town and called from someplace, but I was in a hurry to get here." He looked around at the sparse furnishings and added, "God only knows why."

So Martin didn't know that Conn had called and told him that he wouldn't return to work at the *Probe*. What had his message said? Oh yes. He had told Martin, "Not now, not next week, not ever."

But he had made that statement before he knew how much it was going to cost to install his mother at Catalina-Pacific.

THE NEXT MORNING when Dana woke up it was raining. Not a major storm like the one on the night she had spent at Conn's, but a slow drizzle. Although Dana had no access to weather reports, she thought the rain might herald a cold front moving through the area. She was sure Conn wouldn't fly the hawks in this weather.

He stopped by her cabin at the agreed-upon time, dodging between the drops and stomping the mud off his feet on the porch. She opened the door to him, expecting him to come in, but he shook his head.

"No, I can't stay. I wanted to let you know that we won't be going to Shale Flats today."

"What about tomorrow?"

To her surprise Conn shook his head again. "Not tomorrow."

This stunned her so much that she didn't know what to say. Disappointment rushed in when his face took on a forbidding expression that brooked no protest, allowed no questions.

He took in her crestfallen face, and an emotion flickered behind his eyes for a moment. But he didn't say anything to soften the blow of her disappointment.

He lifted a shoulder and let it fall, almost carelessly. She didn't know what to make of that.

He tightened his lips but offered no further explanation. "See you," he said, and with that he was backing away, then running through the raindrops to his truck.

Bewildered, Dana watched as Conn's truck traversed the ruts toward the road, its exhaust plume trailing behind.

Before he rounded the curve, she thought she made out another person in the truck sitting next to Conn.

Another person? What was that all about? She'd thought Conn had canceled because of the rain, but maybe there was more to it than that.

Her spirits tumbling, she went back inside, facing another long day of counted cross-stitch.

"So," MARTIN SAID cheerfully as he propped his feet on a crate he'd dragged in from the mews and pressed into use as an ottoman. "You given any thought to coming back to the *Probe?*"

Conn let out an impatient huff of breath and stared at the rain steadily drumming against the windowpane. "Not much," he said. It wasn't true. He'd thought about it much too much, ever since two days before when Martin had shown up at his house.

"So what are you doing to make a living? Freelancing?"

Conn thought guiltily about his laptop and how he hadn't even booted it up once in the months since he'd arrived. "Some," he said.

"Jim Menoch asked me if you were writing. He's still over at *Nation's Green,*" Martin said, naming a prominent nature magazine. "You might try sending him a piece or two."

"I might," Conn said noncommittally.

"I read some of those extracurricular things you used to

write years ago when we were both working at *Newsweek*,'' Martin said.

Conn scoffed at this. "I hardly remember them at all." Conn vaguely recalled hammering out a few nature articles and some essays that had eventually been published in a couple of journals, one of them edited by Jim Menoch. "Most of them are still unpublished," he added.

Martin pursed his lips judiciously. "No reason why you couldn't polish them up."

Conn tried to remember if those pieces he'd written were actually any good. They had been so far off the hard news track that they hadn't seemed important at the time. He'd virtually blown off a couple of magazine editors who had called him at *Newsweek* saying they wanted to see more, so maybe the articles had been better than he thought. One of the published pieces had been about an endangered species of fish in North Carolina, and it had drawn raves from environmentalists. He'd been surprised, considering how difficult it had been to make the subject interesting, when it was, well, boring to most people including himself. He'd enjoyed the challenge, though.

"I'd never win a Pulitzer writing stuff about the environment," Conn said. It had been his goal once—a Pulitzer Prize in journalism. If he hadn't quit the *Newsweek* staff in a snit over story credits, he could have been a contender. But he'd been younger then, and he had been half-crazed with loss. Add to that the problem that during the *Newsweek* years, he'd waxed arrogant and cynical. He'd thought he had the world by the tail in those days, and it had been a rude awakening to find out that he hadn't.

Martin studied him seriously. "Listen, Conn, a Pulitzer isn't everything. You don't have to beat yourself up over the road not taken."

Conn laughed ruefully. "Is that what I'm doing?"

"Damn right. I can see it in your eyes. There isn't one of us in this business who didn't have his eyes on the high road, but let's face it, there aren't enough golden rings out there to go around, and I've learned not to look back. Most days it's enough to get paid for typing one word in front of another and coming up with the kind of stuff people like to read.''

"I got burned out, Martin."

Martin eyed Conn meaningfully. "There's no such thing as burnout, my friend."

"You couldn't prove it by me," Conn shot back.

"You're a good writer."

"*Was* a good writer."

"You've still got what it takes."

"You need ambition and incentive and the fire in your gut. You need passion. I don't have that anymore." Conn watched Martin for his reaction, which was instantaneous.

"You don't lose talent, man!"

"That's what you said when you rescued me after the *Newsweek* debacle," Conn retorted.

"I didn't rescue you after you left *Newsweek*. You rescued yourself."

Conn recalled the sleepless nights, the consuming regrets about quitting a job that any reporter would covet. "I would have been out pounding the pavement looking for another job if you hadn't snapped me up and hauled me kicking and screaming to the *Probe*."

Martin thought this over. "And because you've worked there, because you know the ropes, I'm sure you understand that the *Probe*'s not a bad place to work, especially now. That's what I told you then, and I'm telling you again. A regular paycheck, a great retirement plan, stock options—"

"I know, Martin." Conn waved the words away.

"I need you at the *Probe* as much as I ever did."

"Ahh, Martin, I doubt that I'd fit in anymore. If I ever did."

"You were the best investigative guy I ever had on my team. But that's not the kind of job I have in mind for you this time around."

This was a surprise. "So what else is there?"

"Bentley Howser is retiring."

"Bentley Howser! The celebrity circuit?" Conn was astounded that Martin would even suggest that particular job to him. Bentley wrote straight gossip laced with a dash of syrupy and mostly phony goodwill. In Conn's opinion, the celebrity column was about as low as you could go at the *Probe,* and that was really saying something.

"You'd be a fantastic celeb reporter," Martin said defensively. "Get you out of the rat race."

Conn took a slow swig of beer, let it slide down his throat. "Wrong. It would only be a different kind of rat."

"The job has its perks. Expense account, the stars you'd meet."

The celebrity circuit! Hobnobbing with insufferable Hollywood types! Eating at the restaurants where he'd be most likely to run into movie and television stars! Escorting the trendiest blond bimbos to all the "in" nightspots in hopes of gathering news nuggets for next week's *Probe!*

"When is Bentley retiring?" Conn asked. Bentley Howser was in her late fifties and had long been promising to write a tell-all book about the celebrities she'd been chasing for the past twenty-five years.

"She's got a nibble from a publisher. More power to her. She knows more about Demi and Madonna and Bruce and Mel than anyone else in the world. If she can brew that into a bestseller, if she can cop a megabuck contract from some publisher, she has my blessings."

"And mine. But I'm not Bentley. I would never be able to hit the snide gossipy tone that made her famous." Conn wasn't sniping at her, far from it. He was obligated to Bentley for vigorously defending him when Martin fired him.

Martin smiled. "I want to put a different spin on our celebrity coverage. Make it more believable, more real, less tattletale. Your reputation as a solid reporter would move the column more toward center."

"My reputation as a solid reporter didn't help much when I laid claim to it before."

"That was different. In my opinion—"

"Which was wrong, Martin, you've got to see that."

"In my opinion you should have dug up the goods on Senator Bridlingame in any way necessary."

"Including pawing through his garbage at one o'clock in the morning," Conn said in disgust.

"The guy was aiding and abetting illegal Chinese arms dealers," snorted Martin.

"There were other ways to prove that."

"I didn't think so, not before the election." Martin leaned forward. "Sometimes you have to get down and dirty to find out what you want to know. In this case, it would have been for the good of the nation."

"Please, Martin, don't wax overly patriotic. And you did uncover the truth about Bill Bridlingame before the election."

"No thanks to you," Martin tossed back. One of the senator's junior aides had come forward with the information of the man's skullduggery on the eve of the election. Afterward, Bridlingame had been trounced at the polls.

Agitated, Conn stood up. He meant to offer Martin another beer, but Martin stood, too.

"Conn, Conn, I like you too much to argue about what happened. It's water over the dam, under the bridge, whatever. Let's start over. We want you back as part of the *National Probe* team."

"I've still got a sour taste in my mouth over the Bridlingame episode. You fired me, remember?"

Martin made a disparaging gesture, then clapped Conn on the back. "I'm ready to hire you back."

Playing for time, Conn walked to the refrigerator, had second thoughts and dumped his empty beer can in the trash. He wished to hell he were anywhere but here. He wished he were at Dana's cabin, sitting in front of the fire with her, admiring the paint job they'd done on the walls. He wondered what she was doing now, what she had been doing for the past couple of days while he'd been busy with Martin.

"Tell me you'll think about it, won't you, Conn?"

Conn wanted to close the subject once and for all. But then his gaze fell upon the letter from Catalina-Pacific tucked into the pocket of the jacket that hung on a hook beside the back door. Catalina-Pacific, the place he couldn't afford for his mother.

In hindsight, he supposed that he had been foolish to tie up most of his funds in this cabin in the wilderness, but his friend Steve had needed the money and he'd wanted to help him out. Also, Conn hadn't been thinking too clearly in the aftermath of the Senator Bridlingame debacle. All he'd wanted was to get out of L.A., and this place had provided the means to do it.

"Conn?" Martin gazed at him expectantly.

"Maybe I'll think about it," Conn said against his will.

"A maybe is good enough for now. Bentley says she won't leave until we find the perfect person to replace her."

The perfect person to replace Bentley was, in Martin's eyes, Conn. Otherwise his former boss and mentor wouldn't have trekked all the way to Arizona to see him. Conn had no doubt that, staunch ally that she was, the well-meaning Bentley had suggested him.

Taking the job at the *Probe* would solve the problem of how to finance Gladys's move to Catalina-Pacific. As Conn's eyes met Martin's, a bleak feeling settled around his heart.

"MY, YES, BUT THIS LOOKS mighty fine, and you finished it pretty fast, didn't you? Have you started on your second piece yet?" asked Esther Timms, the Cougar Creek librarian, in the grating voice that drove Dana nuts. She turned Dana's counted cross-stitch sampler this way and that, admiring it.

"Not yet, but I bought a new supply of embroidery floss

today at the dry goods store, so at least I haven't given up."

Esther's chins wobbled in mirthful good humor. "Oh, I don't figure you for a quitter, Dana. Have a chocolate, why don't you? They're real good."

Esther nudged the yellow box of candy toward her, but Dana shook her head. "I don't want to gain too much weight," she said. It wasn't easy to refuse, not when she could spot a chocolate-covered cherry nestled so beckoningly amid the empty paper frills of the already eaten.

Esther yanked the box back toward her and scooped up a Jordan almond. "Mmm. Suit yourself." She picked up her own counted cross-stitch and began stabbing away at it. "You might as well stop off at my nephew's shop and get him to frame it for you. Billy Wayne Sprockett's his name. He'll frame it for you real cheap."

"Oh, maybe I'll wait until I finish both pieces." Esther's eighteen-year-old nephew was the local jack-of-all-trades. According to her, he could fix tired washing machines, frame any kind of artwork and rid a house of varmints, all with equal aplomb. He also worked part-time as a mechanic at the local Conoco.

"Guess you've been busy fixing up Homer's old place, huh?" Esther asked encouragingly.

"I painted the living room," Dana offered. She set her books down on Esther's table and rubbed her arm. The books were heavy.

"Oh, honey, that's nice. What color did you pick?"

"It's called whisper blue."

"Well, I always say, if it's going to be blue, I'd rather have it whisper than shout." Esther chuckled at her own humor.

Dana managed a feeble grin.

"You ready to check those out?" Esther inclined her head in the direction of the books.

"I suppose so," she said. She really didn't feel like going back to the cabin, though she didn't have anyplace else to go. "But, um, I was wondering, Esther. Do you have any books on falconry?"

"Falconry? Nope, not a one. Sorry, but we don't have a lot of nonfiction here. Sounds like you must have met our resident falconer, Mr. McTavish. He's a mystery, that one." Esther took pride in knowing everything about everyone in Cougar Creek, but so far she had no clue that there was more to know about Dana, a fact for which Dana was fervently grateful.

"I'm slightly acquainted with Connor McTavish, yes. He's my only near neighbor." Dana hadn't seen Conn for several days, and it seemed like a very long time. She figured that he must still have company, and she'd wondered more than once if he had a female friend visiting him.

"Hmm. Seems like everybody's only slightly acquainted with that man, but hey, that's okay." Esther heaved herself up from her chair and, her slippered feet slapping on the tile floor, she made her way over to the desk. Dana followed, depositing the books on the wide green blotter. Esther laboriously checked out each book in turn, which meant stamping each one with a hand stamp. Automated equipment was not yet a feature of the Cougar Creek Library, nor would it be, according to Esther.

"There you go," Esther said cheerily. She slid the books across the desk to Dana. She added as if in afterthought, "You know, honey, you ought to stop in at Susie's Pow-wow Diner and get you some of their taco soup to take home for your dinner. It's real good, and they'll pack it up in a nice container so it'll still be hot when you get it home. That's what I'm going to do for dinner tonight." Esther lived above the library and didn't like to cook for one; she and Dana had discussed it before.

"Thank you, Esther, maybe I'll do that. Yes, I just might." She smiled at the librarian, who beamed. Esther might be a busybody, but she meant well.

One thing for sure, if Dana had wanted to get more friendly with the locals, they would have welcomed her with open arms, if Esther was any indication of their interest in strangers. After hanging around show business types, it was good to meet someone who was unfailingly forthright. But Dana didn't dare become close friends in Cougar Creek with Esther or anyone else. It was too dangerous, and she wouldn't be around long.

She jaywalked across the street to the diner and placed her order for the soup, waiting while the waitress spooned it into a takeout container. On a portable television set behind the counter, screen credits rolled for one of the shows at Dana's old network, GBN. She did a quick double take when she saw Erica Soderstrom listed as producer.

Producer? Erica had been an assistant's assistant when Dana was there. Erica Soderstrom, her rival for Philip's affections, clearly owed her meteoric rise at the network to something other than talent.

"Anything else, ma'am?" asked Susie, the part-Navajo owner, who manned the cash register.

Dana pulled herself back from her thoughts. She wasn't jealous of Erica, which surprised her. "No, nothing," she said distractedly. It was amazing that she couldn't summon up even the slightest bit of envy of Erica, whose life now seemed far removed from hers.

Susie was in the process of counting change into her hand when Conn McTavish approached the counter. Today he was wearing snug-fitting jeans and a dark-green sweater over a white T-shirt. He didn't seem to notice her until he sauntered up to the cashier's desk, and his face registered surprise when he realized who she was.

"Dana," he said, and he flashed her a smile that must have melted the hearts of countless women.

"Hello, Conn," she said, but despite her appreciation for his heartily male good looks, she was already angling so that she could get a good view of the person behind him. She had so convinced herself that Conn's companion of the last few days must be a woman that she was surprised to see that the person with him was decidedly male. He was a distinguished-looking man whose big-city patina fit him as comfortably as his impeccably pressed khakis and highly polished loafers. His clothes were so expensive and well coordinated that he looked like an ad in *GQ*. The ten-gallon hat he wore was at odds with his image and worn, she suspected, only for effect.

Conn cleared his throat. "Dana, this is my house guest, Martin Storrs. And Martin, Dana is my neighbor. She lives over by the creek."

Martin inclined his head in acknowledgment. "It must be your place that we stopped off in the rain the day after I arrived."

So it was this man she had seen as Conn drove away from the cabin! It hadn't been a woman in Conn's truck after all. Dana surprised herself by feeling a wash of relief so strong that it almost bowled her over.

Conn slapped a twenty-dollar bill down next to the cash register. "I haven't forgotten that we're going to fly the hawks again," he said to Dana.

"I hope not," Dana said. She was clutching the soup to her chest, feeling foolish for her fears about Conn's visitor. It seemed as if she couldn't stop smiling at Conn, couldn't stop grinning. "Well," she said. "I guess I'd better be going. I'm taking soup home for dinner, and there's no point in letting it get cold."

"No point at all," Conn agreed, and he smiled down at her. That smile infused her with a pleasure and delight that she couldn't fathom. Was she so lonely that she was grateful for any little crumb of interest? But this was more than a crumb. More like a bite, she'd say. And why did she care so much?

She'd better be on her way before she made a fool of herself. "Goodbye," she blurted hastily to Martin. "It was nice meeting you."

"Nice meeting you," he replied, looking slightly puzzled and more than a little perplexed. Did he recognize her? She wasn't sure. Maybe she was being too paranoid. No one in

Cougar Creek had made the connection between Day Quinlan and Dana Cantrell yet, not even Esther.

She edged past the two men, as well as three other customers waiting to pay their checks, before walking rapidly to her car. Once inside, she settled the container of soup so that it was not likely to spill on the rough road out of town and caught a glimpse of herself still grinning when she glanced in the rearview mirror.

Conn's visitor was a man! She still couldn't get over her relief. And, secondary in importance but still not negligible in the scheme of things, Conn had mentioned flying the hawks.

Though she wasn't in the mood to stop, she checked her box at the post office. Her mind was still focused on thoughts of flying the hawks again when she saw the letter from Philip. It had been forwarded to her from Chicago with her other mail.

It was the first time he had written her, or at least it was the first time a letter had been forwarded from him. She turned it over in her hands, thinking about the rage she still harbored in her heart after that last awful day, the day that should have been one of the happiest in her life.

The letter had been mailed in a General Broadcasting Network envelope, and it had probably been typed on a GBN letterhead by Philip's administrative assistant. A slow-burning rage burgeoned behind her eyes, and without a qualm she tore the letter to pieces and crumpled it into a ball, which she aimed toward the trash can outside the post office. It was a perfect slam-dunk shot.

So much for attempts by Philip to reach her. She never wanted to have anything to do with that self-serving jerk again.

It wasn't until she was lying in bed that night recalling the episode in the diner that she recalled how Martin had looked at her with slightly more interest than most people around here did. That fact raised danger signals, but she honestly hadn't felt he was any kind of a threat.

As she waited for sleep, she tried to remember Martin's last name. Scores? Shores? Storrs? Yes, that was it.

The name seemed vaguely familiar to her, but perhaps that was only because in her line of work she'd met a lot of people. She was quite sure she'd never seen this man before, and his name was probably similar to that of somebody she'd encountered once upon a time.

ON THE DAY the phone installer installed the phone line, Dana woke up feeling achy all over. After breakfast her throat started feeling scratchy. Once the man left, she nestled down into the cushions of her father's green chair, pulled a brightly patterned afghan over her knees and stared at the new phone. She had the urge to call someone, but she wasn't friendly with anyone but Esther, who, though she seemed to be a kind person, was immured in a world bound by books and needlework and good things to eat, scarcely needing or wanting anything else.

Dana, chafing to know when she could fly the hawks again, wanted to pick up the phone and call Conn. But she wouldn't feel right about it. She didn't know if he still had a houseguest, for one thing. For another, she thought if they were going to get together, Conn should make the first move.

It was like high school all over again, when her mother had cautioned her against calling boys first. "Let them call you," her mother had said. "If they have any interest, they will."

She knew now that she should have followed that advice with Philip, but she'd thought that since she was an adult, she wouldn't have to abide by her parents' rules anymore. She'd pursued him after she caught his eye at a network party. And Philip had responded, and she'd thought he loved her, but in the end he'd found someone else. After more than a year together, he'd taken up with Erica, who had known what Dana hadn't—that if you played hard to get, you'd eventually get your man.

Dana had known about Erica Soderstrom all along, had heard that Philip had the hots for her, knew that Erica kept pushing him away. She had thought that Erica was only a passing attraction and that their love—hers and Philip's— was safe. She and her friend Noelle had speculated whether Philip had any interest in Erica, and the answer had always been no. It was clear, Noelle said, that Philip only cared for Dana. Wasn't Dana smart and beautiful, and hadn't Philip said she was a tiger in bed? So how could Philip like someone like Erica, who didn't even encourage him?

Well, as it turned out, both Dana and Noelle had been wrong, wrong, wrong. Erica had capitulated in the end, and Philip must have felt something for her or he wouldn't have risked his relationship with Dana to do something so stupid as take Erica for a tumble. In Dana's bed, no less.

Dana would have liked to talk to Noelle. She wanted Noelle to know she was okay. But Noelle was a programming executive at the same network where Philip was a vice president, and what if after she and Dana talked, Noelle let down her guard, somehow gave away Dana's hiding place? Dana didn't want Philip to find her. She didn't want him to know about the baby until it had been born. Philip was too powerful, too manipulative and too controlling by far. He would want the baby, if only to keep his mother from badgering him about getting married. "Do you want to be the last of the Granthams?" Myrtis had said to her son more than once. "If you don't pass on the family name, it dies with you, and we're too proud a family to let that happen."

And Myrtis would insist on raising the child, imbuing it with all her outmoded notions about the importance of being a Chicago Grantham, descended from the Boston Granthams, don't you know, who were offshoots of the Cabots and the Lodges. Philip's son, and of course it would be a son because it had to carry on the family name, would be sent to some snobby Eastern prep school and expected to matriculate at Harvard. The child would be raised by servants, because it was a sure thing that Myrtis wasn't going to give up her extensive social life for a baby. As for Philip, once he had provided the world with little Philip Exton Grantham III, his responsibility would be over. He had never exhibited any real interest in children. No, once he'd provided Myrtis with a grandchild, he'd be on his merry way, chasing beautiful women from one bed to the other.

Before Dana would allow her baby to be brought up by someone else, particularly under the supervision of Myrtis and Philip, she'd die first.

The baby chose that time to send out one of those little rippling notices of its presence, and Dana laced her fingers over her abdomen. This was her way of hugging her child, and it would have to do until the baby made its appearance.

"I wonder if it's good that you seldom hear my voice," she said out loud to the baby. "I wonder if it would be better if I talked more."

She knew that babies could hear before they were born and that muffled tones penetrated her abdomen and the watery cradle where her son or daughter awaited being born. She knew that hearing her talk would accustom her baby to her voice.

"I'll never leave you in the care of someone who doesn't love you, never." For an answer, the baby kicked her hard in the stomach. "Now that's not nice," Dana chided, but she couldn't help laughing. This was going to be a feisty kid.

Her friend Noelle had borne two children and knew all about matters of pregnancy and childbirth, claiming to have had a difficult time with both. She would be a valuable resource, someone Dana could call up in the middle of the night if she had a question about the changes in her body.

But Noelle didn't know she was pregnant. No one from her former life did.

And her present life sometimes seemed very lonely.

She pictured Noelle in her office at the network, businesslike and impeccably groomed with her gleaming pale hair and conservatively applied makeup. Philip had always said that Noelle was the most beautiful of all Dana's friends. Dana remembered the many lunches that she and Noelle had shared. They'd gone skiing together once a year on a women-only jaunt to Vail, and they'd laughed and cried together time and time again throughout their seven-year friendship. In the course of that friendship they'd talked over the foibles of their various boyfriends, discussed the pros and cons of schools for Noelle's children and debated whether or not to get tattoos. Noelle had been against tattoos, but Dana had been in favor of the idea, if only to annoy Myrtis. Even though they never actually went through with getting them, it had been fun to speculate about Myrtis's reaction. Oh, Dana missed Noelle. She missed her very much.

Without giving herself time to think about it any longer, Dana scooped up the phone and punched in call-blocking numbers so that Noelle wouldn't be able to trace the call to Cougar Creek. The phone on the other end rang four times, five. Dana was ready to hang up when Noelle answered.

"Noelle?"

A stunned silence greeted her voice. Then, cautiously, "Day? Is that you?"

The name fell upon her ears as if it belonged to a stranger, as now it did. Dana no longer knew the woman who had been known to the world as Day Quinlan. She was Dana now, and perhaps that's who she would be for the rest of her life.

"It's me, Noelle."

Noelle sounded frantic. "Day, where are you? Are you okay? Everyone's been talking of nothing else, and Philip is—"

"I can't tell you where I am. I wanted you to know that I'm fine."

"Philip is so upset, Day. How could you run off like

that, how could you leave all of us wondering what on earth is wrong?"

"It's over with Philip, Noelle."

"Because of Erica?" Noelle asked cautiously.

"You could say that."

"Well, Erica's broken off her relationship with him."

So Philip had been dumped by the woman he'd dumped her for!

Noelle went on talking. "Erica and Myrtis didn't get along. I promised Philip that if I heard from you—"

"No!" Dana said sharply. "Please don't tell Philip I called. I don't want him to know anything about me."

"He loves you, Day. You know he does."

"Noelle, it doesn't matter. I don't love him. I called to talk to you. Can't we just chat?"

Noelle hesitated. "About what?"

"About the things we used to talk about. About cooking. Or…or…" For the life of her, Dana couldn't think of any other mutually acceptable topic. Work was out of the question, since Dana no longer worked. Clothes would seem to be a useless subject, since, of necessity, Dana's taste now ran to shapeless smocks while Noelle presumably was still into Hermes scarves and designer suits. Noelle's children? At the moment it was as if Dana had never known them, never met them. She couldn't even recall how old they were.

Noelle picked up the conversation, biting off her words sharply so that Dana knew right away that she was harboring resentment and possibly anger. "You disappear for a couple months after shocking everyone by walking off the set of your hit talk show and you want to talk about cooking?" Her voice rose on an incredulous note.

"I guess I do," Dana said.

Noelle laughed, sounding more like her own self. "Oh, Day, that's funny. I've missed you, you know. And so have Tricia and Raymond. The tabloids have been having a field day with this disappearance of yours. There's not a day that goes by that I don't hear from a reporter from *Celebrity World,* the *National Probe,* or *Tattletales Weekly.*''

All she needed was for some reporter to get wind of her whereabouts and she could kiss her privacy goodbye. Despite the warmth of Noelle's tone, a shiver of dismay ran up Dana's spine. The uneasy thought occurred to her that she might not be able to trust Noelle the way she once did. "Don't tell Tricia and Raymond I called, okay? And please, please, Noelle, don't give the tabloids anything to work with."

"I won't leak even the slightest crumb to the tabloids, but not tell Tricia and Raymond? They'll want to know you're all right. Speculation is rife, Day. People say that you've got some awful wasting disease, that you're having a complete cosmetic surgery overhaul, that you've eloped with a sultan from an oil-rich island in the Indian Ocean. Which is it, huh?" Noelle was teasing now, and Dana smiled.

"You can cancel the disease, the surgery and, what was it? Oh yes, the sultan. I'll let you know in my own sweet time what's happening, but until then, you'll have to remain curious. And silent, Noelle. No talking."

"Well," Noelle said. She sounded dubious.

"Noelle? I thought you were my friend."

Noelle sighed. "I am. I'll keep it quiet, Day, if you'll let me hear from you from time to time."

"You got it, girl. Now I'd better hang up."

"I'm glad you called. You can't imagine how glad, Day. How about leaving me a number where you can be reached?"

Dana chose not to respond to this. "'Bye, Noelle," Dana murmured before she hung up.

She sat staring at the phone for a minute or two, tears misting her vision. God, she missed Noelle. They'd been best friends since Dana's show was picked up by the network, and their too-short contact only reminded Dana that she had chosen the hardest path of all. There had been valid reasons to choose self-exile over the other options, but even now she still had a hard time coming to terms with her choice.

Anyway, all that talking, short though the conversation had been, had made her throat feel raw. Dana wiped the tears from her face with the end of her sleeve, pulled the afghan up over her shoulders and closed her eyes.

The baby would be here in two more months. That was plenty of time for Dana to decide if she wanted to resume her former life with its in-your-face media attention or try something new.

CONN HAD TO FORCE HIMSELF not to depress the gas pedal all the way to the floor as he drove home to Cougar Creek after delivering Martin to the airport in Flagstaff. The city's traffic, its hustle, were anathema to him after these months spent in Cougar Creek. As the truck ate up the miles between there and Cougar Creek, he went over his last conversation with Martin in his mind.

"Please take my job offer seriously," Martin had said firmly in the few minutes between the boarding call and getting on the plane. "I hope you'll be thinking about it."

Conn hadn't been able to offer Martin much encouragement, but he also didn't close the door on the opportunity. And that's what the *Probe* job was—an opportunity that wouldn't benefit him at all but would certainly ensure his mother's well-being. Conn knew very well that his mother had never shirked, back in Clay Springs, South Carolina, when she'd had to do something unpleasant to improve his lot. So why was he balking?

Clay Springs had been a decent place to grow up. Conn had kept his same friends from kindergarten through middle school, and it was a typical small-town growing-up experience—roller skating on Saturday mornings with the gang and sneaking into the town's only movie theater most Friday nights. But, though she'd grown up there herself, Clay Springs had never been good enough for Gladys McTavish.

Conn had always assumed that he would go to work at Clay Mills, the town's only employer of any appreciable size, like almost everyone else did. True, a lucky few managed to secure employment elsewhere—in faraway Greenville, perhaps, or maybe Columbia.

Everyone in town knew that you could earn a decent living at Clay Mills. You just couldn't advance very far, the main reason being that the company was owned by the Clay family, and they produced lots of offspring. The sons and daughters of the owners grew up, graduated from exclusive private colleges and found positions as upper-level managers; middle managers were considered hired help and imported from elsewhere. Although they were all college educated, there wasn't much chance for a middle manager to progress past that level unless he happened to get lucky and marry a Clay. And as far as being a "linthead," which was the pejorative term reserved for the hourly workers, including Gladys McTavish, his mother soundly vetoed that idea for her only child.

"Son, you're as good as any Clay and as smart," his mother had declared one day when Conn was twelve. "You're going to go to the best college. Not the best college I can afford, Conn, but the best college, period. Someplace where you can rub elbows with the Clay kids."

It hadn't escaped Conn's notice that his mother had scrimped and saved all her life. Instead of shopping at the local Belk store like everyone else in town, she had replenished her meager wardrobe from the racks at Goodwill and at the Salvation Army Thrift Store two towns over. Shopping thirty miles away from Clay Springs meant, Gladys explained, that no one would see her buying others' cast-offs. But for him, for Conn, Gladys had bought the best—new Dockers and Levi's from Belk.

In the eighth grade, when lavish brochures from prep schools began to turn up regularly in their mail, Conn had been mystified as to their purpose until his mother told him that she was planning to send him to Woodfield Hills Academy, a private prep school in Virginia.

"But I want to go to Clay Springs High!" he had said, devastated to think that he wouldn't be joining his friends there the following fall.

"And grow up and work in a cotton mill? I don't think so," Gladys had huffed indignantly. She'd gone strangely quiet after that exchange, and of course Conn couldn't have known what a financial sacrifice it would be for her to send him to Woodfield Hills. He didn't understand, at age twelve, how preposterous her ambition was for a mill-worker. For someone who had spent her life servicing a loom in the mill, who came home covered with white lint every day, a private prep school should have been out of the question. Conn didn't find out until much later that Gladys had been shrewdly investing part of her meager salary and all of her overtime pay since he was a baby and had amassed a nest egg of amazing proportions.

Conn went to Woodfield Hills, all right, where he'd become friends with assorted teenagers from the Clay family, who were duly enrolled there at birth. If his wealthy schoolmates thought it odd that on holidays he went home to a weatherbeaten old house in the mill village while they returned to the sprawling elegant mansions where they had grown up, no one ever said.

At graduation from Woodfield Hills, Conn won a full scholarship to Princeton. "See you there," Rhett FitzAllen Clay had said offhandedly as they walked in procession out of Woodfield Hills' Wade Rhett Clay auditorium, named after Rhett's great-grandfather, a benefactor of the school. And Conn and Rhett Clay had been classmates for four years at Princeton, with Rhett giving Conn rides back to Clay Springs every Christmas and Easter vacation in whatever latest BMW model he happened to be driving.

Rhett FitzAllen Clay had recently been appointed president and CEO of Clay Mills. And Conn, who had once dreamed of winning a Pulitzer Prize in journalism, was currently unemployed.

Which brought him back to the main problem—sending Gladys to Catalina-Pacific. If there was a way to do it without returning to work at the *National Probe*, Conn sure would have liked to know what it was.

The dark outskirts of Cougar Creek were quiet. The town's only trailer park slid past in a blur of squatting single-wides and a sprinkling of satellite dishes a minute or so before the Welcome to Cougar Creek sign heralded his arrival in the town proper. If there had been a bar around, he would have stopped in for a couple of drinks, but there was no place like that. No naked dancing parties, no singles' clubs. He pulled up outside Susie's, thinking that he might stop in at the diner for a light meal, but for once no rusting pickups occupied the parking slots. He could see Susie inside polishing the Formica counter, and he figured that she wouldn't welcome somebody messing it up right before closing time. Down the street, he caught a glimpse through a dusty window of the town librarian sitting at the library's only table and reading a book.

Those were the sole signs of life in the town, and it was only eight o'clock in the evening. The town didn't even have a video rental place in case he'd had a TV, which he didn't. With a sigh, he pulled out of the parking place and, gunning his engine past the Conoco station, where a couple of young fellows were chilling out and shooting the breeze, Conn set his truck on a course for home.

Only he didn't go there. He found that without thinking about it, he had headed down the road that would take him to Dana's place.

I'll tell her we can fly the hawks tomorrow. He knew that stopping in to see her was silly, since, as of this morning, he had a phone and could telephone her more easily than go out of his way. For a moment he thought about backtracking and heading toward his own house, but then he decided against it.

He had this sudden irrational urge to see her. To fix his eyes upon her lovely face and drink in her beauty. He hadn't realized it before, but all the while Martin had been visiting, he had ached to see Dana, had missed her, had longed to hear her voice. And not on a telephone, either.

When he pulled to a stop in Dana's driveway, he noted that the cabin was dimly lit, and he sat for a moment in the truck debating whether or not to go to the door. Then he realized that she would have already heard and possibly seen his truck and that it would be awkward to explain later why he had driven up to her cabin and then left again. He even had an excuse for showing up, a book on falconry from his own extensive library on the subject. He'd stashed it in the truck after their first trip to Shale Flats together, and then Martin had arrived.

He paused for a moment on the shadowed porch. A coyote howled somewhere in the distance, a mournful lament. His knock on the door sounded hollow, and a cluster of dead leaves, driven by some stray remnant of a wind, flurried around his feet. He waited, didn't hear any movement within and began to feel alarmed. Shouldn't Dana have answered the door by now?

He knocked again, louder this time, and glanced at his watch. It was almost nine o'clock, not so late that Dana would have gone to bed. Or would she? He had no idea what her schedule was like.

He heard a rustle, and then the curtain at the window parted and he saw her peering out. Her face seemed two-dimensional behind the glass, a pale, startled oval parting the two sides of the curtain.

"It's me, Dana—Conn," he said.

She didn't smile, just let the curtain drop, and then he heard the *snick* of the lock as she unlatched the door. The door opened, and he shuffled from one foot to the other in front of her, feeling unaccountably out of place.

"I guess I could have called," he said by way of apology for interrupting her evening. "Now that we have phones."

"Oh, Conn," she said wanly, as if with great effort. Her voice sounded husky, weak, but she stood aside so he could enter.

"You weren't asleep, I hope?" he asked as she shut the door behind him.

She shook her head and put her hand to her throat. Her face was flushed.

"I didn't mean to wake you up. I thought it was early enough—hey, is everything all right?"

If he wasn't mistaken she swayed on her feet. Her hand went out, flailing empty air as she reached for support from the wall.

Conn caught her just before she hit the floor.

Chapter Six

When Dana opened her eyes, Philip was hovering over her, a concerned expression on his face, and for a moment she couldn't figure out where she was.

But it wasn't Philip. It was Conn, and she was at the cabin in Arizona, lying on the couch.

"What happened?" she said woozily. Her voice sounded like a rusty hinge, and her throat was on fire. Conn was regarding her with concern, and the sight of him both reassured and, for some reason, annoyed her.

"You answered the door and were so overwhelmed to see me that you keeled over in a dead faint," he said. "What's going on? It's not the baby, is it?"

Conn's tone, though Dana could tell he was attempting to be calm, was threaded through with worry. She stopped being annoyed and started to feel grateful. She, who had been only too aware this evening that she had no one, was not about to throw away a human being who was willing to expend time and effort on her.

"Not the baby. My throat hurts," she said, wrapping her arms around her swollen belly to reassure herself that everything was okay. The baby aimed a few reassuring thumps at her pelvic bone, which couldn't help but make her wince.

"It *is* the baby, isn't it?" Conn said, kneeling at her side. "I'd better call a doctor. Do you *have* a doctor here?"

Dana struggled to prop herself up on her elbows. "I swear it's not the baby. Just my throat. I see an obstetrician in Flagstaff, but I don't have a doctor in Cougar Creek. Please, try not to make me talk." Her teeth began to chatter.

Conn laid a cool hand against her hot forehead. "You're burning up. Do you have a thermometer? Oh, don't talk— I forgot. I'll look around, see what I can find."

Dana fell back against the couch pillows and commenced shivering. When Conn came back with a thermometer, which he seemed to have found in a first-aid kit she didn't even know she had, he sent her a sharp look.

"You're cold. Open your mouth like a good girl, and while we're waiting for the thermometer to register, I'll warm this place up." He went to the wall heater and switched it on before assembling tinder, kindling, and logs for the fireplace.

"Matches?"

She pointed to a small redwood box on the mantel. He found a match and lit it, bending to touch it to the tinder. The flame flared, caught. He stood up again, unmistakable signs of strain in the white lines around his mouth, before gently withdrawing the thermometer from between her lips. She was proud of herself for not biting it in half. He bent and studied it in the light from the nearby lamp.

"A hundred and one temperature," he said, looking none too happy about it. "No wonder you're feeling rotten."

She started to get up to retrieve the afghan from where it had fallen when she'd been awakened by Conn's knock on the door, but he rested a restraining hand on her shoulder. "What do you want? I'll get it for you."

She pointed to the afghan, and he went and brought it back, spreading it carefully over her legs. She closed her eyes, thinking that if she had her choice, she would choose to sleep for a couple of days at least. She would huddle in front of this warm fire, let this man take good care of her, and retreat into...

Conn shook her awake. "Dana! I asked you for your obstetrician's phone number."

She opened her eyes. "Did I sleep?" Now her voice was no more than a croak, and Conn said, "You started to doze, but I woke you up. Don't worry, I don't expect you to stay awake much longer. Just tell me where to find your doctor's number."

Her obstetrician was Dr. Tolliver Evans, and his office was in Flagstaff. She went for regular appointments, but her pregnancy had been uneventful from the first, and anyway, would you call an obstetrician for a sore throat? She didn't want to say all of this at the moment because it hurt too much to talk.

"Never mind, I'll find it." Conn strode to the small desk in the corner of the room. Suddenly Dana felt a stab of panic. If Conn found her little leather address book in the drawer, the one she'd brought with her from Chicago, he'd know who her friends were, would be able to guess where she had lived. Agitated, not wanting him to find it, she sat bolt upright. "Doctor—booklet," she croaked, pointing at the pile of papers on the corner of the desk, and he must have known what she meant because the next thing she knew he had picked up the brochure with a picture of a smiling baby on the front. Dana nodded vigorously. The booklet was a handout from her Dr. Evans, and his phone number was stamped on the back.

Conn found the number. "I'll call him," he said. He pulled the new phone toward him, tapped out a number. Dana closed her eyes while Conn dealt with the inevitable answering service. After outlining the situation to the answering clerk, he secured a promise for the doctor to call back and hung up.

"Well, that wasn't much help." He regarded Dana, a slight frown pleating his forehead. "Would you like anything? You look so weak." Conn eased down beside her on the couch, and she could smell the scent that she identified with him—leather, pine and wide-open spaces. She shook her head.

"I think I'll make you a cup of tea with honey. My mother always gave that to me when I had a sore throat."

Dana attempted a smile. Conn went into the kitchen and dug around in the cabinet under the counter for a teakettle. She wanted to tell him to look in the drawer under the stove, but her throat felt raw and fiery. She knew he would find the teakettle on his own, and eventually he did. She heard him running water in it, and soon he reappeared in the living room. He checked the fire, said that the logs were catching and stood watching her with his hands on his hips. "I wish that doctor would call back," he said, looking agitated.

If Dana hadn't known it would hurt too much, she would have chuckled at Conn's bewilderment. Here he was, so sure of himself, so in command of most situations, and he seemed to be thrown for a loop by a pregnant woman with a sore throat.

At that moment the telephone rang. Unaccustomed to that sound in this place, Dana was startled. Conn, however, strode across the room and scooped up the receiver.

He rapidly explained the situation to the person on the other end, presumably Dr. Evans. "Right," Conn said, and then, "Okay." He listened for a while longer. "I'll tell her. And thank you."

He turned to Dana. "Your doctor says you don't have to drive all the way to Flagstaff to see him. You should have a local doctor take a look at you, but don't try to talk anyone into prescribing medicine over the phone. You'll want a new doctor to understand that you're pregnant so he won't prescribe anything to hurt the baby. He said that you should take a couple of acetaminophen for the pain and get to a doctor first thing in the morning."

"Umm," was all Dana said.

The teakettle whistle blew, startling both of them. Conn went into the kitchen, and soon he came back with tea. She appreciated his pouring it into her favorite cup; it was one of the few feminine things about this place, a remnant of the set of dishes her mother had used when Dana was a child.

He gave her a pill, which she swallowed in a gulp. She drank the tea in little sips, barely able to force the warm liquid past her burning throat. Conn sat in the chair across from her, his forehead furrowed into a worried frown. "I don't like this. I don't like this at all."

She sent him a questioning look. He got up and paced from one end of the room to the other. "What if this is something more than a sore throat? Lots of illnesses start that way. What if it's scarlet fever? Some kind of strange southwestern rodent disease? And what's that other one? It has the name of a fruit." He looked distracted, and his hair, curved into loose waves across his forehead, stood up in front where he had run his fingers through it.

Despite her misery, a bubble of laughter welled up in Dana, and she smiled. "Lyme disease," she said, the words grating painfully.

"That's the one I mean, Lyme disease. How do you know that's not what this is?"

She shook her head and made a face.

"You don't think so? Well, I'm going to make sure you get to the doctor tomorrow morning, first thing."

She blinked at him.

"Well, what do you expect me to do? Let you drive into town when you've got a fever that makes you faint? Someone has to make sure you're okay, and I don't mind being that someone." He glared at her, and if she hadn't known better, she'd have thought he was angry. She tried to telegraph her gratitude to him, and perhaps he understood.

"You can't stay on that couch all night," he said after a time. "I'll help you to bed."

She must have looked alarmed, because he spoke swiftly to allay her fears. "I said I'd help you to bed. I didn't say I was going to bed, too."

She felt a blush spreading to the roots of her hair. She hadn't meant—well, she hadn't thought—but that was the thing. She *had* thought. The fact that he knew what she had been thinking didn't help her state of mind any.

He took the cup and saucer from her and disappeared into the kitchen. She heard him running water in the sink, then the ripping of a paper towel from the roll. His hands were still damp when he returned and pressed a hand to her forehead again.

"Still hot as blazes. Let me help you up." He bent and slid an arm around her shoulders. He levered her up from the couch so that she didn't have to go through the awful spraddling of her feet and knees that was the way her big belly required her to rise from a sitting position these days.

"Everything okay?" Conn asked anxiously.

All strength seemed to have left her legs, but she nodded. He kept a tight hold on her as she turned slowly and made her way toward the bathroom, conscious at every step of the bulk of her pregnancy.

Conn left her at the bathroom door. "If you have any problem, holler," he said as she closed it.

Dana knew he was standing right outside the door, and she wished he wouldn't. She gripped the edges of the bathroom sink and stared at herself in the mirror. Her face was red and puffy, her hair a careless tumble of red-gold. Her eyes were glassy, bright. She hated looking like this for Conn. She hated looking like this for anybody.

When she emerged from the bathroom, she saw that Conn had pulled aside the curtain concealing the sleeping alcove to expose the double bed behind it. There was a window above the bed, and its thin draperies were looped back to expose night-dark panes. Her reflection in them was wavery, watery. *Kind of like I feel,* Dana thought to herself.

She kicked off her shoes. Conn held her arm and eased her down on the bed, and she sat there looking at her bare feet. They had swollen with her pregnancy, and she realized glumly and irrelevantly that the toenails needed cutting.

Her stomach surged. She clamped her hands over her diaphragm, willing it to stop heaving.

"Dana? Are you all right?"

She shook her head. Her stomach continued to churn, and she tasted bile at the back of her throat. She wanted to die of embarrassment; it would be too humiliating to vomit in front of Conn.

His voice came to her as if from a long way away. "You look slightly green," he said. "You're not going to—"

"I might," she gasped. "I feel like I'm going to—"

"Wait," he said urgently and went running to the kitchen. He returned in record time with a small basin, which he thrust under her chin barely in time for her to upchuck in it.

Never mind the fever; never mind her wrenching stomach. She wanted to die right there and then of embarrassment.

Conn brought a cool washcloth and wiped her face, then a glass of water so she could rinse her mouth.

"Okay?"

She nodded, sure that nothing would ever be okay again. But she did feel slightly better now.

"If you think you're able, I'll draw the curtain while you put on your nightgown. Or whatever it is that you sleep in."

"A nightgown," she murmured. "It's hanging on a hook in the closet."

He went and got it. She avoided his eyes, not wanting to see his revulsion.

He pulled the curtain across the opening and went away, and she could hear him bringing in more logs from outside. She could see him, too, through the thin muslin curtain. It seemed like too much effort to shuck her clothes and pull on the gown, too much trouble. She'd rather watch Conn as he moved about, his outline blurred. He went into the kitchen, came out with a glass of water and stood sipping it as he stared into the fireplace.

Poor Conn. This was more than he had bargained for when he'd stopped by, she was sure.

"Dana? Everything okay?"

"Mmm-hmm." She unbuttoned her blouse and shrugged out of it, pulled off her slacks and slipped into her nightgown, a warm one with a high frilly collar and long sleeves. When Conn called to her, she was in bed with the covers pulled up to her chin.

"You can open the curtain," she said.

Conn pulled it back and peered down at her. "Anything you need?" He looked bemused.

She shook her head. "You probably don't know much about taking care of a pregnant woman."

He looked away, then back. His expression had changed. "As it happens, I do. My mother had a problem pregnancy when I was small. My father ditched us, so I took care of her. I was only four years old."

Her lips rounded into an *O*.

"So I'm not leaving you. I'll bed down on the couch for the night. Don't worry, I can find blankets if I need them. It's warm over by the fire." He started to pull the curtain across, but her hand stayed him.

"All right. I'll leave it open." He smiled down at her for a brief moment and went to sit in the green chair, picking up a book and riffling through it.

Dana curled up in a protective ball, her arms holding her swollen belly. The fire crackled and spit in the fireplace, and time stretched out so that Dana had no idea how much of it had passed.

After a while Conn got up to feed another log into the blaze. Dana's eyes had been closed, but she opened them when she heard the springs of the chair squeak, and she pillowed her cheek on her hands as she watched him move about. The firelight cast the planes of his face into shadow and picked out the blue-black highlights in his hair. He seemed quiet and reflective and oddly at ease in her house, although she thought he would probably rather be home.

She wondered how the hawks were, if anything was new with them. She wondered if Conn had thought about her at all during the time that his house guest was in residence. She wondered...

The next time she opened her eyes, Conn was staring at her from across the room. She shifted slightly in bed, felt the baby settle against her hipbone. Her throat still hurt, but the pain had dulled, probably because of the pills. Her stomach was only slightly queasy.

"Dana?" Conn stood and walked slowly to the bed.

"I'm okay," she said, her voice a mere whisper. Her throat didn't hurt as much if she whispered.

"What's wrong?"

She didn't want to explain about the baby and how sometimes its movement kept her awake at night, nor did she want to complain about her throat, since he already knew it hurt.

"Can't sleep," she said.

"Anything I can do?" His eyes were pools of deep concern.

She shook her head. Without saying anything more, he went away and brought a damp cloth. He bathed her face and arms, and the cool water felt good on her hot skin.

He left for a moment, came back. "When I was older, my mother sometimes liked me to read to her when she was sick," he said. He paused. "I brought you a book about falconry."

He must have been reading her mind. After all, she'd asked Esther for such a book earlier in the week.

"No, don't talk," he said comfortingly. "I'll go ahead and start with chapter one." He went back to the green chair and adjusted the reading lamp. She saw that he'd unbuttoned his shirt and pulled it out of his jeans, affording her a tantalizing view of a well-muscled torso. Lot of good that did her, she thought muzzily.

As he opened the book, Dana shoved a pillow under her stomach and tried to get more comfortable. No one had read to her since she was a little girl, and she'd almost forgotten how her father had introduced her to the classics—*Alice in Wonderland, Huckleberry Finn, Little Women.* She'd sat on his lap, and he'd always liked her to give him butterfly kisses—flutter her eyelashes against his cheek—when he finished the chapter for the night. She smiled at the memory.

Conn cleared his throat. *"The Joy of Falconry,"* he began, and his deep voice soothed her mind the way the honey in the tea had soothed her throat. He read with expression, his voice flowing around the syllables mellifluously, and she found the subject matter fascinating.

If she hadn't been sick, she would have treasured this moment.

But before Conn reached chapter two, Dana was asleep.

HE STOPPED READING out loud when he realized that she was sleeping. He stood, stretching out his muscles, thinking that he didn't mind being here. He might have, once. He had resented her when he first met her.

But now it was different. Her interest in his hobby had drawn him closer to her than he'd felt to anyone in a long time. And this bond, this attraction, was different from anything he'd felt before.

Women? Oh, he'd known women. Rosalia of the laughing dark eyes and long-flowing hair, who had loved him but eloped with a pilot for Mexicana Airlines. Ginger, a public relations flack for a movie studio, whom he had loved but who never loved him back. Carolee, who had short blond curls and breasts that exactly fit his hands. Kristyl, latter-day flower child, who had absconded to Idaho with his best CDs. Terri, his college sweetheart, now blithely traversing the country presenting seminars on personal improvement and dropping him post cards from places like Dubuque and Kenosha. And Lindsay, lost to him forever—but he would never stop loving her.

Except for Lindsay, he had never been touched to great

depths by any of them. But now here was Dana, who had eyes as blue as the bottom of the ocean on a sunny day and who shared his interest in his hawks. And about whom he knew very little other than the fact that she was alone and pregnant with someone else's child, not his.

He decided to check on her. It was dark in the alcove, so he went back and turned up the brightness of the bulb in the reading lamp by the chair. When he came back, he saw that her face was even more flushed. Her breathing seemed shallow, her chest barely rising and falling with each breath. When he touched her forehead, his fingertips felt seared by the heat, and he jerked them back abruptly. Bending over her in alarm, he touched her again. She was burning with fever.

It was like his mother when she became sick while she was pregnant. His mother had fallen ill one night, and he hadn't known what to do. After all, he had been only four.

Apprehension clamped around his heart like a vise. "Dana! Dana?" He knew he'd better wake her up, take her temperature again.

Her eyes opened groggily, seemed not to know him. Recognition flared after a moment or two, and she moaned.

"Your fever seems higher. I'd better find out what your temperature is." He went to get the thermometer and shook it down with a flick of the wrist. Not that he'd had all that much experience with these things, he thought uneasily.

"Open your mouth like a little bird," he instructed, and that elicited a slight smile. He slid the thermometer under her tongue, and she closed her mouth over it and shut her eyes.

While he was waiting for the thermometer to register, he went to the bookcase and looked for a medical guide of some kind. Even a first-aid book might help. But there was nothing.

When he checked the thermometer, he was stunned. Dana's temperature had risen to almost 103. He might not know much about these things, but he knew that such a high fever was dangerous, and he had no idea of its repercussions for a pregnant woman.

His mind raced. Here they were in the middle of nowhere, Dana was maybe seven months pregnant, and she was clearly very sick. The nearest hospital was many miles away. Outside, the wind howled.

He glanced at his watch. It was three o'clock in the morning. In his mind, it made no sense to call Dana's obstetrician in faraway Flagstaff. He'd have to tackle the answering service again before Dr. Evans would even return his call, and the obstetrician had, in effect, told him to take his business elsewhere, albeit in a kindly way. Conn knew a doctor in Cougar Creek, an elderly general practitioner who hung out at the Powwow Diner. Did he make house calls? That was anybody's guess.

Dana moaned, and he saw that she was trying to shift positions.

"Dana, you have a really high fever. I'm going to call the local doctor and see if I can talk him into coming out to see you."

She opened her eyes, and she looked scared when she saw his face. He was sure his expression registered his doubt and fear. She tried to sit up, and he thought that if her throat was closing, if she were actually have trouble breathing, perhaps he should prop her up on pillows. He brought a couple of throw pillows from the couch and placed them behind her head, and she tried to smile. Her lips were cracked, her eyes sunken.

"I think you'd better try to drink something," he said. "Do you think you can?"

Eyes closed again, she made a negligible motion with her head, and he didn't know if it meant yes or no. He went into the kitchen and poured some of the leftover tea in a glass with ice cubes. He thought that a cold drink would be better than a hot one if he were going to try to bring that fever down.

He raised the glass to her lips, and she managed several

swallows, but swallowing was painful for her. More worried than ever, he went to look up the local doctor's telephone number.

The man's name was Jeb Nofziger, and no one answered at either his home or office number. Conn ran a hand through his hair, trying to think, trying to remember what his mother used to do for a high fever. Once he had had some childhood illness—measles, he thought—that had struck suddenly with a very high fever, and his mother had given him three aspirin and sat him in a tub of tepid water to bring down the fever.

Was that the right thing to do for Dana? He didn't know. But he did remember that a person could go into convulsions if a fever got too high, and that would seem to be a serious complication indeed, especially if the patient were pregnant.

He stood for a moment staring down at her. She lay with her eyes closed, her chest barely rising and falling with each breath. The mound of the baby rounded the bedcovers over her abdomen, and Dana's fingers were interlaced protectively over it. A frightening sense of discovery welled up inside him as he stood there, a certain knowledge that he cared about this woman and what happened to her. From the first he had sensed a vulnerability in her, and even though she had tried to prove to him that she was capable of caring for herself, she could not manage alone in this circumstance. It was up to him to take care of her—and her unborn child.

He knelt beside her. "Dana, I want you to take another acetaminophen. Do you understand? We need to bring this fever down."

She opened her eyes and looked directly into his. He thought for a second or so that she was going to object, but all she did was nod an almost imperceptible yes. He went and shook the pill out of the bottle. She opened her mouth, and he put it on her tongue. Her hand trembled as she raised the glass to her lips, but she managed to swallow.

After she handed the glass back to him, she fell back against the pillows.

Conn went into the bathroom and turned on the water in the tub full force. The tub took a long time to fill, and he cursed the inefficiency of wells and water pumps in this place so far away from city conveniences. Finally, when the tub was full, he tested the water with his hand. It was too cold. He added some hot water to balance it. That would have to do.

He returned to her bedside and took her hand in his. "Dana, I want you to listen to me. We have to get this fever down, the sooner the better. Do you understand?"

She opened her eyes. In them he saw a bleak despair, and he saw that she understood how sick she was.

"I'm going to have to get you into a lukewarm bath. To bring the fever down."

As his words sunk in, despair was overtaken by disbelief. She closed her eyes again as if to shut him from view, which wouldn't do. It didn't help that he wasn't sure that he was doing the right thing. He didn't know anyone he could phone at three in the morning to ask this question; also, the Cougar Creek doctor hadn't called back.

He threw back the covers. "Put your arms around my neck, Dana," he told her. She twisted her head from side to side, and he didn't know if she was trying to tell him that she didn't want to get into the tub or didn't want him to take her out of the bed.

He wasn't about to let anything she did stop him from helping her. He took both her hands in his, placed them around his neck. She made a noise, but he couldn't tell whether it was meant to be protest or assent. He slid one arm under her shoulders and one beneath her legs. She was surprisingly light, even with the added weight of the baby. He tried not to look at the ripe curves of her breasts as they shifted under the thin white cotton nightgown she wore. He wasn't supposed to be relating to her as a man to a woman, only as a human to another human in dire need.

The bathroom was barely big enough for one person, much less two. He maneuvered her in through the door, and she opened her eyes wide.

She started to speak, but he said, "Hush. Try to relax. This will probably work, and then I can get you back to your nice warm bed." He sounded more confident than he felt.

Dana had removed one arm from around his neck and was plucking at the nightgown. He couldn't figure out if she meant to take it off or if she wanted him to leave it on, but he figured there was no time to waste with explaining either option. Instead of trying, he lowered her into the cool water. The nightgown billowed up, then settled down, clinging to her body as it became wet. Her breasts shone smooth and pink through the transparent cotton fabric, and so did her belly. If she was embarrassed at his scrutiny, she gave no sign.

Keeping one arm around her shoulders, he dampened a washcloth and sponged her face. Her eyes were open now, still sunken, still glittering with the heat of the fever. To distract her, he started to tell her about the effort he had made to contact the local doctor.

"It's a guy named Jeb Nofziger, I've met him once or twice at the Powwow Diner. If he calls back, don't worry, I won't leave you alone in the tub. I can bring the phone in here, tell him about your condition, and if you want you can speak to him."

Her eyes darted to him in alarm, and he knew she was telling him that her throat hurt too much to talk to anyone, even a doctor.

"You don't have to try to talk. I can convince the guy you're pretty sick. And don't worry—if I don't hear from him tonight, then I'll rustle him up in the morning. You'll be okay, Dana. I'll do everything I can to make sure of it."

She listened, bit her lip. Again that gesture, the weaving of her fingers across her swollen abdomen.

"The baby will be fine, too."

She nodded. "Kicking," she whispered, the words barely audible.

His gaze slid down to her belly. The wet gown was stretched tightly across it, and he was amazed to see a tiny ripple of the skin under the transparent fabric.

"See?" Dana asked him, and he nodded, dumbfounded.

"Do…do they all do that?" he blurted.

She attempted a thin smile and nodded yes.

"Sorry," he mumbled, recovering a bit from the astonishment of actually seeing evidence of a little arm or leg that wasn't actually born yet. "I didn't mean to make you talk."

She shook her head, and if he wasn't mistaken, there was a gleam of pride in her eyes. He took that to mean that Dana didn't mind his asking stupid questions and that she didn't mind him seeing what appeared to be something so intimate that only an expectant mother was ever privileged enough to see. And her doctor, of course, and the father of the child.

If the father was around. He wished he knew the circumstances of Dana's pregnancy, why there wasn't a man in evidence. But this was not the time to pursue that line of thought.

"Feeling any better?" he asked hopefully.

Dana nodded yes.

"Maybe the acetaminophen is working, and this bath, too," he said.

Her lips moved. "Maybe," she mouthed without sound.

Conn had no idea how long she should stay in the tub. Half an hour? More? He sponged her face again, and she gripped his arm. It wasn't a strong grip by any means, but to him it meant that she had some strength left.

"What do you want?" he asked.

She blew a strand of hair out of her eyes.

"Oh, I know—you'd like me to push your hair back." She nodded yes, and he brushed her hair off her hot face.

Her skin didn't seem as hot as before, though. He thought the bath was working.

He lifted water with the hand that wasn't supporting her back and sluiced it over her arms. He kept talking, not knowing what to say or how to say it.

"When you get well, we'll go fly the hawks again. Would you like that?"

Her eyes opened, communicated their interest without really smiling.

"We'll drive to Shale Flats early in the morning, and I'll start you out by letting you fly Demelza. You know, the kestrel that you found on the trail? She wasn't hurt that day at all, you know. Maybe a little frightened and confused by something. She flew away that day, flew away from me. My fault. I should have tied her to my wrist faster when I took her out of the cage."

Dana reached for the washcloth, wiped her own face.

"I think the book I brought last night will teach you a lot about falconry. When you're well enough to read it, I mean. And—"

He didn't know how long he went on talking. He chattered aimlessly, covering a range of topics until Dana put a finger to her lips. She didn't want him to talk anymore? He knew he'd been babbling, and maybe she was too sick to listen.

"I feel better now," she whispered. "Can you take my temperature?"

He reached for the thermometer, which he had left on the sink, and popped it into her mouth. When he removed it, he saw that her temperature had fallen to a hundred degrees.

"That's better," he said with satisfaction. "Only a hundred. What do you say we get you out of here?"

She nodded vigorously, and he reached over and pulled the plug up for the drain. "Hold on to me," he told her as the water began to swirl away, and she put one wet arm around his neck as he eased her to her feet in the tub.

But what to do with her now? She was standing there in a nightgown heavy with water, and the fabric was so fine and thin that it left nothing about her body a mystery. He could see it all—high, round breasts; swollen belly; underpants that did little to hide the nest of curls beneath.

"You can't wear that gown back to bed," he pointed out, hoping for some guidance here.

"Dry one. In the dresser," she whispered.

"I don't want to leave you. I can't have you falling and hitting your head or…or something."

"I won't," she said. "Legs are steady. I'll hold on." She grasped the towel holder over the tub for support.

He didn't like the idea of leaving her for even a few moments, but he knew it was necessary for her to get out of the wet gown. He draped a large towel around her and then went and opened every drawer in the dresser before he found a stack of gowns and pajamas in the bottom one. He chose one—it was pink flannel—and hurried back into the bathroom.

She was grimly hanging on to the towel bar, dripping water into the draining tub. She looked like a drowned rat—a drowned *pregnant* rat—but it was clear that she was a real trouper.

"Now how are we going to do this?" he asked her. His own take on this situation was Modesty Be Damned, but he didn't know how she would feel about that.

"Help me," she said.

He only needed her to ask once. He unbuttoned the neck of the gown she wore, discovered that it had a long concealed zipper in front, and, keeping his eyes averted, he peeled the wet fabric away from her body until it puddled around her feet in the now-empty tub. He handed her a dry towel and waited until she had dried herself as best she could, and then he held the pink flannel gown up and shimmied it over her head, pulling it down to cover the rest of her. If she was embarrassed, she didn't let him know.

And the odd thing was, he wasn't embarrassed, either.

He had thought he would find her misshapen body ugly or repulsive, but it wasn't at all. It struck him as a fine thing that women had the capability to carry a child within for the months it took to grow big enough to survive outside the womb, and it seemed like something miraculous to him, now that he was aware of how the body accommodated the changes of pregnancy. He had once thought that pregnant women were awkward and ungainly. But now he realized that carrying a child was one of the most graceful things, one of the most exalted things, a woman could do.

He helped her out of the tub and kept a tight hold on her while, with her slow gait, she made her way back to the bed. When she was tucked under the covers, her eyes held his for a long moment. "Thank you, Conn," she whispered, and gratitude shone from her eyes.

"You're welcome," he told her. "Now hush, and try to sleep."

She smiled through cracked lips. Bemused, wondering how he had become so nurturing, he found some petroleum jelly in an old jar in the bathroom cabinet and spread some of it on her lips with his finger. He had an idea that those lips would be soft and pliable when kissed. Before he had a chance to consider the ramifications of this discovery, she smiled, and he said, "Want me to leave the curtain open again?"

She nodded.

The idea of kissing her took root and grew in his overly fertile imagination. It might not be such a great idea to kiss her on the lips while she felt so sick. Still, he found himself wanting to lean over and kiss her chastely on the forehead, as if she were a little girl.

But he didn't. Because he was overly aware that Dana was no little girl. She was a mature woman. And she had stolen her way into a heart that he'd closed to all comers some time ago.

Chapter Seven

"Flu," said Jeb Nofziger. "I've seen a lot of it in the past two weeks. When the weather gets cooler, people get sick. You can count on it."

Dana perched on the doctor's examining table, and Conn had settled uncomfortably on a hard plastic chair in the corner, dwarfing it with his large frame.

"Plenty of liquids, here's a prescription. I'll let you know what the lab says about your strep test." Dr. Nofziger scooted on his wheeled stool to a desk where he scribbled a few lines on a prescription pad, tore it off and handed it to Dana.

"How about you? Got any symptoms?" He peered at Conn over the tops of his half-lens reading glasses.

"Nope," Conn said. "I hardly ever get the flu."

"Lucky guy. You ever figure out how other people could avoid getting sick, you could make a million dollars. Say, young lady, do you have someone who can stay with you? I don't like your being all the way out at the Cantrell place alone while you're pregnant."

"I'll be there," Conn said quickly.

The doctor blinked lashless blue eyes. "Oh. Good thing, that. Okay, any other problems, you call me. Got that?"

Both Dana and Conn nodded. Dr. Nofziger stood and headed for the door, his wispy stoop-shouldered figure made even more negligible by the huge white lab coat he wore. He half turned and waggled a finger. "Plenty of liquids. Don't forget. Can't get dehydrated." With that he was gone, the lab coat flapping behind him.

Dana and Conn stared at each other in the harsh fluorescent light.

"You don't have to—" she whispered. She was going to tell him he wouldn't have to stay with her, but he didn't want to hear it.

"Don't be silly. You need someone on the premises until you're feeling better. Let's get going. I want to stop at the drugstore and pick up this stuff right away." He reached over and appropriated the prescription form.

"I—"

He grinned at her and placed a finger over her lips. "It hurts to talk, remember? Come on, let me help you down."

Dana thought that she would be forever in this man's debt for the way he had taken care of her last night. What if she had fainted while she was all alone? What would have been the effect on the baby of a high fever that she hadn't been able to break? She didn't want to think about it.

While Conn went into the drugstore, she sat in the car watching the traffic as it meandered along Main Street. The pace was so slow here that she had to laugh when people acted as if they were pushed for time. They knew nothing about being pushed for time if they hadn't been backed up on the notorious traffic tie-up near Chicago known as the Hillside Strangler, where traffic from three major thoroughfares had to squeeze onto I-290. She'd been stuck there more times than she could count.

When she went back home—

But *would* she? Suddenly Chicago was the last place she wanted to be. Since walking off her show, she'd assumed that she would eventually return and pick up the threads she had dropped, but now, having experienced the ease and simplicity of life in a small town, was that what she really wanted?

Conn chose that moment to swing out the door of the drugstore, and as she watched him sauntering across the street, she thought what a kind man he had turned out to be. This surprised her, and she hadn't known it until last night. But he was.

He slid into the truck. "Everything all right?" She nodded, her throat still so sore that she didn't want to talk.

"This medicine should fix you up. By the way, how are we doing for food at your place?"

"Okay," she whispered.

"Enough to last a week?"

She nodded.

"Well, if we run out of things to eat, there's plenty of stuff in my refrigerator. I stocked up while Martin was here."

As Conn headed the pickup onto the highway, Dana leaned her head against the back of the seat, and Conn turned up the radio. When they passed the road that would have taken them to Shale Flats, he glanced over at her.

"We'll go there as soon as you're well enough," he promised.

She wanted to tell him she was looking forward to it, but her throat hurt too much. She closed her eyes and let her mind drift.

She opened them again when she heard the crunch and pop of gravel beneath the truck's wheels. They were at her cabin, and it suddenly sank in that Conn intended to stay there with her until she could manage by herself. If she became sick to her stomach, he would be there to see. If she looked like hell, he'd be there to see that, too. Last night he'd seen her looking even worse than hell, and naked to boot.

But she didn't have anyone else.

"Here we are," Conn said as he switched off the ignition.

She hated herself for feeling weak. For being weak.

And the smile she gave him was weak, too.

She'd better work hard at getting well. She needed Conn, but only as long as she was sick. After that, she'd go back to not needing anyone.

"I'VE TAKEN CARE of sick birds before," Conn assured Dana three days later as he poked through the food in her refrigerator. The pickings were slim. "One difference, though. Even a sick bird eats more than you do." He tried to glare at her and failed entirely.

Ensconced on the couch, wrapped in a quilt, Dana grinned. "I told you this morning I'm feeling better."

He'd been relieved to hear this claim, but he remained concerned about her. Still, the pallor of the last few days had been replaced by her normal color, and she claimed that her throat didn't hurt nearly as much after dosings with the medicine from the doctor. Her fever was down, and though she had developed a cough, the circles under her eyes were fading.

"It's time for you to get off this invalid food and eat a decent dinner, but I think I'd better make a quick run over to my place and dig a couple of steaks out of the freezer," he told her.

"I don't—"

"Yes, you do. Steaks, baked potatoes with sour cream, and you've got a can of green beans in your cupboard." He recited the menu in hopes of tantalizing her. "Anyway, I'm supposed to meet a kid named Billy Wayne Sprockett at my place in half an hour or so. He's interested in the hawks."

She perked up at this. "He's Esther's nephew. Esther is the misguided person who got me into cross-stitching. You know, the librarian?"

"Well, Billy Wayne drove Martin out to my house when he first arrived in town, and one day when Martin and I were at the barber shop, Billy Wayne walked in and said that he'd like to see the falcons." At one time Conn would have gruffly told Billy Wayne that the falcons weren't for gawking, but something about the kid had impressed him. It hadn't been the two-tone hair.

"Probably a lot of people are interested in the birds. I get the idea that you may be the talk of Cougar Creek."

He scoffed at this. "If that's true, it's probably because they don't have anything else to talk about." He shut the refrigerator door. "I'll be back in a while," he said.

"Maybe I'll pick up where I left off on my cross-stitch," Dana said. She reached down beside the couch for her needlework bag, but where it should have been, she groped empty air. "Oh, Conn, I think I left my cross-stitch in my car. Would you—well, would you mind bringing it in before you go?"

"No need to act so apologetic." Conn shrugged into his jacket. "Is your car locked?"

"The key's in my purse. In the outside pocket."

He went to get the key, and as he reached into the outside compartment of her purse, he dislodged a bit of paper. It fell to the floor, and he picked it up. It was only a scrap, the corner of an envelope containing what appeared to be a return address. He couldn't help but read it.

"Philip E. Grantham," it read. The address was in Chicago.

"Conn? Are you finding my keys?"

He jangled them in her direction as he stuffed the bit of envelope into his jacket pocket. "Anything else you need from your car?"

"No, Conn. And thanks."

He took her the needlework bag and left soon after, still puzzling over the scrap of paper. All his investigative instincts surged to the fore. Not that he wanted to stick his nose into all the intimate details of her life, it certainly wasn't that. He simply wanted to know more about her. Their relationship had undergone a subtle change since he'd helped her through her bout with the flu, and he was becoming more fascinated by her every day.

Why did she know Philip Grantham? What was he to her? A relative? A business acquaintance?

Or—and this was probably a long shot—the father of Dana's child?

For some reason he didn't like to think about the man who had fathered her baby. He wasn't able to stop at the fact of the guy's fatherhood; his mind was fertile ground for imaginings about what they'd had to do for Dana to get pregnant in the first place. It was disturbing to picture Dana making love with anyone, to think about someone else sliding close to her in bed and curving his fingers around her breasts. Or breathing in the sweet perfumed scent of her hair or—

Stop it, McTavish, he warned himself sternly. *Stop it right now. It's none of your business what Dana Cantrell does with anyone. None at all.*

When he pulled into his own driveway, he wanted to feel a rush of pleasure at being home, but he didn't. He turned his key in the lock and pushed open the front door, realizing that the place seemed empty, lonesome. The only sign of life there was the answering machine he'd unearthed and hooked up to the new phone. The message light was winking at him, and he checked his messages. There were two.

The first one was from the administrator of Catalina-Pacific. "You haven't let us know if your mother is going to be transferred here," said the slightly accusatory voice. "There are many other people on our waiting list, so if you don't intend for your mother to take advantage of this wonderful opportunity to be part of our Catalina-Pacific family, please let us know."

He grimaced and hit the playback button again. The second message was from Martin.

"I meant what I said about wanting you back at the *Probe,*" Martin said, his hearty voice sounding tinny on tape. "I had a great time visiting. Maybe I'll come back to Hicksville for a visit soon, and my door in L.A. is always open to you. Keep in touch."

Keep in touch? Well, maybe. If he couldn't figure out a way to increase his income, he might need to reconsider Martin's offer.

Conn shut off the machine and went to the freezer to get the frozen steaks that he was planning to take back to Dana's. Which he would no longer be able to afford if he put his mother in Catalina-Pacific. Anyway, he'd thought he'd have a couple more weeks to make up his mind, a couple more weeks to figure out where he was going to get the money that would make his mother's move possible.

While he was considering this, it occurred to him that the steaks would taste best if cooked on a charcoal grill, and he didn't know if Dana had one. He went to the phone and dialed her number.

It was busy. He hadn't expected that, but it was no big deal. He located a small hibachi that Steve had left in the shed years ago. It was portable, and if Dana didn't already have a charcoal grill, he'd suggest that she keep it.

On the spur of the moment, because the packing box that contained it was also in the shed, he unpacked his computer. He was pretty sure he knew where to find the floppy disks containing those nature articles he'd written, too. He might have time to find them before Billy Wayne of the exuberant hair showed up to see the hawks.

AFTER PRICKING HER FINGER again, Dana threw the counted cross-stitch sampler across the room in annoyance. It was the first day since the onset of the flu that she'd felt like doing anything, and now here was this stupid needlework and she couldn't concentrate on it.

She wished Conn would come back from his meeting with Billy Wayne. She wished she could convince him that she was well enough to go somewhere, anywhere. She wished—

But every time she wished she wasn't pregnant, she felt as if she should bite her tongue. Not be pregnant? She couldn't imagine it. The trouble was that when Conn looked at her in a certain way, when their gaze held for a fraction too long, when she wanted an excuse to reach out and cup her hand at the nape of his neck—then she couldn't help but imagine what life would be like if she weren't with child.

If she weren't going to have a baby, she wouldn't have come here in the first place. She never would have met Connor McTavish to begin with. There was that.

But this baby was a wanted child. Dana had given up her whole life so that she could bear the child in peace, away from the glare of the media spotlight. Away from Philip and his maneuverings and manipulations. And away from Myrtis, his mother.

Except now she wanted more. She wanted *something*. Oh, maybe not what she'd had before, the hoopla and fame, but it was hard to exist on her rare trips to town, Esther's attempts at friendship and counted cross-stitch. She needed more.

She needed Conn.

The words as they materialized in her head fairly took her breath away. She hadn't expected to need anyone, and she'd thought she was getting along fine. Yet the past few days of Conn's companionship had taught her how much she was missing by sequestering herself away from people.

She and Conn had learned much about each other in the past few days while he was nursing her back to health. She had found out that he didn't like raisins and that during his childhood he'd read most of the same books that she had.

And as for what he had learned about her, he knew that she worked counted cross-stitch to pass the time but hated it, that she'd grown up reading the same books he had, that she was a lost cause as far as learning to play poker, and that she was allergic to shellfish.

She made herself pick up the book on falconry. Conn had insisted on reading a chapter to her every night, and she had learned a lot. Leafing through the pages, she saw that it had pictures, lots of them, of birds of prey looking fierce with their hooked beaks and outstretched talons. That was, she supposed, the way raptors were perceived by most people, but definitely not by her. Not anymore. She well remembered Aliah's golden eyes as the peregrine swooped toward the lure and the softness of the falcon's wing when her feathers had inadvertently brushed Dana's cheek. It had felt like the wing of an angel, she had thought at the time.

It was a totally new experience, this flying of the hawks, and a way of expressing herself that she had never known before. Suddenly jittery with her inactivity, Dana got up and went to the phone. She would call Noelle, that's what she'd do. Maybe she'd tell her about the hawks.

On second thought, that would be foolish. She might slip and give away her location. But she wanted to call Noelle anyway.

She picked up the phone and carried it back to the couch, then drew a blank when she couldn't recall Noelle's phone number. And it was a number that she used to call several times a day. That showed her how far removed she felt from her past life.

It took only a minute to retrieve her address book from the back of the desk drawer and to enter the numbers on the keypad of the phone. When she heard Noelle pick up on the other end of the line, she said, "Surprise, Noelle! It's me."

"Day! What's the matter? You sound terrible."

"Oh, just the flu. I'm better now."

"I hope so," Noelle said doubtfully. "Have you seen a doctor?"

"Yes, and don't worry. He says I'll be fine. I don't want to talk about me. How are you?"

"Okay, but Timmy had the flu, too. He's finally back at school, and I worry that Katie might get it. I've been wondering, Day—are we going skiing this year the way we always do?"

This caught Dana by surprise. She regarded her swollen belly and smothered a wry chuckle. "Not likely. Maybe next year.'' How young could a child be and learn to ski? Could she take the baby with them next time she and Noelle went? Maybe Timmy and Katie could go, too. With three children between them, she and Noelle could make it a family outing.

Noelle went on talking. ''Tricia asked if I'd heard from you. It made me uncomfortable to lie to her.''

A pang of regret rocked Dana; she'd always liked Tricia, who had lived in the same apartment building.

''You can tell her I've been in touch if you like. Any more flack from the tabloids?''

''I had a call at work this week from someone at *Tattletales Weekly*. And Bentley Howser of the *National Probe* left a message. I can't stand that woman.''

''That makes two of us. I hope you didn't call her back.''

''No way. Philip said—''

''You've seen Philip?''

A small hesitation, and then Noelle said, sounding defensive, ''I work for Philip, Day. As we all do here at General Broadcasting.''

''Of course. I meant socially.'' Dana regretted her sharp interruption.

''Oh well, Philip stopped by my office one day. He said he'd heard from Bentley Howser, also. He didn't know anything to tell her, he said. He wanted to know if I'd talked to you.''

''You haven't. At least as far as Philip is concerned.'' Dana tried and failed to keep the bitterness out of her voice, but with the lingering image still clear in her mind of Philip's bare pink buttocks pumping—in Dana's bed, no less—and Erica's subsequent shriek and scramble for cover, Dana felt less than kindly toward either one of them. Especially Philip, because he had betrayed her.

It was at that moment that the door to the cabin swung open and Conn said, ''Hey, I didn't know if you had a charcoal grill or not so I—''

Dana hurriedly muffled the phone, but it was too late.

"Day?" Noelle was saying. "Is someone there with you? It sounds like—"

Dana broke the connection before Noelle finished her sentence, and her eyes met Conn's. Guiltily, she thought, though she wasn't sure why. He wouldn't care if she talked to someone, but it wouldn't do to have him find out who it was.

Conn cocked one eyebrow and went to set down the bags and boxes he was carrying on the kitchen table. He glanced over his shoulder as he began to unpack them.

"Sorry, I didn't realize you were on the phone," he said.

"I was just hanging up," Dana said.

His keen eyes bored through her as he came to stand in the doorway. "Was it anyone I know?"

Dana felt her cheeks coloring under his scrutiny. "A friend. No one from here."

"Not that it's any of my business," he said dismissively as he went back to his unpacking. "I brought a hibachi so I could grill the steaks tonight. I didn't think you had a charcoal grill here."

"I don't," Dana said, laboriously getting up from the couch. She lowered herself to one of the chairs at the kitchen table. "How are the birds?"

"I'll work them tomorrow. Billy Wayne wants to go with me." He crumpled up the plastic bag. "Where does this go?"

"In the closet. So you liked Esther's nephew?"

"Seems like a decent kid once you get past the orange-and-purple hair. He used to keep pigeons for racing, so he was excited to see the hawks. He'll be a good one to come and feed them if I ever have to go to L.A."

Dana said very carefully, "Are you thinking of going soon?"

"I like to visit my mother from time to time," he said.

"You haven't seen her for a while, I take it?"

"Not for several months. She doesn't know me, but I

always feel better if I check in once in a while to make sure that everything is okay.''

''When will you be going next?'' She didn't like to think of his leaving.

''I'm not sure. Say, do you want potatoes or rice with your steak tonight? I brought potatoes,'' he said, indicating two large russets on the edge of the sink, ''and you already have rice in your cupboard.''

''Potatoes. I'll wash them.''

''Fine. I brought my laptop computer so I can work, and I can use the time to sort out some things on it while you take your nap.''

Conn went into the living room and sat down in the green chair with the computer on his lap. She peeked at him once while washing the potatoes, and he seemed absorbed in whatever it was, studying something on the computer screen with an intensity that begged no interruption.

She wondered what kind of work he was doing and why he had chosen to take it up now. She had seen no evidence of his doing any kind of job before.

A daily nap had become a necessity since her bout with the flu, so she didn't intend to skip it today. When she headed for the sleeping alcove and pulled the curtain across the opening, Conn seemed not to notice. He was still intently peering at the computer screen when she fell asleep.

THE ARTICLE HE'D WRITTEN about the Florida panther, an endangered species, seemed like a halfhearted effort. That was probably because he had never pursued the freelancing aspect of a writing career; there had been no room in his life at that time for halfhearted endeavors. But as he read, he realized that all he needed to do was juggle some paragraphs around and update it a bit. Then the piece would be ready to send to Jim Menoch, his friend at *Nation's Green*.

He stood up, energized by the idea of readying the article for publication. After grabbing an apple from a bowl on the coffee table, he sat down on the edge of the couch. That's when he spotted the small leather address book tucked down between the couch cushions. Thinking that he didn't want it to get pushed any farther under the cushions, he wedged his fingers down next to it and pulled it out. Idly, because he was still concentrating on the Florida panther article, he thumbed through the pages of the little book.

It had lots of entries. The name of someone named Raymond was underlined, two phone numbers crossed out and replaced with new ones. Tricia Phelps didn't have an address, only a phone number, and Noelle Hassler had her children's names listed under hers. He was on the verge of closing the book when a name leaped out at him—Philip Grantham, the same name that was on the scrap of the envelope he had found earlier.

Philip Grantham had no address, either, but there were three phone numbers—home, office and mobile.

He heard the yank of the curtain behind him, and he dropped the book back onto the couch. He nudged it under one of the pillows.

He stood up, turning to find Dana looking all rosy with sleep.

"Feeling okay?" he asked.

"Mmm. Feeling lazy is more like it."

"We settled that a couple of days ago. You're to sleep as much as you like. We have to get you in shape so that you can fly the hawks with me again soon."

She smiled at that. "Can't wait." She glanced at his computer. "Did you get much work done?"

"Enough."

"What is it you're doing?"

"I've decided to do a bit of freelancing. Nature articles, that kind of thing. Say, since you're awake, I'll go light the charcoal in the hibachi. I thought I could set it up on the old picnic table out back."

"Fine. I'll toss the potatoes in the oven."

He nodded, wondering if he would ever feel comfortable

asking her something about her life before she came here. All the while he was piling the charcoal and squirting it with lighter fluid, he debated whether to broach the subject over dinner.

SHE COULDN'T HELP HERSELF. She leaned over the back of the chair and read the words on Conn's computer screen. He'd never mentioned that he was a writer.

From what she could figure out, the document she was reading had something to do with the Florida Everglades. It wasn't a part of the world that she associated with Conn. When she searched her memory trying to recall if he'd ever said anything about being in Florida, she came up with nothing. She leaned closer and realized that the writing pertained to the Florida panther.

If she had dared, she might have scrolled down the screen to find out more. But she was saved from that decision when a screensaver popped up on the screen, and the Florida panther information was obliterated by cartoon fish swimming.

She reminded herself that she should be doing something besides trying to figure out what Conn was up to. For lack of anything better to do, she went and dug the toenail clippers out of the basket in the bathroom where she kept them.

When Conn came back inside, Dana was sitting on the side of the bed with clippers in hand, trying to figure out how to cut her toenails. With mounting despair, she realized that they never told you that in any of those pregnancy handbooks. They told you about massaging your nipples so they wouldn't crack when breastfeeding, they told you to eat saltines for morning sickness, but not a word about toenails. She couldn't bend over—the baby was too big now for her to be able to reach her toes. She couldn't even reach her toes with her knee bent and her foot on the edge of the bed, mostly because her big stomach kept her knee from bending much.

Conn went over to his computer and turned it off before closing the lid. "Anything wrong?" he asked mildly.

Dana glared at him. "Only everything," she snapped. She didn't know why she snapped; it just happened. It occurred to her that she had endured a surprise pregnancy, a faithless lover, and self-exile only to be done in by toenails.

He looked as if the hinges on his jaw had given way. "Could you explain that?" he asked cautiously. Her eyes couldn't help following the indentation on his upper lip and admiring the curve of it.

She swallowed, a big gulp. "It's—it's—I hate counted cross-stitch. And I hate being p-pregnant. And I hate not being able to cut my toenails." She waved the toenail clippers in the air for emphasis and ending up throwing them against the wall. They fell with a clatter, and in horror she realized that Conn was staring at her with an expression of dislike. Or was it disgust? Or what?

Tears burned the back of her eyes, and one slid off the end of her nose and fell onto her shirt. She hadn't realized that she was crying.

"It's the hormones," she said, holding back further tears with difficulty. "When you're pregnant, they go berserk. And then *you* go berserk. Not you, I mean me. Oh, what am I saying? I can't even piece together a coherent sentence." Another tear started its journey down her cheek. "I'm going to cry and get my nose all stuffed up again. I think I hate myself. I shouldn't hate myself, though, cause I'm not even *me* anymore." How true this was, Conn would probably never know, and her whole crisis of identity made her want to wail. She'd *liked* being Day Quinlan.

"Dana," Conn said, coming and kneeling beside the bed. "I don't know what started this. I thought we could have a nice dinner, like we have the past few nights. You're supposed to be feeling well enough to enjoy it."

"Well, I'm not," she said stubbornly, refusing to look at him. She was fat and ugly and would never look like Day Quinlan again. No one would believe she was Day

Quinlan, not in a million years. She didn't have to worry about being discovered. About Philip giving her a hard time over the baby. About taking the baby from her.

"Do you want to talk about this?" Conn asked gently, taking her hand.

"No. All I want is to be able to cut my toenails," she said.

To her surprise Conn tossed his head back and laughed. He laughed long and hard, but she couldn't join in.

"I didn't think you could be so mean," she sniffed. "You're making fun of me because I look so awful." The minute the words were out of her mouth, she regretted them. She knew she was being childish and petty, but she couldn't help it. It was as if some evil genie had come along and forced the words out of her mouth.

Conn sobered quickly. "No, you don't look awful," he said solemnly. "Except for your toenails being too long," he added with a sly twinkle.

"Ohhh, you!" she said, and socked him with a pillow.

He fell back on the floor, pretending to be stunned. He sat up again. "Point your foot in my direction. I'm a pretty good toenail groomer. I trim the birds' talons, you know."

She yanked her foot away in horror. "No way. I'd be too embarrassed. It's too personal."

He reached for her foot and pulled it toward him. "So? You don't think vomiting all over my hands was too personal? And we made it through *that*, didn't we?" He retrieved the clippers from where they'd fallen when she'd thrown them.

Dana blushed. "Conn—"

"Keep still, or you'll end up with one less toe." He clipped the first toenail, then the next one. "Was that so bad?"

"No," Dana said, clutching a pillow to her chest. "And you didn't have to bring up the fact that I tossed my cookies that first night."

"I wouldn't have if you hadn't been so ornery." He

finished with the first foot and took the other in his hand. His hands were warm, and Dana tried to relax. She could, if only she hadn't felt so undignified.

"Have you felt the baby move today?" He asked this every day.

"Yes, and quite forcefully too."

He finished clipping the toenails of the second foot, and Dana hastened to pull both legs up onto the bed. "Um, thanks," she said. "I'm still embarrassed, but—well, thanks."

Conn sat down beside her on the edge of the bed. "Dana," he said, "is there anyone you want me to call to come stay with you while you get over the aftereffects of this flu bug? If I were you I'd think of someone—a friend maybe—who could stay here with you." His tone had shifted and become more serious.

"No," she said sharply, too sharply. She didn't add that the sweet domesticity of their situation was beginning to grow on her and that she didn't want to depend on him too much.

She didn't want to need Connor McTavish.

At the same time and with growing dismay, she realized her own helplessness and vulnerability. And she was scared—scared of being alone, scared of—scared of *herself*. With sudden clarity she admitted for the first time that she wasn't the person she had been before all this, she wasn't strong, confident Day Quinlan anymore. She was the frightened and defenseless Dana Cantrell, at the mercy of her hormones and barely recovered from the flu.

It made sense that Conn wanted her to find someone to stay with her because he was fed up. Who could blame him after what he'd been through with her the past few days? And with growing panic she realized that she didn't want Conn to leave. But what did *he* want? She lifted her eyes to his, searching for reassurance that he wanted to be with her despite the problems she presented.

But to her dismay Conn looked edgy. He looked miffed.

While she groped for words that would express her appreciation to him for all he had done for her, and offer her apologies for her sharp retort when he'd asked her if she had anyone else to stay with her, he stood abruptly.

"I'd better get those steaks going," he said gruffly. And then, keeping his face a blank mask, Conn walked purposefully out the back door.

Chapter Eight

Conn stepped out into the cool dusk and inhaled a deep breath of fresh air. His patience was fraying rapidly. After that little scene inside, it seemed to him that he had bitten off more than he could chew. Taking Dana to the doctor, cooking for her, spending the past three nights on her couch, even cutting her toenails, for Pete's sake! He hadn't known he was signing on for a long-term stint a few nights ago when he'd stopped by to talk to Dana about flying the hawks. And it wasn't as if she appreciated it.

On the other hand, what else could he have done but stick around? As sick as she was, he couldn't have left her alone. He'd been brought up to accept responsibility and to help others when necessary. It was his mother who had molded that aspect of his character. Gladys was the type who was always going to the aid of sick neighbors, helping out with either food or care. Once she'd even sat up all night with a kid down the block who had measles when his mother couldn't stay home with him because she had to work third shift or lose her job. And Gladys had dragged herself to work at the mill the next morning, never complaining.

But, he reminded himself now, that was Gladys. He wasn't his mother, nor did he want to be.

And it wasn't as if Dana didn't know anyone who could help her, despite her assertions to the contrary. There was that phone conversation he'd interrupted—all very hush-hush. She had friends. Her address book proved it. She knew other people besides him. All this made him want to bail out of this situation ASAP. Unless...

Unless. There was always the "unless" factor.

The grill sizzled when he threw the steaks on. He was doing a slow burn, too. Slow, but picking up speed. He told himself that what he needed was to get out of here. What he needed was—

His freedom back.

And something else, too. He needed a woman to whom he wasn't mightily attracted. Dana didn't qualify.

The "unless" factor in this case was that he wanted her. How this could be, he couldn't imagine. His imaginings had taken on forms that he couldn't have anticipated when he'd first seen her on that path near the mesa when she'd been awkwardly trying to rescue Demelza. Dana had looked so fiery and upset and concerned, and then she'd lit into him with gusto when she'd thought he hadn't shown the proper concern for the kestrel. He'd countered by treating her to a gruff countenance, and all the while he'd been charmed by her.

As he continued to be, even though he probably had no right to be thinking about her in the way that he was now unless—there was that word again—unless she wanted him, too.

It took a while to cook the steaks. He spent the time figuring out a scenario for when he went back inside. He'd talk to Dana calmly and in a matter-of-fact way. It was time that she knew the feelings he was beginning to have for her. After all, the last time he'd fallen in love—with Lindsay—he hadn't made that final all-important commitment. And then it had been too late.

"What I want," Lindsay had told him then, "is happily-ever-after. Babies and a minivan and a vine-covered cottage with a picket fence. You know, the whole works."

"The whole works?" he had replied, reaching for her

and pulling her close. "I'll show you some works. Fireworks," and he'd kissed her passionately. He had loved Lindsay, and she'd loved him. But he hadn't known how much he loved her until it was too late.

Lindsay had been tall and beautiful with jet-black hair flowing down her back in a rippling cascade and startling blue eyes that sparkled with laughter. He'd met her at *Newsweek* where she'd shot the photos for some of his articles. He admired her work and told her so at a cocktail party at which she'd shown negligible interest in him, surrounded as she was by a bevy of slavish admirers. Conn had expected her to be permanently busy when he called to ask her out for a drink the following week, but to his surprise she'd said yes.

And she had never stopped saying yes. Yes to accompanying him to his loft apartment that night, yes to making love, yes to traveling with him on vacations. But when she had expected *him* to say yes to a permanent commitment, the relationship had hit a stall. He wasn't ready, he told her. He needed more time. But, oh, he had been mad about her from the moment he'd first set eyes on her.

Lindsay possessed all the attributes he'd ever wanted in a wife, but at that time he'd been excited by his career prospects and caught up in his life as a man-about-town in the Big Apple. So he'd waffled and postponed, all the while assuring Lindsay that he would settle down soon.

Not soon enough, as it happened. After a year or so, Lindsay tired of his promises and accepted a permanent assignment in a troubled outpost of the former Soviet Union. He had begged her not to go, pleaded for more time, but she'd been adamant. Without a ring on her finger, she'd said, she was out of his life.

Conn had received the phone call on a peaceful Sunday morning in May while he was working his way through the *New York Times* editorial page and wishing that Lindsay were there to offer help with the crossword puzzle as she had been wont to do. Her bureau chief regretfully informed him that Lindsay had been caught in a rebel ambush on a country road outside the capital and had been severely wounded while shooting pictures of the action.

Conn flew out on the next plane from New York, but by the time he reached the understaffed and ill-supplied hospital where they'd taken her, Lindsay was dead. He hadn't been there to hold her hand or deal with the doctors, few of whom spoke English. There hadn't even been a chance to tell her one last time that he loved her.

His grief was exceeded only by his regrets. If it hadn't been for him, if he hadn't kept putting off his commitment to her, they would have been married and she never would have taken that eastern European assignment.

He had gone slightly crazy in the months afterward, getting wrecked at parties, descending into long periods of depression, which was why he'd flown into a rage over story credits at *Newsweek* and subsequently resigned. That wouldn't have happened if he hadn't been out of his mind with grief. Afterward, his friend Steve had helped out with an offer to come to Arizona for a visit so he could renew his interest in falconry. Subsequently Martin had offered him the job at the *Probe*. With his friends' help, Conn had made his way slowly back from the hell that his life had been after he lost Lindsay. There had been no women since. It was almost four years since she'd died.

Yet now there was this woman, Dana. She was as different from Lindsay as it was possible to be. Even so, for the first time since Lindsay, he felt that same excitement, that same curiosity about another human being with whom he felt a certain rapport. There had sprung up between them an undeniable electricity that neither of them had acknowledged in so many words.

The corners of his mouth quirked upward as he thought about Dana's embarrassment when he'd cut her toenails for her. It was funny, the way she'd hugged that pillow to her chest for comfort while he did what had to be done.

He had never shirked from doing what had to be done.

It was time, he thought, for a confrontation of sorts. He slid the steaks onto a platter and went inside.

He was taken aback to see that there were candles on the table. Dana had positioned the philodendron from the kitchen windowsill in the middle of the kitchen table and put some kind of lacy doily under it. A glass of wine awaited him beside his place mat.

"Conn?"

She appeared in the doorway between the kitchen and living room, the hollows and planes of her face gilded by flickering candlelight. "I mixed the green beans with some canned mushrooms from the pantry. I hope you don't mind." He saw that she had lit a fire in the fireplace.

Already thrown off balance by the unexpected ambiance, he merely stared at Dana. He was dazzled by the look of her, the sweet voluptuousness of her softly rounded body beneath the long, flowing thing she'd put on—a robe of some sort, but not the worn chenille one she usually wore. She'd brushed her hair back behind her ears so that it curled gently along her neck, and she wore makeup. Not just lipstick, but something that enhanced her eyes and made them look even larger than they were.

She took the platter with the steaks from him. "I'll deal with this while you wash up."

He looked down at his hands and realized they were grubby from handling the charcoal earlier. He went over to the kitchen sink and ran the water noisily, telling himself that he was a grown man who was accustomed to the manipulations of women, that he shouldn't be thrown off course by candlelight and eye shadow, that he was entitled to ask questions and have them answered.

Dana went to the CD player she kept on one of the kitchen shelves.

"What kind of music shall we have? Any preference?"

He found his voice. "Whatever you like." She selected a disk from the stack on the top shelf and slid it into the player. The soft strains of Celtic music filled the air.

She had sat down at the table and was unfolding her napkin. She gazed at him expectantly.

He walked across the room and sat across the table from her. She passed the steak platter over to him, and he transferred one of the steaks to his plate.

"I can't eat such a large steak," she said. The hoarseness of her voice, which had been brought on by the flu, was overwhelmingly sexy.

"How about half?"

"That's good."

He cut the other steak in two and lifted it with the fork to put it on her plate.

"Thanks," she said, and proceeded to describe how she'd mixed the mushrooms with the beans, why she'd decided to do it in the first place, how pleased she had been to find a can of mushrooms on the pantry shelf behind the stewed tomatoes, and so on. He didn't know how anyone could get so much conversational mileage out of a side dish, and he didn't want to hear any of it.

"Dana," he said. Something in his tone must have caught her attention because she stopped talking and shot him a startled look.

"Conn, before you say anything else, please understand that I'm sorry for biting your head off earlier. I wanted to make amends and this—" she gestured at the plant, the wine on the table, the vegetables "—this was the only way I knew how to do it." Her gaze was plaintive, beseeching.

Damn! He didn't know how to deal with this. With her. His relationship skills were rusty to say the least. That is, if he'd had any to begin with, and he wasn't sure he had.

He chose his words carefully. "It's all very nice," he said. "It's just…" He stopped talking, unsure how to proceed.

Her gaze met his levelly. "Just what?"

"That I've been living here with you for several days and I hardly know you any better than I did before."

"Conn, I don't blame you for being angry. Since I've

been pregnant, my emotions have been on a roller-coaster ride, and I apologize if I—''

''That's not what I mean. Well, not exactly. Don't you understand that I care that something might happen to you? You don't seem to have anyone who checks on you regularly.''

''But I do,'' Dana said softly. ''I have you.''

''Well, what if I didn't? What if I'm not here?''

''I have a phone now. That should set your mind at ease.''

''It does somewhat. Not completely, though. Would you please pass the salt?'' It struck him as slightly incongruous that they were attempting to continue with dinner even though the conversation—if you could call it that—had swerved into what had by tacit agreement become forbidden territory.

She handed him the salt. He polished off a few more pieces of steak, all the while waiting for her to say something.

Dana looked uncomfortable. ''I have a friend I check in with from time to time. Someone in Chicago.''

Chicago? That was where this Philip person lived, the one who had written to her. His ears perked up, but she didn't look as if she wanted to say anything more about it.

''That's good,'' he said, and paused in case she felt like elaborating. Dana picked at her food, looking distinctly upset. ''Look,'' he said doggedly, ''I'm sure you think I'm overstepping my bounds, but what I'm saying here is that I don't know what I'm dealing with. What's worrying me is that I'm beginning to have feelings for you. And I don't know if it's okay for me to have them. I don't know if you're free, Dana.''

Her expression changed from one of bewilderment to sudden comprehension. A faint flush spread slowly across her cheeks. ''You're the one who told me that we're all captive in some way,'' she said.

''I said it, sure. But I'm not talking about that now. To

put it bluntly, what I want to know is if there's another man in the picture. Because if there is, I'll bundle up those feelings and put them away.''

"Conn, I can't talk about this," she said in a strangled tone. She started to get up from the table, but Conn caught one of her hands and pulled her back down again.

"So there is someone," he said. "Who is it?" But he was asking himself, who could it be besides the father of her baby?

She closed her eyes, opened them again. "You're wrong. There isn't anyone.''

He called on the skills of persistence that had enabled him to succeed as an investigative reporter. "You're going to have someone's baby," he said doggedly. "Whose is it?''

"It's not important. It doesn't matter. Not to you or to me.'' She pulled her hand away but didn't move to get up again. She rested her hand on her belly, reminding him all over again why he had initiated this discussion.

It also reminded him that she wasn't one of his usual interview subjects. She was his friend, not a quarry to be run down in the course of his job.

He looked away, making himself back off. "God, Dana," he said. "You don't make this easy.''

His head snapped back around when she spoke. "Easy?" she said. "When was life ever easy?" She got up again, and this time he didn't stop her. He merely watched her as she moved to the sink and rinsed off her plate and silverware.

He stood and began to clear the table.

"I'll do that," she said.

"We'll both do it," he told her firmly, and he carried the rest of the dishes over to her as she rinsed them and then put them in the dishwasher. By this time he knew where she kept the plastic wrap and the aluminum foil, and he wrapped the rest of the steak in foil and put plastic wrap on the dish with the beans and mushrooms. She flipped the switch over to start the dishwasher and began wiping the counter with a sponge.

"You know, I've been planning to leave tonight. Go back to my own place."

"You're free to go," she said carefully. "No cages here, no ties."

"I know that."

She glanced up at him from under her eyelashes. It was one of her most winsome expressions.

"If you—"

He had no idea how she intended to respond, because in that moment he heard a rush of water under the sink and before two seconds had elapsed, a veritable Niagara was shooting out the bottom of the cabinet door.

"It's the dishwasher," he shouted. "Turn it off!"

She reached out, flicked the switch back to the off position, and the dishwasher motor stopped. But greasy water continued to pour out from under the sink.

He opened the cabinet door and saw immediately that the problem was in the drainpipe from the dishwasher, which fed into the sink drain. The pipe was made of rusty metal and there was a gaping hole in it from which water still dripped.

Dana brought several towels, and because she couldn't bend over very well, he blotted up the water. He explained rapidly what he thought had happened: the drainpipe had been almost rusted through, and now that the dishwasher was in use every day, it hadn't been able to withstand the pressure from the draining water and had given way.

"So the problem's not serious," she said.

"Not at all. I can fix it." He found a bucket in the kitchen closet and got down on his knees before removing drenched boxes of detergent and cleanser from the cabinet below the sink. He reached underneath the sink to check out the pipe. It had a hole in it big enough for three fingers.

"I'll call Billy Wayne Sprockett tomorrow," she said.

"No, you won't. Anyway, Billy Wayne's going to be

with me first thing in the morning up at Shale Flats. I'll stop by afterward to replace the pipe, but for now I'll slide this bucket underneath to catch drips. And the dishes will have to wait to be washed." He positioned the bucket under the leak and rose to his feet before rinsing his hands off in the sink. Dana handed him a dish towel.

"We have dessert," she said apologetically. "I almost forgot about it." She pulled a plate across the counter. "Have some?"

She'd baked a yellow cake topped with toasted coconut frosting. He took one of the pieces and bit into it. "This is good," he said. "I like a woman who knows her way around a coconut."

She stared at the piece of cake in her hand and, after a moment's thought, set it aside. Her eyes met his. "I'm ready to tell you about what happened to me. Some of it, anyway. If you want to listen." Her flicker of a smile didn't disguise her tension.

He hadn't expected an explanation, but by this time he was eager to hear it. "We could sit in front of the fire," he suggested.

"Okay." He followed her into the living room. She sat on the couch—he wondered if she had put away the little address book that he'd so carefully replaced there—and tucked her feet up under the afghan. He sat down beside her. She seemed slightly nervous, and he waited for her to start talking. She didn't, at least not right away.

After a while she shook her hair back and turned slightly to face him. The fire provided a backdrop for her beauty; her hair glinted in its light.

She drew a deep breath. "My baby's father was an executive where I worked. I met him the first day on the job and fell head over heels in love. Or at least that's what I thought." She managed a rueful smile. "It took a while for him to notice me. We didn't progress past polite hellos at the elevator for months.

"At a company party, he was standing beside the cocktail buffet, and because he was next to the shrimp dip and I wanted to keep talking to him, I ate more shrimp dip than I've ever eaten in my life and broke out in hives.''

''That's one way to get a guy's attention,'' Conn said with a laugh.

''Right. Especially when you're all puffed up with welts and you have to rush to the hospital. He went along with me to the emergency room, had his driver take me home afterward, held my hand in the back seat, and made sure I was settled for the rest of the night with my girlfriend who lived down the hall. He even called the next morning. But he didn't keep calling, so I found out his office schedule and managed to station myself beside the elevator when he was likely to be getting on or off. It took a huge box of profiteroles to bribe his administrative assistant for the necessary information.''

''Good thing you can cook,'' Conn said.

''Oh, I didn't make the profiteroles myself. I was too busy shopping for new lingerie. You see, I was sure this guy would tumble eventually. Still, it took six months to get a date with him.''

''It speaks well for your patience, anyway.'' He couldn't believe she'd wait so long for anyone. He wouldn't have.

''We fell in love. For me it was instantaneous. For him— I'm not so sure. He's from a prominent family, and he liked taking me out, being seen in all the right places.'' She wore a faraway look, and she caught her lower lip between her teeth. She seemed to see something that he couldn't, seemed to be caught in a scene from the past.

''Anyway, we were engaged for almost a year. I was stunned when I found out I was pregnant. I'd bought a home pregnancy test, and it tested positive, but I didn't let him know. I wanted to save the news for a surprise because I thought he'd be happy. We'd talked about kids, and his mother was pushing for him to get married and have a son who could carry on the family name. So when I got the

call at work, I was ecstatic. My doctor told me that I was
going to have a baby.''

She inhaled a deep breath and continued. ''At the place
where I worked, I had a contract that was up for renewal,
and I knew then that I wouldn't sign it. I'd quit my job,
stay home and gestate. We hadn't planned on getting married so soon, but we could push the wedding date up. I was
overjoyed.

''At the time, my fiancé was having some remodeling
done at his house, so I'd given him a key to my apartment.
He liked to take paperwork there in the middle of the day
because it was close to our offices and no one would disturb
him.''

''So what happened?''

''I never got the chance to tell him the news,'' she said
in a low tone.

Conn's heart plummeted. The man she'd loved—had he
died?

She seemed to be steeling herself, then plunged ahead,
the words coming in a rush. ''After the call from my doctor,
I decided to go home for lunch. I knew my fiancé was at
my place, his assistant told me that's where he'd gone. I
couldn't wait to share my excitement with him. I opened
the front door quietly so as not to disturb him. I'd brought
Thai takeout, one of our favorite foods when we ate in.
And then,'' and she swallowed. Her hands were clenched
in her lap, and Conn reached over and took one of them in
his.

''And then,'' she went on, ''I heard sounds from the
bedroom. I thought maybe he was talking on the phone,
but as I drew closer, it became clear that the sounds weren't
of people talking. I set the food down on the hall console
and walked into my bedroom. They…they were making
love. In my bed. He and an assist—a colleague of mine
from work.''

''Dana, you don't have to tell me any more.'' He stroked

his fingertips along the top of her fingers, meaning to comfort her, but she didn't seem to notice.

"I stood there. I couldn't move. It was as if my feet were stuck to the floor. And then he...he saw me. And she screamed. And the room erupted in flying bedsheets and clothes and explanations—but I only stood there."

She closed her eyes and it was a long time before she opened them again. "I didn't tell him about the baby. I couldn't. I didn't want to share anything with him again, ever, and most particularly, I didn't want him to know about our child. Our child," she said. She unclenched her hands and spread them over the mound of her belly. She looked at him bleakly. "My child, now."

"He never tried to contact you?"

"I ignored it."

"Do you think that's fair to him?"

"No. Neither do I think it was fair that he brought another woman into my bed."

"What if he tries to claim parental rights?"

"He'll never know he's the father."

"I understand why you don't want him to know, but it's his baby too."

She lifted her chin. "You don't understand. His life is only about him, about what he wants, what he likes. He would fight for custody in order to get his mother off his back about providing someone to carry on the family name, and then both of them would ignore the child."

"You have your rights, too."

"Do you think I could be satisfied with visitation now and then? His family has vast political connections, they know all the judges, and I'm afraid I wouldn't stand much of a chance in a Chicago courtroom."

"What happened to the woman you caught him with?"

"She's history. Myrtis—my ex-fiancé's mother—didn't like her."

His eyes held hers. "If you want to know what I think, your former fiancé was a very stupid guy."

"From your mouth to God's ears," Dana said in an attempt to bring humor into this tale, but he wasn't fooled. She'd been devastated by the discovery that her fiancé had been unfaithful, and she was slowly working her way back from that misery. He knew what it was like; not that Lindsay had been unfaithful, but he had loved and lost someone, too. He wanted to tell Dana that, but he never talked about that period in his life. Never had and probably never would. The more he thought about it, the more he ached for Dana. He couldn't imagine seeing what she had seen, being faced with incontrovertible evidence of a faithless lover. No wonder Dana had retreated to this place—she needed somewhere to lick her wounds and recover.

So had he. They had more in common than she knew.

Suddenly restless, he stood and threw another log on the fire. When he turned back around, she had pulled the afghan up close to her chin and was shivering.

"Is it too cold in here for you?" he asked. "I can build the fire up more."

"It's hard for me to talk about what happened. I get all trembly and emotional over it." She smiled apologetically.

Conn sat down beside her again, and she shifted over to make more room for him. In the process one of her feet was uncovered by mistake. She wore socks; she'd kicked her slippers off earlier. She was surprised when he took her foot between the palms of his hands and rubbed it gently. "Let me have your other foot," he said.

"Okay, so are you trying to tell me you have a foot fetish? First the toenails and now this?"

"I can see why you'd think that, but what really turns me on is your knees." He was joking, she knew that.

"You've never seen them. I'm always wearing jeans."

"Not always," he said, and suddenly, with embarrassment, she remembered the night he'd helped her into the tub. He'd seen all of her. Too much of her. Her face felt hot, and she buried her face in her hands.

"No point in hiding now. I've seen all there is to see. So you might as well give up that other foot."

Knowing when she was beaten, she edged it out from under the afghan, and he rubbed that one, too. "Feel okay?"

"Feels good," she said.

"Warm now? Want me to stop?"

"They're warm, but I don't want you to stop."

He kept rubbing her feet, and she closed her eyes and leaned her head back against the couch.

"So you came here to get away from your fiancé?" he asked after a time.

She opened her eyes. "He's not my fiancé anymore," she said.

"I guess that means you've answered my question," he said. "About whether you're free."

Glad that they were no longer on the topic of her body and how it held no mystery for him anymore, she said, "You didn't expect such a complicated story."

"In a way I did."

"Conn?"

"Hmm?"

"The steaks were good tonight. Thanks for bringing them and the hibachi."

"It was a delicious dinner. Even if it did get slightly off track. Toes toasty enough?"

She nodded, and he moved his hands higher to massage her instep.

"Do you think I'll be well enough to fly the falcons in a couple of days?"

"We'll go when you feel strong enough."

"I talked with Jeb Nofziger yesterday, and he says I should be feeling stronger every day. Thank goodness it wasn't strep throat."

He moved his hands higher to her ankles. "I wish you could go with Billy Wayne and me tomorrow. It would be fun."

"I know. But I'm making great progress with my counted cross-stitch."

He chuckled. "And progress with other things, too."

She blinked at him. "Like what?"

"Like our relationship," he said.

"Do we have one?"

"I'm guessing that we do."

"You mean now that you know there's no one else in the picture?" she asked. She watched his face, waiting for his reaction.

He nodded. She thought about how long it had been since she'd enjoyed the company of a man this way. To be honest, she had loved Philip, but she hadn't particularly liked being around him. He seldom paid any attention to her, he'd never had time to do the things she liked, and his mother had been a constant thorn in Dana's side.

If this man was thinking in terms of a relationship, there was something Dana needed to know. "What about the baby?" she said, holding her breath, waiting to see what he would say.

"What about it?" He seemed genuinely puzzled at the question.

She allowed a slight playfulness to creep into her tone. "I'm going to have one. You must have noticed."

"So it's not a bowling ball you're carrying around under those big shirts you wear?" he asked, completely deadpan.

"And it's not a watermelon either," she retorted solemnly.

He became more serious. "I guess your pregnancy should matter, Dana. But it doesn't. In fact, what I'm thinking about is not the baby. It's you."

"Me?" The word came out in a kind of squeak.

He seemed amused. "Yes, as in if you want to be kissed."

She sounded the retreat, though she was effectively imprisoned on the couch until he chose to let her up. "I may be germy," she cautioned.

"I never get sick. And if I've been around you for days and still haven't caught anything, I'm probably not going to catch it now."

"But if you did—"

"If I did, you'd have to take care of me. Turnabout is fair play."

"I'd make you chicken soup," she promised, feeling her breath catch in her throat.

Conn leaned closer so that his mouth was directly in her line of vision. It was a generous mouth, the lips finely sculpted and firm. Or at least they looked firm.

She went on talking. "I'd drift a cool hand over your brow if you had a fever, just like you did for me. I'd bring you aspirin and—"

"If I got sick, would you talk this much? Or would you merely minister to me in a kind and generous way?" He smiled, making the corners of his eyes crinkle.

"I'd minister," she murmured.

His lips brushed hers, only a whisper of a kiss. "Would this 'ministering' include kissing me?"

"I'm not sure," she said.

"I'd get well faster if you did," he cajoled.

"Maybe I would, too. If you kissed me, I mean," she said, and then, because she thought if she didn't he would never get around to it, she slid her hand up and around the back of his neck and pulled his lips down to hers.

Conn was startled, but relaxed almost instantly. Her lips were soft and pliable, and the scent of her in his nostrils was headier than all his imaginings. He drew the kiss out, savored it, decided to end it, then changed his mind. It went on for another minute or so, the heat rising in his blood, his heart thudding in his ears.

He knew he'd better go home. He'd outstayed his welcome as it was. He'd come back in the morning to check on her before he met Billy Wayne up at Shale Flats, maybe boil her an egg for breakfast as he had done for the past two days.

He pulled apart from her only to be caught and held in her gaze. Lips parted and slightly moist, she stared at him.

"I'd better leave," he said, but when he moved to get up, she only pulled him closer.

She didn't want him to go. She wasn't sure she wanted more than a kiss, but the thought flashed through her mind that it would be nice to cuddle up to a warm body in the middle of the night. He was already tucking his shirt in. Next he would put on his jacket, and then he would drive home to a bed as lonely as hers.

Outside they heard a car approaching, and as the headlights swung across the window, they exchanged surprised glances.

"Someone's coming," Conn said. "Are you expecting anyone?"

"No," Dana said. They both scrambled to their feet.

The car engine died. In the light from the porch they could see someone getting out, opening the car's trunk and removing a box. As the figure started toward them, Conn said, "It's a woman."

"Esther," Dana said, recognizing the librarian's rotund figure as it drew closer. "I can't imagine what brings her out here in the dark."

Dana wrapped the afghan around her shoulders like a shawl and was right behind Conn as he stepped out onto the porch. Esther labored toward them, toting the box and slightly out of breath by the time she reached the steps. She stood there blinking in the yellow circle of light from the porch fixture.

"I brought a sick bird," she said without ceremony in her not-so-dulcet tones. "It's an owl that can't fly. I don't rightly know what's the matter, but Billy Wayne was sure you'd know what to do with it."

Chapter Nine

"We'll take the bird to my place where I can examine it thoroughly," Conn said.

"Billy Wayne said he found the bird on the side of the road. Said it acted stunned," Esther said as she handed over the box from which emitted a hearty *bump, bump, bump*. "I went to your house first, and when you weren't home, I thought I'd better check to see if you were here. Billy Wayne said you were over here earlier." Her eyes caromed curiously from one of them to the other, clearly trying to figure out the relationship.

Conn lifted a corner of one of the cardboard flaps and said, "Seems like this bird is moving around all right."

"It's not so disabled that it can't eat. Billy Wayne fed it some leftover hamburger he had in his Jeep. That boy is always eating, I tell you," Esther said.

Conn set the box down on the porch and went inside to get his jacket. Dana followed. "I'm going with you," she said.

Esther called through the open door, "Billy Wayne said I should go along and make sure the bird is okay. I don't know much about birds. But I promised."

With his back still turned to Esther, Conn raised his eyebrows. "Does she always talk so much?" he mouthed.

"I'll keep her out of your way if you take me along," Dana said. "I feel well enough to go, really I do." He looked skeptical and as if he were about to offer a vociferous objection.

"I'm going stir-crazy in this cabin," she hissed desperately. The truth was that with her lips still tingling from his kiss, she didn't want to be apart from him. "I'll bundle up in my warmest jacket. I'll take extra vitamins tomorrow. I'll—"

He raised his hands as if to ward off a barrage of more words. "Okay, okay. How long before you can dress in something more sensible?"

She looked blankly down at her robe. "Thirty seconds," she said, and she almost made it, too, hurrying into the sleeping alcove and scrambling into a pair of jeans and a warm sweater.

When they set off for Conn's house, Esther followed in her own car. But once they were there, she pulled up behind Conn's truck and remained in her car, letting the engine run. Conn got out of the hawk wagon and went around the back to take out the box with the owl.

Esther rolled down her window. "Dana?"

The wind was whipping around them, the temperature dropping. Dana, taking care not to stumble on the rocky driveway, walked over to see what Esther had to say.

Esther wrinkled her brow up at her. "Sure is getting cold for this time of year, isn't it? I think we're going to have an early winter. Anyway, I told Billy Wayne I'd make sure the owl is okay. Do you think I can leave now? You two don't want me around, I suspect."

"Oh no, it's not like that," Dana hastened to say, a statement that was greeted by a slightly skeptical lifting of Esther's eyebrows. Then, knowing how relieved Conn would be if Esther decided to take herself elsewhere, Dana mustered a weak smile. "I'd love for you to stay, but I'm sure Conn will take good care of the bird, so if you have something else to do…" She let the sentence dangle tantalizingly.

Esther took the bait. "Just so you'll know, I'm reading

something really good. It's about a duke and a lost princess, and she's pregnant with a sheik's baby. She—''

"Dana? I need you," Conn called peremptorily from the back of the hawk wagon.

"I'd better help him," Dana said.

"Can one of you stop by the library tomorrow and let me know how the owl's doing?"

"We both have phones now."

"Oh, good. I'll jot down the numbers." Esther pulled a pad of paper out of her car's glove compartment and scribbled on it while Dana dictated Conn's number, then hers.

As Esther's car pulled away, Conn told Dana to go inside and get a pair of leather gloves while he went around back with the box containing the owl. Dana was happy to let herself into the comparative warmth of the house. A fire had been set in the fireplace, ready for Conn's homecoming, she supposed. Magazines were strewn here and there, and the place had a comfortable lived-in look.

Poor Conn—no sooner had his houseguest left than he had been saddled with her. No wonder he was ready to return home.

Conn opened the back door and stuck his head in. "Can't you find the gloves?"

"I haven't had a chance to look."

"They're in a bag next to the wood box. Make sure they fit."

The phone began to ring.

"Are you going to answer that?" she asked.

"No, I'll return the call later. I have to get back to our fine feathered friend. He's making a mighty fuss inside that box." Conn ducked out the back door again, and Dana went to get the gloves. They were of heavy leather, the kind Conn wore when he handled the falcons.

The answering machine picked up the call as she was shoving the bag back into place. She recognized the caller's voice immediately. "Conn? Conn, it's Martin. Where have you been lately, my pal? I've got somebody else here who is lobbying for this job, so you need to let me know if you're interested. Call me.''

Martin hung up, and Dana stood staring at the machine's blinking light for a moment. Conn hadn't mentioned that Martin had offered him a job.

''Dana?''

Dana roused herself to action and let herself out the back door to join Conn in the shed adjoining the mews.

He looked up. He was pulling on his own heavy leather gloves. ''The gloves are for protection,'' he said as he flexed his fingers. ''These guys can be vicious when they're hurt. Esther decided not to stay?''

''She had other things to do.''

Conn shook his head. ''There's an old Southern saying that fits her. Back in Clay Springs, we'd say that her tongue's hung in the middle so it can rattle at both ends.''

Dana laughed. ''She's a sweet person, but I know what you mean. I think she's just lonely.''

A thrashing ensued from the box, which was still closed. The bird inside let out a harsh cry of protest at its plight.

''Anything I can do?'' Dana asked.

''Close the door to the outside in case our little patient takes it into his head to fly the coop.''

Dana complied while Conn opened the box. Dana moved closer and leaned over to peer inside. Beady eyes blinked up at them quizzically out of a heart-shaped face, and small ear tufts stuck out from the owl's head, giving it a slightly comical appearance.

''It's a screech owl, full-grown,'' Conn said. He reached in the box and picked the owl up, but not without a brief scuffle. ''Put the gloves on. I'll want you to help me hold him.'' Dana did as Conn asked while he stroked the bird soothingly, murmuring to it in a low tone. The owl glared at Conn apprehensively, once breaking the gaze to dig his beak into the leather glove. Then it let out a series of raucous cries.

''This fellow can't be hurt too seriously, or he wouldn't

be so feisty," Conn said. He set the bird on a small plat-
form, motioning Dana closer with his chin. "Come and
hold him steady."

Dana advanced slowly so as not to scare the owl, and as
Conn eased away, she cupped her hands around the bird's
body. "That's right," he said approvingly as she maneuvered for a better grip. "Hold his wings close to his body
so he can't struggle and injure himself even more."

Even through the thick gloves, Dana felt the bird's heart
beating. Conn ran a gentle exploratory finger down the
owl's chest and back. When the bird didn't object to this
treatment, Conn spread its wings and felt the bones carefully. The owl tried to get away when he touched a certain
spot, but Dana tightened her grip.

"Do you have any idea what's wrong?" she asked.

"His wing doesn't seem to be broken, only swollen. I
think he may have been hit by a car. A glancing blow off
a windshield, perhaps, which can leave a nasty bruise. A
car can be the worst enemy of a bird of prey."

At that point, the owl grabbed Conn's gloved thumb with
its beak. "Hey, stop it," he said, but he laughed. After a
moment, the owl released him and sat glowering at both of
them.

Dana was relieved that the bird's injuries weren't worse.

"I can manage him now," Conn said. "Go have a seat
on that box in the corner if you like."

Dana sat down on the box and wrapped her arms around
herself for warmth, watching Conn intently as he handled
the bird.

"Cold?" Conn asked sharply.

"Not exactly." The sweater under her jacket was warm,
and she'd worn a long-sleeved shirt beneath it.

"You can go in the house if you like. No sense in court-
ing a relapse."

The empty house held no appeal for her, and it was much
more interesting to watch Conn. She liked the way he handled the bird, his movements sure and economical. He

knew what he was doing, and the bird seemed to sense it. It no longer struggled; it seemed to trust him.

Conn set the owl on a scale and weighed it. Then he gave it some water. "Birds that have been injured are often hungry and thirsty. Sometimes they haven't been able to hunt for days. This little guy seems pretty much okay, but I'll keep him under observation for a while." He opened the door of a cage and set the owl inside.

Dana watched as Conn took some meat from the refrigerator and cut it into pieces for the owl. He put the food into the cage. After a suspicious look at Conn, the owl sidled over to the meat. Without even a moment's pause he began to tear at the pieces.

Dana laughed in delight at this sign of normalcy in what they had thought was a seriously injured bird. "I think he needs a name," she said.

Conn shook his head. "I don't want to get attached to this bird. The goal is to release him back into the wild, which is why we don't want him to get too accustomed to humans. He needs to retain his normal healthy fear of us in order to survive out there."

Dana considered this and decided Conn was right. "I'm going to call him Oscar anyway. I won't get attached to him. But he needs a name."

Conn regarded her with amusement. "All right. But why Oscar?"

"I had a dog once named Oscar." She didn't remember much about the dog, since her mother had banished him from the house the first time he'd tracked in mud when he was a puppy. Later, over her tears and objections, claiming that she didn't want to keep cleaning up after him, Grace Cantrell had given the dog away. "I don't like pets. They're too messy," her mother had said. Dana had mourned Oscar for a long time, and she vowed that if she ever got another dog, his name would be Oscar. Living in the city as she had all her adult life, she'd never felt comfortable about getting a pet of any kind.

But this owl, this bird that was not to be a pet—well, Oscar seemed like a fitting name for him.

They watched while the bird finished eating, and then Conn picked the cage up and set it in a darkened closet. "I want him to settle down and rest," Conn said. He turned on the faucet at the small sink and began to wash up.

"Mind if I take a look at the other birds?" Dana asked.

He dried his hands. "Of course not. You can come here to see them any time you like."

She liked the idea of being able to visit the hawks. They went out into the cage area, and the first one she saw was Demelza, the kestrel.

"I can't wait to fly her," she said. Demelza blinked at her, but she didn't seem scared. "Maybe she knows who I am."

"Probably," Conn said.

Dana moved up closer to the mesh. "Soon," she told Demelza. "Soon, I hope."

They moved on to Roderic's cage, and Aliah's, and Suli's. Maybe it was because she was with the falconer, but they seemed to accept her. She recognized a trustful intelligence on their part; it shone from their eyes. It struck her that it wasn't so different from the expression in the eyes of audience members or interviewees when they realized that they had nothing to fear from her after she had taken the time to put them at ease.

"How about a hot drink?" Conn asked when they had made the rounds of all the cages. "Martin bought a whole gallon of cider while he was here, and there's some left."

She smiled up at him. "Great idea."

Dana followed Conn into the house and watched while he tossed a few cinnamon sticks into a pan before adding the cider. "I'm not too sure what I'm doing here," he said. "This is how Martin prepared this stuff. He's given up coffee and tea, says he's into juicing and tofu big-time. I might as well warn you that I have no idea how this is going to taste."

When he'd heated it on the stove, he poured the cider into a mug and handed it to her. She took an experimental sip. "It's good," she told him.

Conn, who had watched carefully for her reaction, grinned. "I'll have to take your word for it. I'm sticking with the tried and true." He poured himself a glass of wine and took her hand to lead her into the living area.

Dana sat down and sipped the cider while Conn lit the fire. "So you and Billy Wayne are still going to Shale Flats tomorrow?" she asked.

"Yeah. I think he's got the bug."

"For falconry?"

"Looks like it." Conn stood up as the fire began to blaze and came over to the couch. She scooted over to make room for him, at ease with him in his house in a way she hadn't been the first time she came here.

"You know, Conn, if you need someone to take care of the hawks while you're gone, I'll be happy to help you out."

"You? While you're pregnant? I wouldn't think of asking."

She stared at him steadily. "You've got to get over thinking I'm this delicate little petunia who can't even—"

"Who is getting over the flu. Who shouldn't have to deal with a bunch of screaming hawks."

"They don't scream," she said hotly. "Not a peep out of them tonight."

"I fed them earlier, so they aren't hungry at present," he retorted. He got up and rearranged the logs to produce more heat.

"Conn, you've been a big help to me. I'd like to help you too. Anyway, when are you going to California next?"

Conn considered this. "Pretty soon, I suppose. I need to check on my mother. I need to get her out of that place she's in, get her into Catalina-Pacific. And I also need to figure out where I'm going to get the money to swing it."

"Is the new place expensive?"

"Very. I didn't expect to have financial problems, but buying this place cost more than I thought, and my tech stocks took a dive." He didn't want to talk about this now, didn't want to worry about Gladys at the moment.

When he turned back around, Dana was swirling the liquid in the bottom of her cup. "This was good, but I guess I'd better go home. It's getting late." She spoke regretfully, and he thought of their kiss earlier before Esther had shown up with the owl.

He reached out to take her cup, but at that moment, Dana lurched to her feet, and he didn't have enough warning to move out of the way, which, come to think of it, would have only tripped him up on the legs of the coffee table. They stared at each other eyeball to eyeball, almost nose to nose.

Almost lips to lips.

Dana tottered, looked as if she might fall backward onto the couch. He quickly reached for her and—

And slid his arms around her. It seemed so natural to hold her that way, so right to be looking down into her eyes, which widened perceptibly. Her lips parted, and he knew in that moment that she wanted him to kiss her again. Kiss her now or forever hold his peace, he thought, or he could kiss her now and—

Hold her forever?

The thought came to him out of the blue, struck him like a bolt of lightning. His lips descended inexorably toward hers, and she gripped his arms. And he would have kissed her, too. Except that the phone chose that inopportune moment to ring.

Disappointment registered in her eyes, and Conn said, "I can ignore that. The answering machine will pick up." It was the second interruption in a night that had seemed to hold such promise.

"Martin Storrs is the person who called earlier. Maybe he's calling back." She uttered the words breathlessly. She

wanted him as much as he wanted her. He was sure of it
now, as sure of her as he was of himself.

But it occurred to him that Martin was likely to mention
the *National Probe,* and he didn't want Dana to know that
he had ever worked there. It would scotch any budding
romance, he was sure. So when Dana reached out and
picked up the phone, handing it to him without comment,
he pushed away thoughts about how soft Dana's lips would
feel and barked out a hello. He kept hungry eyes on Dana
as she brushed past him and headed into the kitchen area.

"Hey, Conn," said Billy Wayne's affable voice in his
ear. "Did my aunt Esther bring you the owl?"

Conn raked a hand through his hair, wishing now that
he'd let the answering machine pick up. "Uh-huh," Conn
said.

"I found the owl over near the bluffs when I was running
my dogs there after I left your place today. The dogs might
have got him, but I saw what they were barking at before
it was too late."

"Great, Billy Wayne." Dana turned around and raised
her eyebrows quizzically. He raised one shoulder and let it
fall in answer. After an answering small shrug accompanied
by a thin smile, she turned away to rinse her mug out in
the sink.

"Well, is the owl all right?"

"I think he's bruised from a dust-up with a passing car,
but other than that, he seems fine."

"That's cool, man. Sounds like he'll be okay. I'll see
you up at Shale Flats in the morning, right?"

"Sure. I'll be there."

Conn hung up, and Dana came around the end of the
couch. Their previous mood—moods, if you counted the
one that Esther had interrupted—had disappeared, only to
be replaced with resignation. He might as well face it. This
just wasn't their night.

"Come on," Conn said. "I'll drive you home."

Dana faced him squarely. "I don't want to go home," she said.

"You—what?" He must not have heard her correctly.

"Well, I don't want to go home yet, anyway."

"It's late."

"I know. Couldn't we sit by the fire for a while and relax? You've been working frantically with the owl."

He had forgotten that she was getting over the flu. The fact was emphasized when she tried but failed to suppress a cough. He shouldn't have let her come with him tonight. He should take her home and make sure she got to bed right away.

To bed.

While he was holding that thought, she sank down on the floor, her back against the couch.

"That doesn't look comfortable," was all he could think of to say.

"It's going to be," she said. She pulled a couple of couch pillows down and stuffed one of them under her knees. The other one she slid behind the small of her back. She patted the floor beside her.

After only a moment's hesitation he sat down and stretched his feet toward the fire.

"Do you think we need to check on Oscar?" she asked.

"Not at the moment. I'll call the Raptor Center over in Toluran tomorrow and find out if there's anything else we need to do." He used the "we" unconsciously, not realizing until after he said it that he had naturally included Dana. "I mean, that *I* need to do. I didn't mean to involve you."

She turned her head and focused wide eyes on him. "I want to be included. It was so gratifying when I felt Oscar quiet under my touch. I didn't expect to have such a calming effect."

"You were good with him."

"It was the first time I'd ever held a wounded animal between the palms of my hands. I could feel his little heart pumping against my fingers, and it was—well, it was incredible to know that I was responsible, or partly so, for his life.''

For some reason Conn recalled Dana's abdomen rippling with the movement of her baby and what he'd felt when he'd observed it. It had been a sight so moving, so beautiful, that it too had called forth emotions that impressed upon him the preciousness and importance of life.

Conn laced his fingers through hers, suddenly serious. ''You're going to make a wonderful mother, Dana,'' he said.

She blinked at him. ''Why do you say that?''

''The nurturing side of you was very much in evidence as we worked with Oscar,'' he told her.

''A baby is different.''

''Of course, but the feelings are the same. Protectiveness, and a willingness to do whatever it takes. You have those qualities, you know.''

''So do you.''

He squeezed her hand and let his gaze fall upon the fire. It was a considerable blaze, and along with the wine, it had warmed him through and through. A glance at Dana revealed that she was quiet and pensive, lost in her thoughts.

When she saw him watching her, she smiled. ''I've been thinking about a friend of mine. Tricia doesn't have a fireplace in her Chicago condo, so she bought a video of a fireplace, complete with all the crackling and sputtering of wood burning. It plays for about thirty minutes, and then it rewinds. I saw it one time and thought it was silly. But then, my mother would have loved it.'' She laughed.

He laughed too. ''I prefer the genuine article.''

''So do I.''

''On the other hand, if I had a television, I'd order one of those videos just to see what it was like.''

''Why don't you have a TV?'' she asked.

''People who get caught up in them experience vicarious pleasures. I'd rather be out there somewhere living them.''

"Is falconry one of those pleasures?"

"Yes," he answered, but at the moment he was thinking of other pleasures too long unfulfilled. He slid his arm around her shoulders, and after a moment or two she leaned her head back against it.

"You know, I gave up earlier," he said.

"On what?"

"On us. It didn't seem like we were getting anyplace."

"You mean with, um, kissing."

"Right."

"The first time at my house or the second time here?" Her head swiveled toward him.

"Both. I didn't think it was in the cards."

"At my house I thought you couldn't wait to get home to the hawks."

"That," he said succinctly, "wasn't necessarily true. Especially after we kissed."

She turned back around again. He caressed her shoulder through her sweater.

When she didn't speak, he said, "I think I want to do it again."

"You didn't do it in the first place," she pointed out. "I kissed you. And here Billy Wayne phoned before I could even pucker up."

"Any chance you might make another attempt?" he asked hopefully.

"No," she said, her tone light. "It's your turn."

He bent slightly toward her and slid his free hand up the side of her neck. She looked up at him through her lashes. He saw uncertainty in her eyes and liking, and underlying all of that was something that he couldn't quite peg. Courage? Defiance, perhaps?

He supposed it did take courage to leave a relationship as she recently had done, and certainly she was defying society's expectations when she'd come here to make a go of her pregnancy all alone. But she wasn't alone anymore. She had him.

Just how true this was hit him like a ton of bricks. *She had him.* He wasn't going to hurt her the way that jerk of a fiancé had, nor was he going to back off. His heart twisted at the thought of what the guy had done to Dana. She hadn't deserved such treatment.

He kissed her cheek before angling her head so he could reach her lips. She leaned into him, and he felt the relaxing of tension in her body as he pulled her close. He deepened the kiss, teasing her with a lazy sweep of his tongue. She let out a little sigh, or was it a moan? Her hands moved across his chest, her fingers light, paused briefly at his nipples and continued up and around his neck.

Desire flared, and he felt himself growing hard. This woman knew how to kiss; she was practiced and experienced and so was he. He knew he should stop—she was pregnant with another man's child—but at the moment his brain didn't seem to be working properly. Other parts of him certainly were—his lips, which fit so neatly with hers, and his tongue, which dared to explore the warm sweetness of her mouth, and his hands—

His hands, which wouldn't stay put. As she eased down against the floor, they moved naturally up under her sweater. Lost in sensation as he was, he still managed to restrain himself for a few moments, but his restraint was overruled by lust. It didn't help that she was pressing against him, sliding her leg between his.

He reluctantly stopped kissing her. "Dana? Should we be doing this?"

"Why not?" she murmured against his neck. "Why on earth shouldn't we?"

"Because," he started to say, but then she silenced him by placing her mouth over his. If there was any doubt, it faded when she guided his hand up to her breast. He felt the roundness of her belly—how could he not?—but somehow it only made her more desirable. His fingers cupped her breast, his thumb circled her nipple, and she opened her mouth even wider. His desire for her went beyond the usual, beyond sex. For the first time since Lindsay died, he wanted to know a woman, heart, mind and soul. And not just any woman. This woman.

He feathered a chain of kisses down the side of her neck, inhaled the musky woman-scent of her from the hollow in her throat, pushed aside the vee neck of her sweater and kissed the pulse throbbing there. Her breathing was hot in his ear, and he felt his own breath coming in sharp pants. She pressed closer, whispering his name.

She slid her hand inside his shirt, and it rested warm against the hair on his chest. If they were skin to skin, body to body, nothing would be between them.

But something was. He felt a slight jab to his midsection and, stunned, he fell away. Dana's eyes, a complex range of blues, widened in alarm.

"Was that—"

"The baby. It kicked," she said. She sounded breathless, whether because of him or because the baby's kicking hurt, he couldn't say.

"It kicked *me*," he said. He felt wonder mingled with annoyance. He certainly wasn't in a mood for lovemaking anymore.

"I'm sure it didn't mean to," Dana reasoned.

"Well, it certainly knocked me down. So to speak."

Dana looked at him. She blinked. "You look so...so disappointed."

"I am." But he felt his lips curving into a grin. He didn't think he was the only disappointed one. She seemed as perplexed as he was.

"I guess little whozit doesn't want his mommy to fool around."

"I don't think the baby knows what's going on out here," she said reasonably.

He had to laugh. "Come on, Dana, I was only joking. Don't take everything I say so seriously."

"I guess I'd better remember that," she said.

"You're doing it again! I'm only making light of a moment that has no parallel in my experience. I've never tried to make love to a pregnant woman before.''

"We weren't exactly making love. We were only kissing.''

"A little more than that," he reminded her, his eyes involuntarily dropping to her breasts.

She moved slightly away. "I, um, well, I liked it.''

"I gathered that. So did I.''

"Do you want to resume where we left off? Or is that the end of it?" She looked so funny, so comical in that moment that he couldn't help laughing, at which she seemed crestfallen.

"What is this, twenty questions?" Then, seeing that she wasn't trying to be funny, he sobered. "As it happens, I think that's enough for tonight.''

"It really turns you off, doesn't it? That I'm pregnant?" she said quietly.

He let out a long exhalation of breath and leaned back on the couch pillow. "No, it doesn't. But when little whozit—''

"Please stop calling my baby 'little whozit.' I've chosen names. If it's a boy, it will be named Blaine, after my favorite uncle. If it's a girl, her name will be Rosemary. It was my grandmother's name.''

"Well, when little Blaine or Rosemary aimed a dropkick at my navel, that quelled any lusty feelings I was having at that moment. It also sparked my curiosity. Does it hurt?''

She tipped her head to one side, assessing him. "You're serious, aren't you?''

"Of course I am," he said. He couldn't imagine something inside him pushing and shoving like that.

"No, it doesn't hurt. I think they do it to make more room. I can feel it, but there's no pain.''

"And does it go on for the whole nine months?''

"You start feeling the baby move when you're about four or five months along. I felt my baby move on the day that I quit—" She stopped abruptly, paled and regained her composure. He thought she must have felt it move again. "I first felt it on the day I quit my job," she said more carefully.

"You quit? I thought maybe you were on a leave of absence."

He'd wondered about her, how she managed to pay her bills, if she would be going back to Chicago after the baby was born.

"I quit," she confirmed.

"It takes a lot of guts to quit a job when you're pregnant. Unless you have a healthy trust fund, that is."

"I thought it over carefully. I have some money."

"But not from the baby's father," he said.

"Not from him. Look, I really don't like talking about it." She edged away, turned on her side and pillowed her head on her arm.

"Okay," he said affably. He knew it had been a miserable period in her life, so he wasn't at all surprised she preferred not to discuss it. He wondered where she got her money. It's not as if she lived an elaborate lifestyle here, though. Maybe she didn't need much.

When he looked down at her, she had closed her eyes.

He glanced at the clock. It was nearly midnight. "I think I'd better run you home."

But Dana was fast asleep, looking unfathomably mysterious and womanly as she lay there, a slight flush on her cheeks, a tiny smile gracing her lips.

He didn't have the heart to wake her up, so he stretched out beside her. He watched her as she slept, one arm tucked under her hand and the other curved around her abdomen. The fabric of her sweater was pulled so tautly over the rise of the baby that he thought that if he watched carefully, he might see little Blaine or Rosemary kick again.

But he fell asleep before he saw anything.

Chapter Ten

Dana awoke to the glow of the fading embers in the fireplace and to Conn's hand flung across her midsection. Through the windows with their undrawn curtains, she could see a gray dawn stealing over the landscape. She eased away from Conn and sat gazing down at his face for a moment. Even in sleep he exerted a powerful primal sexuality from which she'd been sidetracked by the fact that he had nurtured her while she had the flu.

Last night she had trembled beneath his touch, had melted in his arms. Had they gone too far?

Her doctor, who thought she was married because she had made her first appointment with him as Mrs. Cantrell, had not prohibited sex. In fact, he had urged her to express her sexuality with her husband throughout her pregnancy. Dana hadn't clued Dr. Evans into the fact that there actually was no husband. It hadn't seemed important when she was reeling from the breakup with Philip and trying to come to grips with the necessity of bearing and raising this baby all alone.

Now she wished she had paid more attention to her doctor's discussion. Did expressing her sexuality include intercourse? She thought it probably did. But she had never entertained the possibility of a man's wanting to make love to her while she was pregnant. And not just pregnant, but hugely pregnant.

She wanted Conn to make love to her. The thought, which had been lurking in the back of her mind for days, wouldn't go away. When she had kissed him, she'd known that she didn't want him to stop, no ifs, ands or buts about it. She wanted to feel his hands caressing her body, all of it, to feel the heat of his sex pressed against her belly, to know him in every way.

She immediately dismissed these thoughts as the strange meanderings of a pregnant woman's mind. Imaginings that could never happen. Crazy, deluded longings.

Except that Conn had made no secret of the fact that he was powerfully attracted to her, pregnant or not.

If the baby had not kicked out at that precise moment, then what?

There was no doubt in her mind that they would have made love—wholly, completely and satisfyingly.

Conn's lips twitched slightly, and he smiled in his sleep. Perhaps he, too, was dreaming of what might have happened. She smiled at this and, because she couldn't resist touching him in that moment, she tipped a finger along the hairs on his arm. They were dark and curly, springing up under her touch. She pictured the pattern of dark hair on his chest, the tapering of it down his belly to the nest of curls below. She wanted to savor the scent of him, the taste of him, all of him.

Which meant that she was over her bout with the flu, *really* over it.

He shifted position and pillowed his head on one arm. He didn't wake, and she supposed that was just as well. She needed time to think this over, time to integrate their relationship into her reality. Using the arm of the couch for support, she laboriously pulled herself to her feet and padded to the bathroom. She might be over the flu, all right, but she still felt a little shaky in the knees.

When Dana emerged from the bathroom, Conn's eyes followed her as she made her way across the room.

"Good morning," he said, his voice rough with sleep.

"Yes, it is," she said. She glanced out the windows, where the rising sun was sending golden rays up and over the mesa. "I think I've overstayed my welcome." She sat on the edge of the couch, mostly because it would have been too difficult to get down on the floor and up again.

"No, you haven't," Conn said. He yawned and raised himself to a sitting position. "If I'd known you were going to stay the night, I would have made sure you were more comfortable, instead of letting you sleep on the floor." His hair was mussed, falling endearingly over one eye.

"I was fine," she said, not saying that it had felt wonderful to be cradled in his arms all night.

"Dana," he said, looking as if he were going to make some momentous pronouncement, but then his gaze came to rest on the mantel clock. He groaned. "I'm due to meet Billy Wayne in less than half an hour," he said, scrambling to his feet.

"We'd better check on Oscar," she said.

"You go take a look, and I'll toss some cereal in a couple of bowls and—say, are you all right? Really, I mean?"

"Yes, Conn," she said. She gazed up at him, wondering what he would say if he knew her lustful feelings at the moment.

His knuckles grazed her cheek. There was a tenderness in his eyes that she hadn't noticed before, or perhaps she hadn't been ready to see it.

"I'll drive you home on the way to Shale Flats," he said, and treated her to a pat on her derriere as she headed for the mews.

DANA INSISTED on taking Oscar back to the cabin with her.

"Why?" asked Conn. "He's fine. Just fine. He'll be fit to fly in a week or so from the looks of him."

"I can keep an eye on him all day. You can't." To her it was simple; she was the best qualified to be the bird's caretaker.

Conn hadn't put up much of a fight, and now, back at

her cabin, Oscar regarded her balefully from his cage, which Conn had set inside the lean-to behind the cabin where her father had kept his fly-fishing equipment. The owl seemed calm, and he sidled over to the side of his cage where she stood after Conn drove away.

"I'm not supposed to get attached to you. I promised," she told the bird. He winked at her in a way that was almost human, as if to say, "Well, we both know you will, but that's okay with me." The owl then let out a howling shriek as if to dissuade her.

The cabin seemed empty without Conn. During the time he'd taken care of her, he had been a fixture around the place, and she had grown comfortable with him and around him. She missed looking over and watching him hard at work with his computer propped on his lap. She missed having someone to chat with, to eat meals with, to make love with—although she supposed that technically they had not quite made love. Little Blaine or Rosemary had taken care of that.

But she didn't want to think of what might have been. Besides, she needed to phone Esther and give her a progress report on Oscar.

Esther sounded pleased to hear from her. "Dana, how are you this morning? And how is the owl?"

"He's okay. Conn thinks he has a bruised wing, which isn't very serious."

"So is our resident falconer coming out of his shell, do you think? You seem mighty friendly with him." Esther was clearly fishing.

"Conn? Well, we're getting to know each other," Dana said cautiously, knowing that whatever she said was likely to be reported widely by Esther, who was shaping up as the town gossip.

"That's a good thing. He's a nice guy. I can't imagine why he prefers to keep all to himself like that. Or why you do, either, by the way. You could join the ladies' club at my church or play bridge with my sister."

"Conn *is* nice," Dana murmured, not adding that she wasn't interested in becoming more sociable.

"Well, I've got to get back to my book. The princess and the sheik are having a big fight, and the duke asked her to marry him. I can't wait to find out what happens."

"Be sure to let me know," Dana said charitably.

"You bet. 'Bye, Dana."

Dana chuckled as she clicked the phone off. Esther reminded her of Raymond, her friend from Chicago. He was a set designer, much in demand, but he loved gossip, too. She hadn't talked to Raymond since she'd learned she was pregnant, knowing that if somehow he managed to figure it out, he'd spread the word so fast that she wouldn't have a chance to get out of Chicago before word reached Philip. But now there would be no harm in talking to him.

She took the phone, which in the past week or so she had come to regard as her lifeline to the world she'd left behind, into the kitchen. When Raymond's number rang at his studio, his assistant first told her that he was busy, but once Dana informed the man that Day Quinlan was calling, he scurried off to find his boss.

"Raymond, it's me," she said when Raymond answered.

"Day! Why, you little minx! How could you run off like that?" He sounded delighted to hear her voice.

"Sometimes you have to do what you have to do," Dana said, smiling even as she resorted to a stock phrase.

"Yes, I know. Which is why I went to Acapulco last week."

This statement made it easy to urge Raymond to report on his adventures in Mexico. He'd bought a leather coat there, and he'd found some delightful carved-wood furniture that he was having shipped to Chicago for his apartment redecorating project.

"You must come and see me, darling, when you get back," he told her. "You *are* coming back, aren't you?"

"Not just yet," Dana said, hedging. At that moment the baby elbowed her in the ribs and rolled over. She wished she could share this major development in her life with Raymond. She knew he would be interested and supportive, but he also saw Philip at the health club several times a week, and with Raymond's propensity for passing along interesting tidbits, she knew it wouldn't be a good move to take him into her confidence.

"So where are you?" Raymond demanded.

"I'd rather not say."

"Oh, being cagey, are you?"

"Yes, I suppose you could put it that way."

Raymond adopted a teasing tone. "Darling, don't you know you can't keep secrets from me? And by the way, if you haven't spoken with Noelle, you should give her a call."

"I have." Dana was surprised that Raymond didn't know this. He and Noelle were close friends.

"And Tricia?"

"No, but I'll be in touch with her soon."

"I hope so. We miss you, Day. Are you sure you don't want to tell me where you are? I could come to see you. You sound a little down today, dear. I'd love to cheer you up."

"No," she said too quickly. "I mean, I have some things to do. Important things." Like giving birth, she thought. Perhaps later she would ask Raymond to be the baby's godfather. He'd think that was a hoot.

"When you're ready for company, give me a buzz. Okay?"

"Okay. I'm glad I caught you in the studio," she said.

"Me, too. Ta-ta, darling."

"Ta—I mean goodbye, Raymond."

When she hung up, she sat and thought how great it would be to reconnect with Raymond when this was all over. Dana tried to imagine showing up at his apartment with a baby in her arms, but she couldn't. Raymond's apartment was done entirely in white—walls, carpet, everything. A baby most definitely wouldn't be welcome there, although she knew Raymond was fond of children. But let's face it—her life would be different from Raymond's once she had a baby. It would be impossible to pick up their friendship right where she left off. She'd better get used to the idea.

Tears of self-pity flooded her eyes, and she lowered her head to her crossed arms on the kitchen table and let them flow. She missed her friends, she missed her show and she missed her former life. She missed the emotional equilibrium that she had once had long ago, in the days before she became pregnant. These days it seemed as if every little thing upset her. Usually she didn't give in to her fluctuating emotions, but today she couldn't help it.

After a while she sat up straight, wiped her eyes and blew her nose. Everybody had problems, not only her. Conn, with his financial worries, and Esther, with her loneliness. At least she, herself, wasn't lonely. She had her baby.

"In spite of everything, I'm still glad I have you," she said out loud to the baby. It might be a silly habit, this talking to Blaine or Rosemary, but it gave her great comfort. She had an idea the baby could hear her.

And maybe it could. It chose that moment to flip over, its little hands or feet fluttering against the inside of her womb like butterfly wings. Like butterfly kisses, only inside.

CONN STOPPED BY Dana's cabin that afternoon to fix her drainpipe. She opened the door before he knocked, her eyes and nose suspiciously red.

"You're not getting sick again, are you?" he asked in a sharper tone than he intended.

"No, and Oscar's doing fine. I fed him some chopped liver that I had in the freezer."

"Let's take a look at him." He walked through the house and out the back door to the lean-to. When he went in, the owl eyed him with annoyance and emitted a screech or two.

"How are you, guy?" Conn said. He opened the cage and reached in for the bird, which had the temerity to peck his thumb.

"Hey, cut that out!"

"That must mean he's feeling fine," Dana said from behind him.

Conn set the bird on top of a barrel. Experimentally he palpated the owl's back and stomach, then spread its wings out. This provoked a squawk and another peck, but he satisfied himself that he had been correct in his assessment of the injury last night.

"In a few more days Oscar's going to be soaring high. We'll set him free once I'm sure he can fly."

Dana followed Conn back into the cabin and watched while he got down on the floor to remove the section of pipe that was rusted. It didn't take him long to replace it with the new one.

"Do you have time for lunch?" she asked as he was packing up his tools.

"No, I have to go home and see if I can fix my hawk wagon. It's leaking oil." He had acquired the truck from Steve when he'd bought the house, and this was the first time it had given him any trouble.

Dana seemed about to ask him something when the phone rang and she answered it.

"Hello?"

Conn wasn't paying much attention, but he sensed an immediate shift in Dana's posture from relaxed to tense, and his eyes flew to her face. She had gone ashen, and for a moment he thought that it must be bad news.

"I...I can't talk right now," she said. "I'll phone you back in a while." If he wasn't mistaken, her voice shook.

A silence, and then Dana turned her back abruptly and went into the living room, which afforded her some privacy although he could still hear every word she said.

"No. No, I can't. Later, I said!" He heard her click off

the phone and waited for her to come back into the kitchen, but she didn't.

He cleared his throat, reminding her that he was there. He grabbed his toolbox and walked past her to the door, picking up his computer on the way. Dana stood with the phone in one hand, clutching the back of the desk chair with the other. She looked as if she had seen a ghost.

"Dana, is everything all right?"

She seemed to pull herself back from someplace a long way away. "Y-yes. I think so."

He tried again. "It must be bad news."

She blinked. "Not exactly." But he noticed that she looked down and to the right the way she did when she wasn't telling the truth. Sometimes he hated this ability of his to know when people were lying. It made his life more difficult than it needed to be.

He forced himself to be polite even as he felt a certain anger that Dana wasn't being straight with him. "If you're sure you're okay, I'll be on my way."

"Sure. I'm fine." She came to the door to bid him goodbye and treated him to a faint smile when, after a moment's hesitation, he bent and kissed her on the cheek.

When Conn drove away, Dana was still standing on the porch. He wondered who it was that had called her, had provoked such a profound response. From what he could tell, she wasn't friendly with anyone in town other than Esther. And he was pretty sure that if it had been Esther on the phone, Dana would have told him.

So it was someone from her past life, probably. Someone that she preferred not to tell him about. Philip, perhaps, and by this time Conn was convinced that Philip was the name of her former fiancé, the baby's father.

But perhaps, he thought, extrapolating as he used to do when he was on the trail of an article, there was more to this than a saga of love gone wrong. Maybe Dana was involved in something nefarious. As odd as it would seem for Dana Cantrell to be part of any shady dealings, maybe she wasn't only hiding from the father of her baby. She could, he reminded himself with all the cynicism of a jaded reporter, be on the lam from organized crime. She could be a criminal herself. She could—

Oh, damn. She couldn't. Not Dana. At least, not the Dana he knew.

He went home and checked his truck, deciding that he needed to add more oil. He didn't have any, so there was no choice other than to drive back into town. By the time he pulled into a parking space at the Conoco station, he was still steamed that Dana wouldn't tell him the truth. Oh, the part about how she'd found out she was pregnant and her subsequent flight was true. He was sure of that. There had been none of that shifting of her eyes, no reticence, no waffling. If she trusted him enough to tell him that much, why didn't she spill the rest of her story? Again, he had come full circle around to the possibility that she was hiding something more.

A feeling of futility settled over him, and it was exceeded only by his anger—at Dana, and at himself for being such a chump. Suddenly he wanted to put some space between himself and this situation, and soon. A visit with his mother was long overdue, and while he was in L.A. he could stop in at the *Nation's Green* offices to see Jim Menoch.

Walking into the gas station, just to let off some steam, he kicked a crumpled beer can that happened to be lying nearby, and it flew up and hit the side of the building with a clatter.

A small boy stuck his head out the window of a rusting small compact car. "You mad about something, mister?" he asked with interest.

"Yeah," Conn growled. "You might say that."

When he went back to his truck, something out of place on the ground caught his eye. A credit card was what it looked like, so he bent and picked it up. He thought he might have dropped it when he got out of the truck earlier.

He turned it over with interest. The name embossed on the front wasn't his. "Day Quinlan," it said.

Conn doubted that he'd ever watched *Day Time* in his life. Yet he knew vaguely what the woman host of the program looked like. Short, blond, cute.

Like Dana, only not pregnant.

With dawning comprehension, with hard-hitting astonishment, he realized who Dana Cantrell really was. She was Day Quinlan, and she'd probably lost her credit card in his truck. Dana was the woman that people all over the country were trying to find, and here she was, living less than a mile away from him in Cougar Creek. Suddenly all the contradictions made sense—a beautiful woman, alone and pregnant; the expensive boots worn with beat-up cast-off shirts from her father; the prissy cloth napkins on the old table.

The thought occurred to him, though he tried hard to fight it, that Martin Storrs would pay a good deal of money to learn where Day Quinlan was. Not only that, but if Conn chose to take the job at the *Probe,* exposing Dana would be a hell of a debut. It would blow all the other tabloids' celebrity columns right out of the water.

DANA WAITED until Conn's truck had disappeared from view before she called Noelle back. The phone rang, and Noelle picked it up on the first ring. For once the sound of her best friend's voice didn't lighten her heart or give her a warm feeling. "How did you find me?" Dana asked without preamble.

"Why, Raymond gave me your number," Noelle said airily. "You must have forgotten to block the call return when you called him. After the two of you hung up, he pushed a button, and a robot at the phone company recited your phone number, just like that. Neat, huh?"

Dana rubbed the bridge of her nose with her thumb and forefinger. Noelle was right. When she had called Raymond, it had been on impulse, and she had neglected to block the call return function on her phone. How could she have been so stupid, and with Raymond of all people? She'd be lucky if he didn't plaster her name and telephone number on billboards all across Chicago.

"Day?"

"I'm here," she said wearily.

"I checked the area code. What ever possessed you to take off for some godforsaken place in Arizona?"

"I can't explain it," she said. "Don't even ask."

"Well, of course I'm asking. Philip said—"

"You haven't told *him?*" Dana asked sharply, her stomach taking a swan dive toward her feet. "I don't want Philip to know where I am." Or Myrtis, either, she might have added.

"Honestly, Day, this is so inconsiderate of you. Did it ever occur to you that the man might need closure?"

"He had closure when I caught him in bed with Erica," she yelped in spite of herself. "Whose side are you on, anyway?"

"I consider both you and Philip my friends," Noelle informed her.

"Since when?" Noelle had always been primarily her friend. Hadn't they laughed together, cried together, consoled and encouraged each other for the past seven years? Hadn't they bonded, truly bonded, as only girlfriends could do?

"Oh, Day, you should have seen how brokenhearted poor Philip was when you left without a word. Take pity on him."

Dana greeted this request with a stony silence. Take pity on the man who had betrayed her so cruelly? Who had had no qualms about breaking her heart?

"Day?"

"I don't want to discuss Philip with you, Noelle. Not now and not ever."

"But Day—"

When Dana clicked the phone off, Noelle was still talking.

CONN FOUND HIMSELF with plenty to do over the next few days, what with preparing for his trip to Los Angeles, deciding that the hawk wagon's oil leak required a new gasket, and further polishing the Florida panther article.

He kept Dana's credit card on a shelf below the bathroom mirror to remind himself why he hadn't called her. He couldn't help it; he thought of her differently now that he knew who she really was.

And every time he saw her name in front of him, he was reminded of how easy it would be to let a few words slip to Martin. Or to Bentley, to whom he owed a favor after she'd spoken out on his behalf over the Senator Bridlingame incident. It would make sense to divulge his information only after negotiating a suitable rate of payment, of course. The money could provide the down payment for his mother's entry into Catalina-Pacific.

Of course, after he'd blown the whistle on her, Dana could expect an avalanche of reporters, photographers and cameramen to descend on her. Neither she—nor the town of Cougar Creek—would ever be the same.

But how could he do this? How could he betray this woman, whom he had come to know and like? And it was more than like, he had to admit that. He was crazy about her, but not about Day Quinlan. No, it was Dana he cared about.

He cared too much about her to blow her cover, especially in light of all the recent emotional upheaval in her life. True, Conn needed money. But he didn't need it that desperately. Yet.

When Dana called him the day before he was to depart for L.A., he was slightly surprised to hear her voice, and he was happy, too. Keeping away from her was an exercise that had sorely tested his resolve. He'd wanted to pick up the phone any number of times, but he wouldn't have known how to make conversation with something as major as her true identity sitting between them, looming large and ominous over their whole relationship.

"Oscar is ready to be released into the wild, I think," she said brightly after a few pleasantries. "I've been letting him out of his cage, allowing him to move around in the lean-to for exercise. Do you think you could come over and take a look at him?"

Conn immediately felt guilty. He'd almost forgotten about the screech owl, and he needed to release him before he left on his trip. He told Dana he would be over that afternoon.

But when he arrived at Dana's place, despite working up a heady sense of anticipation over seeing her, instead of knocking on her door, he went around to the shed and checked on the owl. After a few minutes Dana came out to investigate the bird's screeching. She leaned against the door and watched as he spread Oscar's wings and checked for swelling.

When he had finished, Conn slammed the door of the cage. "I think he's ready to fly," he said, looking back over his shoulder. Dana looked especially pretty today. She had brushed her hair back behind her ears and was wearing a fuzzy blue sweater, a bright blaze of color against the trunks of birches shining silver in the sun.

He made himself stay on track, refusing to be distracted. "The longer we keep Oscar pent up, the weaker his muscles will be. We can walk down the creek to a place where there aren't a lot of trees and release him right away."

"You don't mind if I go with you?" The bracelet Dana wore gleamed golden against her skin, and he saw that it was the one he had returned to her on the morning after he'd met her. The initials on it had been *D. Q.* If he'd watched television more regularly, he might have caught on way back then.

"Of course I don't mind," he said.

"I'll go get my jacket," she said as she started back toward the cabin.

"You'd better wear boots," he called after her when he saw that she was wearing a pair of flimsy flats. "It can be rough going if there are a lot of rocks on the ground."

He had to carry the owl's cage, so he wasn't able to help Dana over the difficult spots in the terrain as they made their way along the edge of the creek. The brassy gleam of autumn was everywhere, a panoply of color. The wind-scoured air felt cool on his face, and above them the sky was a blazing blue. Dana said very little, looking down as she walked and concentrating on where she put her feet. He was glad that he didn't have to talk to her.

Now that he knew who she was, it seemed as if he was dealing with a different person altogether. After getting to know her in this remote setting, it was hard to imagine Dana—Day—on a stage in front of TV cameras. She was famous, a celebrity. People all over the world recognized her from her syndicated show. But he knew things about this woman that few other people did. Things such as the fact that she made really good coconut cake, that she was allergic to shellfish, that she'd been closer to her father than her mother.

That she responded to his kisses as if she'd been set on fire.

When they reached an open spot, he set the cage with the owl in it on the ground. The bird responded with a cacophony of ear-splitting screeches.

"One thing about taking care of him," Dana said wryly. "It's prepared me for the demands of a baby. After hearing what Oscar can do, a baby's crying in the middle of the night will be no problem." Conn smiled at this in spite of himself and opened the cage door.

"Well, Oscar, this is it," Dana said, sounding as though she didn't like it much.

He sent her a sharp look. "I told you not to get attached to this guy."

She let out a sigh and laughed slightly, self-deprecatingly. "I know. I liked taking care of him, that's all."

He tugged a pair of gloves out of his back pocket and pulled them on for protection from the owl's talons. Oscar struggled slightly when he removed him from the cage, then quieted. "Well, guy, you'll be on your own from now on. Godspeed." Conn held the bird aloft for a moment and tossed him into the air. Oscar's wings fluttered, spread and caught the currents before he soared across the clearing. Then, wings flapping and with not even a backward glance, he flew above the tops of the ponderosas on the other side of the creek.

"Goodbye, Oscar," Conn heard Dana say softly in such a heartfelt tone that he couldn't help looking at her. He kept his eyes on her as she watched the bird sail out of sight. He wasn't surprised to see tears in her eyes.

"Well, that's all, folks," she said, blinking them back. "It's sad to see him go, but it's also good to see Oscar flying without a problem. Good to have played a part in his rehab."

Conn lifted the cage and started back toward the cabin. He didn't talk. He didn't know what to say. It seemed as if the only topics he could think of would encourage him to say something that might tip her off that he knew who she really was.

She walked beside the creek with her hands stuffed deep in her pockets. "This experience with Oscar has taught me that I like working with birds," she said after a time. "I like getting them to trust me."

"I could tell that when you flew Aliah," he said, and then wished he hadn't. Sure enough, she latched on to his mention of the peregrine falcon.

"I can't wait to fly her again," she said eagerly. "I'm recovered from the flu now, which is why I'm hoping that we can go to Shale Flats soon. Tomorrow morning, maybe?"

He took his time answering. "Not tomorrow. I'm leaving for L.A."

He happened to glance down at her as he said it and was treated to the sight of her face falling in disappointment. He looked away quickly. He hated disappointing her. He realized that he cared entirely too much about this woman's emotions, about what happened to her, about who she was. And that was very much a sore point that gnawed at the edges of his heart.

"How long will you be gone?" She sounded disheartened.

"I'm not sure yet." He was going to leave his truck at the Conoco station so that Billy Wayne could replace the oil pan gasket, and he had made arrangements for the kid to drive him to the airport.

Dana trudged along beside him, her face devoid of expression. Suddenly Conn wished she'd say she didn't want him to go. He wanted her to miss him, and although he knew that she wanted him physically, that wasn't enough. He wished she would come right out and say that she liked his personality or that she cared what he thought about her. He wanted her to count him as more than a friend.

When they reached the cabin, they crunched through the fallen dry leaves to his truck, where he stowed the cage in back.

"Do you want to come in?" she asked.

He slammed the back of the hawk wagon closed and paused, hands balanced on his hips. He couldn't go on talking to her when he really couldn't talk to her, if that made any sense.

"Who's asking?" he asked abruptly.

She tilted her head to one side. He figured she was trying to decide if he was joking.

"Excuse me?"

"I said, who's asking if I want to come in? Dana Cantrell? Or Day Quinlan?" His eyes drilled into hers even as he hated himself for blurting it out.

He didn't think he could bear the hurt and confusion that he could see his words engendered. A darting flash of fear flickered across her face and settled in her eyes. "You know about me," she said warily.

He dug down into the pocket of his denim jacket and brought out her credit card. He held it up so that the hologram on it caught the sunlight. "You might want this back in case you need to do some shopping."

Slowly her hand came up and took the card from him. She stared at her name until he thought she wasn't going to comment. "You want to sit down on the porch for a few minutes?" she said at last, looking as if she couldn't accept her own helplessness when confronted with the truth.

"Sure." He might as well.

Dana walked over to the porch and lowered herself to the top step, and he did the same. She removed a tissue from her pocket and blew her nose. After that, she lifted her face to the sun and closed her eyes. "I didn't want the tabloids to find me," she said. "They have a way of making my life hell."

He gazed off into the distance where the golden leaves of an oak tree were turning brown and twisting in the wind. Several fell while he watched.

"So," she continued, "before I came here, I took back the name I was born with, Dana Cantrell. I changed it when I went into television, and not too many people remembered it. I figured I'd be safe. The tabloids pay for information, you know. That's why I couldn't get too friendly with the Cougar Creek locals. You never know if they'll turn you in for the notoriety it brings them or for the money or for a whole bunch of other reasons that people have for deliberately ruining other people's lives."

"So I'm the first one around here who knows?"

"As far as I can tell. I didn't even tell my friends in Chicago where I am."

"I thought you said you keep in touch with someone there."

"I do. Or rather, I did. Not anymore. I never told Noelle my whereabouts."

Dana didn't seem inclined to elaborate, and anyway, he was trying to figure out what to do. What to say. Her fingers were systematically tearing the tissue to shreds.

"Dana," he said musingly. He studied the side of her face, which was all he could see. "Or would you rather I call you Day?"

"Dana is my name now," she said quietly, and he thought he caught a note of despair trying to seep out between the words.

"I need to tell you something," he said, knowing that nothing between them would be the same once the words were out.

She lifted her eyes to his. He saw that she was puzzled, and he steeled himself. This was going to get worse, he knew. Much worse.

He drew a deep breath and steadied himself before going on. "Dana, I'm an investigative reporter. I used to work for Martin Storrs at the *National Probe*."

Her eyes widened, and she paled visibly. For a moment she looked wobbly, almost as if she might fall off the step. He came close to whipping out a hand to steady her, but it was only a moment before she stiffened slightly and pulled back a few notches.

"I know this is a shock to you," he began, but before the words were half out of his mouth, she had scrambled to her feet, had awkwardly grabbed the porch column for support, was putting as much distance between the two of them as she could.

"You bet it's a shock," she said, turning on him with barely contained fury. "How long have you known who I was? When did you find that credit card?"

"It fell out of my truck when I was in town a couple of days ago. You could have lost it the first day I met you for all I know."

Her eyes flashed. "I've been paying cash everywhere. I

haven't used my card. I don't know when I lost it. So did you invite Martin Storrs here to check me out? I didn't even know who he was until just now when you mentioned his name in the same breath as the *Probe*."

Her words cut into his heart like a cold, honed blade. He stood. "No, Dana, I swear I didn't know you were Day Quinlan. I'm out of the loop as far as television goes, and Martin didn't recognize you when we ran into each other at Susie's diner. If he had, he would have mentioned it."

"Martin offered you a job. I heard him say so when he called and left a message on your answering machine. Did you take it, Conn?" The naked pain in her eyes was eloquent, more eloquent than her words.

"The man fired me, and now he wants me to come back. But I haven't said whether I would take the job or not." He was sweating bullets under his flannel shirt.

"And you're going to L.A. to talk to him, aren't you? How much money will he pay you when you tell him you've found Day Quinlan? You need money. You told me so," she accused. She was trembling from the force of her fury.

"That's not why I'm going to L.A.," he informed her hotly, chagrined that she would automatically think the worst of him. He supposed he could understand why she would be suspicious, considering her past, but didn't his friendship mean anything to her?

Her face had gone as hard as a block of granite, and her fists were clenched at her sides. He had a sudden memory of how soft and sweet she had felt in his arms when they had slept all night in front of the fire. He made himself stop thinking about it.

"I won't tell anyone. Dana, you have my word."

Her outraged look and the fierce expression on her face told him how much she thought of that assertion. He was suddenly desperate for her to know that he wouldn't do anything to hurt her, not in a million years and not for any amount of money. His powerful feelings for her shook him to his core. He grabbed her wrist, aching for her to understand. "Listen to me," he said urgently.

"I trusted you, Conn." Her words stabbed him in the heart.

"Not enough to tell me the whole truth, apparently."

She wrenched away with one final look of anguish, and without saying anything further, she turned and marched into the house.

Shaken to his depths by the enmity in her eyes, he didn't try to follow her. Anyone else might find Dana's attitude slightly paranoid, but he knew the lengths to which the *Probe* and its sister tabloids were prepared to go to get the goods on celebrities. He felt a heave of disgust for his own participation in such endeavors, and it settled into the pit of his stomach.

He would have pounded on the door and insisted that they talk, if he'd thought it would do any good. But Dana had made it abundantly clear how she felt about him and about the *Probe,* and he didn't think there was any point in trying to change her mind. He felt as if he were made of very brittle glass, and if any more harsh words passed between them, he would shatter into a million pieces. All that was left for him to do, he figured, was to get in his truck and go home.

He didn't look back, but he knew if he did, he'd see her face at the window, peeking out from behind the curtain as she watched him drive away.

Chapter Eleven

Dana had an appointment with her obstetrician in Flagstaff the next day, but it was all she could do to get out of bed in the morning. Sadness had settled over her like a heavy blanket; it threatened to smother her. She'd known all along it would be dangerous to fall in love with Conn. She just hadn't known why.

She was still angry with him and still didn't know if he had somehow, unwittingly or on purpose, managed to blow her cover. She wasn't quite sure what to make of his connection with the *National Probe*. Should she believe him when he said he wasn't going to sell her out? Could he keep his mouth closed around Cougar Creek? Or should she assume the worst and expect the tabloid press to descend on her at any moment? Somehow, regardless of their last exchange, despite the way she'd lashed out at him, she couldn't imagine him betraying her.

Today she'd have to decide whether to leave here or to stay and take her chances. Leaving would mean that she'd most likely never see Conn again. Staying would mean putting herself and the baby at risk. It would be a difficult choice to make.

Finally, when she had pulled herself together enough to get dressed, she thought about the baby. Little Blaine or Rosemary was what this was all about. "We'll get through this," she told the baby. "Together."

One step at a time, she reminded herself wearily. That was the best way. And the first step was to keep her doctor's appointment.

The drive to Flagstaff went quickly because she was lost in thought. It was when she started down the off-ramp from the highway that she felt the contraction, and at the time, she didn't think it was important. She felt it as a brief tightening across her abdomen, a stiffening of the muscle wall beneath the skin.

The first contraction was something to ignore, but the second one definitely was not. *It's not time yet!* she reminded herself, trying not to panic. Uneasily she recalled stories she'd heard of women unexpectedly giving birth on airplanes, in bus stations, at work.

That was a frightening prospect. She told herself that she was almost at her doctor's office, and once she reached there, she'd be fine.

The third contraction was much like the first two, and she couldn't figure out if it was more intense or not. Probably not. But then she had another and another, and soon she lost count.

She found herself on an unfamiliar street and realized that she'd taken a wrong turn when she got off the interstate. She warned herself not to panic. Her doctor's office was on Fillmore Avenue. All she had to do was find the street, and she'd regain her sense of direction.

She pulled into a convenient driveway and backed and turned while a group of small boys watched openmouthed.

"You lost, lady?" called one of them.

"Yes," she said, adding to herself, *In more ways than one.*

She found Dr. Evans's office only a few minutes later. For a moment she sat gripping the steering wheel, trying to pull herself together. Then she slowly got out of the car and went inside, trying not to think about the possibility that she might be going to have this baby now.

STILL TRYING to shake the cloud of melancholy that had hung over him since he'd left Cougar Creek, Conn went to see Jim Menoch the morning after he arrived in L.A. The editor of *Nation's Green* was chubby, disheveled and jovial, and he was quick to ask after all of their mutual acquaintances. Conn had little patience with small talk when what he wanted to know was if *Nation's Green* would publish his articles.

"I liked the Florida panther piece you faxed me," Jim said finally, regarding Conn over the tops of his reading glasses. "I can pay you, oh, two hundred dollars for it."

This seemed like a lowball offer. "Two hundred? Can't you do better than that?"

"Conn, I can't, and I'm sorry. We're operating in the red every month, and we lost a major advertiser last week. The panther piece is great, but the fact is that we're looking for less experienced writers who will accept a pittance to get published."

"You and everyone else in this business," Conn said. There had recently been major shakeouts after a lot of magazines were acquired by multimedia giants, and the Internet was siphoning off advertising money.

"Yeah, but it's the reality," Jim said easily. "If you can take two hundred for the piece, we've got a deal. If not, I can't do a thing for you." His hands moved outward in an expansive gesture of futility.

Conn leaned forward in his chair. "What do you think about the possibility of that article and some of my others that you've published in the past being collected into a book?"

Jim stared out the window. "It's a viable idea," he said finally. "We couldn't publish it, though. We're shutting down our book operation after the first of the year."

Damn, Conn thought after he said goodbye to Jim and was on the way to the restaurant where he was to meet Martin for lunch. *I guess I can eliminate freelancing as a source of any serious income.*

It had only been a hope, and a small one at that. But he hated the idea that his prospects were narrowing.

SEYCHELLES was one of the finest restaurants in the city, a glitzy feed trough where the rich and famous went to see and be seen. When Conn got there, Martin had not arrived yet, so Conn asked to be seated at a table by a window. In five minutes or so he was surprised to see Bentley Howser come waltzing in. She was wearing a bright fuchsia suit, and on her way to the table, she blew a kiss to someone who looked a lot like Keanu Reeves.

Belatedly Conn realized that he should have been suspicious when his former boss suggested that they meet there; Seychelles with its lunchtime martinis and huge cuts of beef was no longer Martin's kind of place. Probably the whole point of this lunch was for Bentley to lobby him to take over her job, he thought sourly.

"Conn!" Bentley crooned. She leaned down for an air kiss and continued to hold his hand even after she had sat down beside him.

"Martin will be late," she said. "He had a meeting. So he sent little ole me to keep you company and give you our spiel."

"Great," Conn muttered, extracting his hand from hers.

"You're not angry, are you, Conn? After all, I wanted to see you. It's been too, too long."

Conn was saved from having to reply by a waiter arriving with menus, and Conn dropped his gaze to the lines of print, all the while seething. His first impulse was to get up and walk out, but that would have hurt Bentley's feelings, and he was fond of her.

He ordered a goat cheese, spinach and sun-dried tomato appetizer, very Californian. Bentley ordered something that looked like a couple of stewed capers on a sprig of radicchio, but then she was always watching her figure.

"So what is it that you do out there in Clutter Creek, Arizona?" Bentley asked.

"Eat dead people," he said with a straight face, just to test her. He didn't think she was paying any attention.

He had to give her credit. She didn't blink. "Like the Donner party. Weren't they holed up somewhere around there?"

"That wasn't in Arizona," he said with feigned patience. "And the name of the town where I live is Cougar Creek."

Bentley waved this information away. "Cougar Creek, Clutter Creek, what difference does it make?"

"Quite a lot to the people who live there and love it." He didn't feel the need to explain that he was fast becoming one of them, especially after his experience on the freeway yesterday when he'd been stalled in traffic backed up for miles on his way in from the airport. He'd forgotten how wearing L.A. could be.

"And you fly those birds of yours quite a lot?"

He thought about his hawks, knowing from experience that it was hard to explain the hold they had on him. "Yes," he said, cutting the word off short. For some reason a picture flashed across his mind: Dana as she flew Aliah and her eagerness and delight in the experience.

"If you move back to L.A., what will happen to them?" Bentley seemed genuinely concerned, which surprised him.

He pulled himself back from thoughts of Dana and started to say that he didn't know, that it most likely wasn't going to happen, but the waiter delivered the appetizer then.

Bentley took advantage of the momentary lull to lean across the table toward him. "Martin and I both hope you will take him up on the job offer. You must know that."

"Martin has mentioned something along those lines," he said carefully, afraid to reveal too much.

"The celeb column isn't hard," she said. "If you don't have anything interesting to report about somebody, you can always make something up. The key is for it not to be harmful. You know, like saying that somebody did something illegal. I would never do that, and I know you wouldn't, either."

"Great," muttered Conn.

"Oh, look there's Madonna," Bentley said, distracted as the star swept past with her entourage. They watched her disappear into an adjoining VIP room, and Bentley whipped back around again, ready to give him her full attention.

"Anyway, you could do such a great job with the column," Bentley said earnestly. "Martin's hoping to give it a different spin altogether, and I believe you're the man for the job."

"I'm not sure the job requires a man," he said. "Readers are accustomed to you and your style of writing."

She laughed. "Naturally. The column was my creation, but with Martin trying to bring new credibility to the *Probe,* I can't expect it to go on the way it always has. It's time for new blood."

"I'm not exactly new," Conn pointed out. He scooped up a bit of goat cheese and tomato on a water cracker and took a bite.

"No, but your style is perfect for hooking readers. And anyway, you know what Martin told me? You're only out on medical leave."

"Medical leave?" How could that be? When Martin had fired him, he'd told him in no uncertain terms to take his belongings and get out.

"Martin never finalized your termination papers. He decided to list you as being on medical leave because he had doubts about your mental state. Upending the trash can on his desk was what made him suspect you were in, I think he said, 'a dissociative state.'"

"Burying Martin's desk in garbage made a point. He had ordered me to comb through the senator's trash. So, Bentley, after I toss a bunch of garbage on my boss's desk, I'm only on medical leave? It might be Martin who's got the mental problem."

"Now, Conn, Martin was leaving your options—and his—open."

"Maybe he still is. Martin says he has someone else in mind for the job, someone who will jump at the chance."

Bentley's expression hardened. "So he told you that, did he?"

"He left a message on my machine."

"Martin didn't mention who it is?"

"Nope." Not that he had cared, nor did he care now. But evidently Bentley did.

She edged her chair closer. "Promise you won't tell a word. Oh, there's Warren and Annette." She yoo-hooed at the couple, who waved back. "Annette looks so soignée after having her last baby," Bentley said with considerable envy. She swiveled back around again. "Conn, I don't want you to tell Martin that you and I discussed the other candidate for the job."

"I won't say anything," Conn told her, not sure that this was wise.

Bentley adopted a conspiratorial tone. "It's Joy-Ellen Bauer. She's coming on hard and fast, and she really wants the celeb column."

Everyone at the *Probe* knew that there was a fierce rivalry between Bentley and Joy-Ellen, starting a few years earlier when Joy-Ellen had arrived on the scene and proceeded to steal Bentley's then-boyfriend out from under her. Worse yet, the boyfriend was the publisher of the *Probe*, a wealthy Australian, and he had ultimately married Joy-Ellen, much to Bentley's distress.

"I think I understand," Conn said cautiously.

"Of course you do. You can see that I don't want Joy-Ellen to take one more thing from me than she already has. So if you'll tell Martin you're considering the celeb job, seriously considering it, he won't give it to Joy-Ellen. There's another slot opening soon, the Weird and Crazy Pet Stories column. You know how Joy-Ellen loves animals. She's bought five llamas for their estate in Napa. Joy-Ellen will set her sights on Weird and Crazy Pets once she finds out it's available, but the present pet columnist is Ron

Fleming, and he's not giving notice until he comes back from vacation in a couple of weeks."

Conn frowned. Despite her pretensions, he liked Bentley, and he would never forget that she had taken his side in the Bridlingame flap. "Bentley, I suppose if it means that much to you—"

"Oh, Conn, it does! You don't know how much. I can't retire in peace until I know that Joy-Ellen Bauer won't succeed me as the celeb columnist. I mean it. And you know, Conn, if there's ever anything I can do for you—anything *else,* that is—please let me know."

Conn let this not-so-subtle reminder of his debt to her sink in as he watched Brad Pitt wend his way out of the restaurant. Bentley seemed to know him because she waggled a finger in the star's direction, and Pitt winked back. Bentley knew everything and everybody famous, even people who didn't live in Hollywood.

His previous debt notwithstanding, it occurred to Conn that Bentley could be useful to him. It might be possible to use the *Probe* for his—and Dana's—own purposes.

"Actually, Bentley, there is something you can do for me," he said slowly.

"What's that, darling?" She focused wide eyes, enhanced by lavender contact lenses, on his face.

"I'll tell Martin I'm interested in the job if it will help you out with Joy-Ellen. But first tell me everything you know about Day Quinlan. Everything," he said, emphasizing the last word. "And then I'll tell you what I need from you."

Bentley tipped her head to one side and favored him with a cool, assessing gaze. "Thanks, Conn, and of course I'll pour out every last little detail. But, Conn, why in the world do you want to know about Day Quinlan?"

"YOU'RE DEFINITELY NOT in labor. These are Braxton-Hicks contractions," said the obstetrician. He stopped palpating Dana's abdomen and stashed his stethoscope in his lab-coat pocket.

Dana stared at Dr. Evans over the mound of her stomach. "In other words, false labor?"

"Absolutely. When is your due date?" He gave her a hand up on the examining table.

She pulled the gaping examination gown around her. "It's still two months away. On the other hand, as I recall, my doctor in Chicago wasn't too sure, mostly because I've always been irregular and I might have given her the wrong date of my last period."

"So possibly your due date could be sooner?"

"I didn't think so when we figured it out. I hope not. I mean, I'm not ready to have this baby."

Dr. Evans chuckled. "Of course you are, Mrs. Cantrell. Or at least you'd better be."

He handed her an information sheet about how to tell if she was really in labor and said goodbye with the admonition to call him at any time if she was in doubt. Dana dressed and proceeded to the counter in the waiting room to settle her bill.

The woman next to her kept staring. "You look mighty familiar," she said. She studied Dana's face. "You kin to any of the Rawlings clan?"

Dana shrank away from her. "No," she said. "No, I'm not."

"Why, you know who you look like? And sound like? I mean, really?"

"Um," Dana said, reaching for the receipt that the young clerk handed across the counter. "I'm really in a hurry, and—"

"You look a lot like that lady that walked off her talk show a few months ago. You look enough like Day Quinlan to be her sister!" The woman turned to the clerk. "Don't she?"

The clerk cocked her head to one side. "If you take away

the reddish hair and make it blond,'' she allowed reluctantly.

Dana backed away. She almost tripped over a baby in a stroller that she hadn't seen behind her.

"You take it easy, Mrs. Cantrell. You didn't hurt yourself, did you?" the clerk said anxiously.

"No," Dana said. As she fled, the woman and the clerk began debating why Day Quinlan, who hosted one of the most popular shows on daytime TV, had left.

"I think she got mixed up in some drug problem. Remember the time she interviewed that drug lord from Colombia about drugs? Must have been drugs, I say."

"She doesn't seem the type," protested the clerk. "Why, Day Quinlan was always speaking out against marijuana and stuff."

It was the first time since she'd left Chicago that anyone had guessed who she was. And it had never happened in Cougar Creek. Suddenly she couldn't wait to get back to the small town and her little cabin where she felt safe.

But her heart sank as she realized that she'd have to leave there soon. She'd better start preparing to move to the apartment hotel in Flagstaff so she'd be near the hospital in case she started labor in earnest. The idea of leaving the cabin near Cougar Creek brought tears to her eyes. She'd fixed the place up, made it her own. She hadn't thought she could grow so attached to it, but she had. Oh, she had.

Still, the thought of the baby's imminent arrival made her smile through her tears. "Not much longer now," she said to it in a conversational tone, though she had felt no more contractions since she had left the doctor's examining table.

Perhaps she could be out of the cabin and far away from Cougar Creek before Conn returned from Los Angeles.

DANA SPENT the next couple of days after her doctor's appointment packing. There wasn't a whole lot to take with her, but she'd ordered some baby things from catalogs—

tiny hats, aqua-and-yellow bootees, sweet little gowns. She folded them with leaden hands before packing them in cardboard boxes. Her clothes, the few she'd brought with her, went into a couple of suitcases. When she was finished, she worked feverishly on the second of her cross-stitch samplers and finally, amazingly, finished it late the next day. Since she was planning to leave early the next morning, she decided to drive into town to show Esther her handiwork, even though she was alarmed to see that the sky was gray and lowering. For a moment she reconsidered. She didn't really have to see Esther before she left.

But she wanted to say goodbye. Esther had been kind to her, and she owed her at least that. She'd be back before dark, anyway, and this night was going to be hard enough. It was her last night in a place that she'd grown to love, and she knew she would be thinking about Conn.

She told herself that leaving Cougar Creek was the best thing for both her and the baby. She only wished she could make herself believe it.

THE NURSING HOME where his mother lived depressed Conn so much that he didn't stay long. It seemed to him that Gladys was dying in the worst way, her mind worn out long before her body. His mother didn't know who he was, of course, and she slept through most of his visit. During that time, her roommate complained that the staff didn't turn her often enough to prevent bedsores. He saw spider webs in the corners of the ill-lit bathroom. And the intercom in the rooms was improperly used to page attendants ceaselessly so that no one trying to sleep could get enough rest.

"I'll get you out of here, Mom," he said to Gladys. He didn't know if she heard him or not. She was awake but kept staring at the ceiling.

The visit, short though it was, made his decision easier. He knew for sure now what he had to do.

DANA, AFTER SHE ARRIVED in town, found Esther alone in the library shelving books. When she presented her needlework, Esther fingered the recently completed sampler admiringly. "Nice job," she said. "Real cute. You want to have Billy Wayne frame both of the ones you did? I could take them over to him."

"Well, actually," Dana began. She stopped, unsure how to tell Esther that there wouldn't be time for this.

"Is something wrong, Dana?"

Dana looked at the floor, dismayed that her eyes were filling with tears. One fell and splashed on the librarian's slipper.

"Dana? Why, honey, you'd better come over here with me and set a spell. We'll have a cup of coffee and you can tell me what's bothering you."

Dana wiped the tears away. "No, Esther," she said, but the librarian steered her across the room where she sat her in a chair and pushed a box of chocolates in her direction.

"I'll get the coffee," Esther said, and Dana, unable to resist, helped herself to a chocolate butter cream mint and popped it into her mouth.

"Chocolate is a mood raiser," Esther said as she returned and set a cup of coffee in front of each of them. "I think it's been scientifically proven."

Dana tried to smile but couldn't. Tears threatened to spill over again, and Esther patted her shoulder comfortingly while she dabbed at them with a tissue.

"I've heard that pregnant women are overcome with all sorts of emotions," Esther said. "Don't worry, I don't mind if you cry your little heart out."

And then Dana was sobbing, her face in her hands, and before she knew it, Esther's arms had gone around her, and she was smoothing Dana's hair. "Shhh, honey, now, it can't be that bad," she said.

"I...I'm leaving Cougar Creek tomorrow," Dana sobbed. "And I like it here, I really do, and Conn's gone, and..." She pulled herself up short before telling Esther that Conn knew her secret and might even now be discussing it with people at the *Probe*. She reminded herself that Esther didn't even know that she *had* a secret.

"Conn's coming back to Cougar Creek, Billy Wayne says. Billy Wayne's taking care of those birds of his."

"I won't be here when Conn comes back," Dana said, adding miserably, "and he wouldn't care, anyway."

Esther considered this. "Do you care about him, dear?"

"I'm going to have a baby," Dana wailed. "It doesn't matter if I care or not. He's not going to want me. I'm…I'm only passing through his life, like Oscar passed through mine."

"Oscar?"

"That's what I named that fool owl. I wasn't supposed to get attached to him, but I did." She sniffed and made a great effort to hold back her tears.

Esther wrinkled her brow. "Look, I'm not looking to pry into your personal life, but I figure your husband walked. So whether you care about this falconer does matter, I think. Maybe a lot. It's okay to find comfort in a handsome man like Conn McTavish. Who wouldn't want to?"

I can't. Not if he's selling me out to the Probe, Dana thought, but she couldn't say it.

"My guess is that Conn cares about you, too. Billy Wayne said that all Conn could talk about when they were up at Shale Flats was you. He said Conn kept relating everything they did to a day when you and he went up there and you flew the birds. Billy Wayne said that Conn talked about how pretty the sun looked on your hair, and how you loved flying that big bird of his, can't recall its name—"

"Aliah," Dana breathed, recalling the brush of feathers against her cheek, the feeling of exhilaration when Aliah stooped and dived toward the lure, the look of Conn silhouetted against the sunrise. She would never go to Shale Flats with Conn again, would never fly the falcons. Would never know that great sense of freedom.

"Yes, the bird's name was Aliah, I remember now. So

if Conn McTavish cares enough to talk with my young nephew about you, I think you can take it for granted that you mean more to him than just any old neighbor. Billy Wayne is a reliable witness, even if he does look a mite unusual.''

Dana wiped away one last tear. "So what do you think I should do about it?"

"Well, what do you say we go over to the Powwow Diner and eat us an early dinner? Susie's blue-plate special today is pot roast with horseradish gravy, and she does a mighty good job with it. This storm that's coming is supposed to be a whopper, but it's not here yet and you and I can have a nice long visit."

"What storm?"

"Oh, I forgot you don't get television or radio weather forecasts out there at the Cantrell place. A big snowstorm blew up out of nowhere, and it's heading right this way. Wait a minute while I go get my purse and close up the library."

"It's a little early for snow, isn't it?"

"Not really, honey, we normally get a few flakes in November. Now where did I put my keys?"

Esther exchanged her slippers for a pair of shoes, shut the library, and Dana allowed herself to be dragged along to the diner.

While they were waiting for dinner, Esther leaned across the table, her eyes bright behind her glasses. "Everybody in town likes Connor McTavish the more they get to know him. They think he's—well, *cool* is the way Billy Wayne puts it. And handsome? Honey, the falconer wrote the book on handsome."

After dinner, Esther would have liked her to stay longer, offering her dessert at her place. But snowflakes had begun to skirl out of the sky on a whippy sharp wind, and Dana told Esther that she'd better be getting back to the cabin.

Esther walked her to her car. "I've really enjoyed knowing you, honey. You keep in touch."

"I will," she said. Sadly, she knew she wouldn't be back to the cabin for a long time, but she promised to send Esther a Christmas card and a picture of the baby.

It was already dark when she rolled out of Cougar Creek. She had tears in her eyes after saying goodbye to Esther, the one friend she'd made here other than Conn, and she was distractedly thinking of all she had to do to shut the cabin up before she left. Another car was behind her as she turned onto the highway toward home, and it continued to follow hers at a respectful distance. It was unusual to see strange cars on this remote road, especially at night. Dana thought about the other car and wondered who would be driving way out into the country at an hour when most people in Cougar Creek were at home with their families, and on a night when a storm was headed their way.

But then she turned on the windshield wipers to clear away the increasing snowflakes, and she didn't think about the car anymore. She wanted to mull over all the things Esther had said about Conn. Maybe he *would* want to seek her out after she'd left here. Maybe he really *did* care.

Maybe. But she'd probably never find out, because she intended to leave no forwarding address.

CONN SETTLED BACK WEARILY into his seat on a 4:15 flight from L.A. to Flagstaff and ordered a martini. Then, on the seat tray in front of him, he carefully spread out a few of the clips from Bentley's column that she had given to him before he left. They were complete with photos.

Dana's pictures stared up at him. "Day Quinlan and her honey, Philip Grantham, at Chicago's Heart Ball," said one. "Day Quinlan and Philip Grantham whoop it up in the Virgin Islands," said another. "Day Quinlan soaks up a few rays on a friend's yacht," said the next. That one showed her reclining on a deck chair in a yellow bikini, sunglasses pushed up to hold her long blond hair like a headband.

Well, her hair was shorter now and not as light in color,

and Dana wouldn't be wearing any bikinis for a while. She had gained a bit of weight in the face, which he found very attractive. No, a correction was in order—he found it beautiful. Since he'd left her, it seemed as if he had thought endlessly about the way Dana looked and the way her skin felt, the sweet smell of her and the sound of her voice.

To his eyes and ears, to all of his senses, Dana was lovely. She merely happened to be a little bit pregnant at present. This separation from her had made him see how crazy he was about her, and he was going to tell her so. His insides clenched when he thought about telling her the rest.

Somehow he had to tell Dana that he was going back to work for the *Probe*. It would make her hate him even more. But once she knew that he hadn't told anyone at the *Probe* her whereabouts, perhaps she would understand that he was loyal to her. Maybe she would appreciate that quality and see his concern for his mother as a manifestation of it. After all, if he could be loyal to other important people in his life, he would be loyal to her. Because of her devastating experience with Philip Grantham, surely Dana would regard his loyalty as a plus.

Conn was more determined than ever not to let this woman get away. He had been foolish enough to let Lindsay go without making a commitment, and he would regret it all of his life. After losing Lindsay, he had fashioned a cage of his own sorrow, and he was ready to spring himself from it now. He was ready to commit to Dana Cantrell/Day Quinlan.

But how could *she* commit to *him* when she hated the kind of work he did?

STILL PREOCCUPIED with her thoughts, Dana cut a hard right off the highway, heading down the winding drive to the cabin. The car following her turned, too.

She was instantly alert. No one else lived on this driveway. The land belonged solely to her with no neighbors closer than Conn, and he wasn't back yet. She blinked and squinted into the rearview mirror, but the car's headlights blinded her. Although it had drawn closer, she still couldn't tell who was driving. Her first thought was that it must be someone from the tabloids and that Conn had done his dirty work, thrown her to the wolves.

But what if it wasn't a reporter? What if it was someone else, someone intending her harm? She wished now that she'd agreed to have a phone installed in her car. Even though a phone might not have worked because of the mountains, she could have tried it. But who would she call when she thought she might be in danger, like now? Esther, who would be ineffectual in a situation like this one? Billy Wayne? The county sheriff, whose headquarters was thirty miles away? Uneasily she sped up. So did the car behind her.

When she reached the cabin, she drew the car as close to the front porch as possible. She intended to make a quick dash for the front door. But she'd have to unlock it before she could get in, so she located the correct key on her key chain and prepared to open her car door. Even as she did so, she knew with unsettling certainty that because of her pregnancy, she wouldn't be able to run very fast.

A man got out of the other car. He stretched, yawned and walked around the front of it so that its headlights cast his figure in sharp relief.

Dana would have recognized that swagger anywhere, and that thin-lipped condescending smile, that pale-brown hair flecked with just the right amount of gray at the temples to make him look distinguished. But she still couldn't believe her eyes.

The ground seemed to tilt sideways. She clutched the car door, trying to maintain her equilibrium.

Her voice quavered when she spoke. "Philip?" she said.

"How touching that you still remember my name," he replied.

Chapter Twelve

As she unlocked the front door of the cabin, Dana supposed she should be grateful that he hadn't brought Myrtis with him.

Philip followed her inside and stood looking around with upraised eyebrows. "Day, this place is a dump. How can you stand it?" he asked bluntly.

She forced back indignation and hurt. She had mopped and painted, scrubbed and rearranged furniture. The cabin was homey now in a way that it hadn't been before, and she was comfortable here. Philip had no right to arrive uninvited and start criticizing. Of course, that's what he'd always done. She hadn't cared before, but now she did.

Willing herself to remain silent, she switched on a lamp and took in the wings of gray hair frosting Philip's temples, his narrow straight nose, the way he looked down it with an air of superiority. She'd once thought he was handsome, but now all she really noticed about him was the cynicism reflected in the narrowing of his eyes as they took in his surroundings. Whatever had attracted her to him in the past held no interest for her now.

She didn't offer to take his coat, but she removed her jacket. Philip stiffened and blanched. "Day?" he said cautiously. "You're—you're pregnant."

She blew out an exasperated sigh. She didn't have any patience for this man, someone she had once loved, someone she had once hoped to marry. She was astonished that she had absolutely no feeling for him at all anymore.

"As it happens, I am," she said curtly. She walked over and hung her jacket in the closet before turning to face him so that he could see the extent of her pregnancy. She felt defiantly proud and firm in her resolve to fight him for this child, fight him tooth and nail with every resource in her power.

"My God." Philip sank down on the green chair, and her first reaction was *No, you can't sit there, that's Conn's place.* Then she noticed that Philip's complexion had turned almost as green as the upholstery fabric, and that made her want to laugh. She'd hold her laughter until later when she could really enjoy it. It gave her a sense of bitter triumph, that suppressed laughter.

"So what happened—did the *National Probe* publish my address for all the world to know?"

"The *Probe?* No."

This poked a hole in her belief that Conn had sold her out, and Philip's denial threw her off balance for a moment.

"So who was it? Was it Raymond, when you ran into him at the health club?"

"Not Raymond. You might as well know, Day, it was Noelle who told me where to find you."

"Noelle?" The walls seemed to close in on her, and she seemed to have forgotten how to breathe. It was hard to believe that her best friend would tell Philip where she was, yet in the light of her last conversation with Noelle, it could be true. With the wind knocked out of her sails, she lowered herself to the couch.

"After she told me your phone number, it was an easy matter to have some of my people trace it to Cougar Creek."

Philip had minions for everything—people to run his household, people to pick up his dry cleaning, people to find other people. It figured that one of his lackeys would have stayed on the case until he located her.

"How did you find out where I live once you got to Cougar Creek?"

"A kid with orange-and-purple hair pointed me in this direction when I stopped at the local Conoco."

Philip had run into Billy Wayne, of course. "Why did you come here, Philip?" She was still numb over Noelle's betrayal.

"To see you," he said reluctantly. He stared down at his shoes, wet and glistening with melting snow.

She closed her eyes and tried to think. Maybe Conn hadn't told Martin or anyone at the *Probe* where she was. Maybe—

"It's not my baby," Philip said flatly.

She opened her eyes and stared at him. "Excuse me?"

"It's not mine."

She dismissed this assertion with the scorn it deserved. "Of course it's yours. You were the only man in my life for almost two years."

His voice rose on a note of querulousness. "You had plenty of opportunity to be with other men when you went on vacation without me. You and Noelle went skiing every year."

"You took vacations without me, too, but I never thought you were unfaithful," she said hotly.

"Noelle said there was a man in Vail."

Sheer incredulity was Dana's reaction to this statement. "What man?"

"Some guy you picked up in a bar."

She racked her brain, trying to recall if there could have been someone, anyone, that Noelle might have thought she was interested in. Certainly she hadn't slept with anyone else from the moment she set eyes on Philip and decided he was the one for her.

She was aware of her anxiety honing down to a fine sharp edge. Her anger grew, burgeoned, spread. "I can't imagine what Noelle was thinking," she said furiously. "There was no one. No one but you. For almost two years,

Philip.'' As she spoke, she realized how stupid she was to argue. If he thought the baby wasn't his, so much the better. He wouldn't want it then.

"No need to go ballistic,'' Philip said placatingly. "I came to tell you something.''

She was instantly suspicious of where he was going with this. "Like what?'' She rubbed her arms through her sweater. It was cold in here. She wanted to turn on the wall heater to get the dampness out of the air, but she suddenly felt a lack of energy for getting up and crossing the room. Her stomach had begun to hurt—heartburn from the horseradish gravy at dinner, she thought distractedly.

Philip went on talking. "I'm here to discuss something important. I want closure, Day. I couldn't believe it when you left Chicago without a word. Not after all we meant to each other.''

"We evidently didn't mean enough to each other for you to stay away from Erica,'' she pointed out. "You're the one who cheated, not me.''

Philip narrowed his eyes. "I wouldn't have been interested in her if you hadn't been such a bitch. You and my mother, hounding me, making my life miserable.''

Oh, that was a nasty cut, but she wouldn't let him get away with it. "Your mother, maybe, but not me. When was I ever anything but kind, Philip? When did I ever start an argument? When did we ever fight, for that matter? I always gave in to you.''

"You're starting an argument now,'' he said smugly.

"I'm not—'' Her stomach was really hurting.

"I didn't come to talk about you and me, actually.''

Did he want to talk about the baby? But no, he wouldn't have come here to discuss the baby if he hadn't even realized that she was pregnant, and she was sure his surprise had been genuine.

Despite the intensity of this scene, she was beginning to feel slightly foggy, as if her thought processes were scrambled. "You want something,'' she said heavily.

"Yes, Day."

"But you said the baby's not yours," she said woodenly.

He looked startled. "It's not the baby I want. It's your blessing."

Totally confused, she could only say, "What?"

"Your blessing. Noelle and I are going to be married, Day."

THE SNOW WASN'T AS BAD when he reached Cougar Creek, but it had made driving on the interstate risky, and Conn was glad to be almost home. By prearrangement, he dropped off the rental car with Billy Wayne at the Conoco station for pickup by the rental company later.

"I fixed the oil pan leak in your truck, and it shouldn't give you any more trouble," Billy Wayne told him. "And, like you said when you called, I put up the extra tarps on the sides of the hawk cages so they'd stay warm in the storm."

"That's fine, Billy Wayne," Conn told him. Quickly, eager to be on his way, he paid Billy Wayne for his work on the truck and for his help with the hawks before heading out of town. He wanted to see Dana, and it was the first time in his whole life that he had experienced such exquisite longing for another person. He had to convince her that he would always be true to her, and he'd make her understand why he was going to go back to work at the *Probe*.

The wind had picked up, and the falling snow was a gauzy curtain that blurred everything but the thin black ribbon of lonely road, marked with tire treads as if someone had recently passed. The weather reports he had heard on the car radio during the drive from Flagstaff had not indicated that the snowfall would be this heavy.

His truck jounced over the bumps in Dana's driveway the way it always did. Here the snow was beginning to stick to the ground, wisping across the dead leaves and rocks in lacy patterns. Tomorrow perhaps they would wake up to a new landscape, pure and clean and new.

At the end of the driveway, the truck's headlights bobbed across Dana's familiar gray sedan and then flashed off the chrome of another car.

Another car? Who would be here at this hour and in this weather?

Mystified, Conn braked to a stop and slid out of his truck. He heard angry voices inside the cabin, and, suddenly worried, he quickened his step. He was at the door in a matter of seconds.

He pounded on the wood. "Dana?"

The voices ceased, and he heard Dana's footsteps crossing the floor inside. When she saw who it was through the window, she threw the door open.

"I heard an argument," he said. "Is everything all right?"

She stood aside so he could enter. "Not exactly."

There was no doubt in Conn's mind as to who the fellow standing behind her was. Nevertheless, Dana introduced them.

"Conn, this is my former fiancé, Philip Grantham. Philip, Connor McTavish. Philip came to see me one last time, Conn, before he marries my very best friend. Now why don't you leave, Philip? Give my regards to your blushing bride."

Conn, his hand extended for a handshake, was ignored. Philip flushed angrily, a nervous tic tugging intermittently at his right eyelid.

"Noelle was a great comfort to me after you left. She is hoping you'll be happy for us," Philip said.

Dana inhaled deeply. "Yes, I guess I am, but I'm even more happy for myself. I'm happy that I won't have to have anything more to do with either of you. I was afraid you'd want the baby, Philip, and I'm really glad you don't. Because you wouldn't get it, not as long as I draw breath."

"Noelle wants to have my children," Philip informed her stiffly.

Dana started to laugh. "Noelle have more children?

That's the first I've heard of any desire on her part to increase the size of her family.'' In fact, Noelle had complained about Timmy and Katie's births so often that Dana
had tired of hearing about it. Timmy had been too big for
her, she said, and Katie took too long coming. Noelle had
vowed many times that she would never have another baby
no matter what. She had even talked about having her tubes
tied.

''She knows my mother is eager for someone to carry
on the family name,'' Philip said.

''Let's hope your first child is a boy, then,'' Dana retorted.

''You won't tell Mother that you had a baby?'' Philip
said, looking worried.

Dana knew what he feared—that his mother would want
the baby, a child that he was clearly not prepared to accept.
''Tell Myrtis? Not a chance. And now, Philip, will you
please get out of my house?''

Philip's jaw worked as if he were ready to fire off another salvo, but Conn stepped forward.

''You heard what she said, Grantham. Butt out.''

''And exactly who are you to tell me what to do?'' Philip
was bristling, but not very effectively. Conn figured he
could punch his lights out without even working up a
sweat.

''Conn is my neighbor,'' Dana interjected.

''And her friend,'' Conn said, not even trying to keep
the menace out of his voice.

''What kind of friend?'' Philip's voice was heavy with
insinuation. ''It could be your kid.''

Conn clenched a fist. ''Listen, you—''

Dana inserted herself between them. ''I only met Conn
a little over a month ago. Philip, you're way out of line.''

''I'll say,'' Conn added.

''I'll go, but not because this big SOB says so,'' Philip
said. He brushed past Conn to the door, but Conn was hot

on his heels. The cold outside was clear and clean against his face, but it didn't dispel his fury.

"Who are you calling an SOB?" As he spoke, Conn's mind reddened with unparalleled rage, and he grabbed the guy's coat. Anger pounded in his veins as Philip whirled, pale eyes hard as agates.

"Get your hands off me," Philip said. The words shot out in short bursts, hanging in the air between them. Philip wrenched away. Behind him, large clumps of snow mixed with sleet were coming down faster now.

Dana stood watching from the doorway. Conn was afraid she might step out onto the porch and try to put an end to this.

Before he could warn her to stay where she was, she spoke, clearly determined to get her own licks in. "Philip, how could you expect me to appreciate your announcement that my best friend is planning to marry you? I confided in Noelle, I told her things I wouldn't tell anyone else in the world. And what does she do? She tells you that I was unfaithful? It was a lie that served her purposes, obviously." Her words rang with indignation and something more. This man had hurt her, and so had her friend.

Philip brushed off the lapels of his coat, which was cashmere from the look of it. "Okay, so we won't be sending Day Quinlan an invitation to the wedding," he told Dana, all but jeering.

"Day Quinlan has ceased to exist," she said, her chin lifting in defiance. "I'm Dana Cantrell now."

"You can call yourself whatever you want. It doesn't matter to me."

"That's enough, Grantham," warned Conn.

"I've said what I came to say." He seemed about to leave. Then, unbelievably, Philip's balled-up fist swing out, aimed smartly at Conn's jaw. Overriding Conn's surprise that this guy would resort to physical violence was his instinct to block the punch with his left, but instead he lunged sideways so that the blow barely glanced his cheek. Then he retaliated with a quick jab to the side of Philip's face and, while he was at it, a satisfying knee to the gut. Grantham let out a surprised *oof!* and, his feet flying out from under him on the slippery porch, he went down doubled over.

Dana screamed, and Philip groaned. "If you don't get back in that car of yours and disappear pronto, I'm calling the sheriff," Conn said, his voice a menacing growl.

Grantham's eyes closed, then opened again. He sprawled with his feet and arms going every which way, his mouth opening and closing as he gasped for air. He looked like nothing so much as a fish out of water. He put a hand to his face and stared at it dazedly when it came away covered with blood.

"Let's get back inside. It's cold out here," Conn said to Dana. With a hand on her elbow, he guided her into the cabin.

After slamming the door between them and her uninvited guest, Dana lifted the curtain back and peered out into the darkness. Philip stumbled off the porch in the general direction of his car. She dropped the curtain and went to the wall heater, flipping the switch to On and standing in front of it while it heated up.

"At least you didn't hurt him so much that he couldn't walk," Dana said into the silence.

"I didn't want to hurt him at all. He aimed the first punch."

Dana seemed distracted. "I suppose he'll be all right going back into town. I wonder why we haven't heard his car starting."

"He's probably still shaky on his feet. At least I left him in condition to drive."

"But the snow." She glanced out the window.

Conn shook his head in disgust. "He's from Chicago and no doubt accustomed to driving in wintry weather. I'm not going to waste any time worrying about that slimeball. I'll kill him if he ever comes near you again."

They heard a car engine start. Conn went back to the window and watched as Grantham's car drove slowly away, trailing a plume of white exhaust, its red taillights reflecting off the falling snow.

He was ready to move closer to Dana, preparatory to upping the emotional voltage of this little scene, but she shot him a curdling look. "So now that you've been to see Martin, should I expect a phalanx of reporters invading my property tomorrow morning? Complete with flashbulbs and TV cameras?"

He'd opened his mouth to reply indignantly when she held up a hand. "No, don't. This has been quite a night for revelations. I'm not sure I can take any more."

What he wanted more than anything was to see her love for him shining pure and lucent from her eyes. This wasn't going as planned, to say the least, but he forced himself to remain calm. He had to make her understand that he would never do anything to hurt her. "Dana, I didn't say anything to Martin or anyone else."

Whether she believed him or not, he couldn't tell. There was a tautness around her eyes that he'd never noticed before, and her lips were compressed into a grim line. He realized that despite her tough facade, tears were on the verge of spilling down her cheeks.

She started to turn away, but he was across the room in two strides. He captured her in his arms, pinning her to him.

"Conn, don't," she said, but he didn't want to let her go.

"Are you all right?" he asked gently. "Grantham didn't hurt you, did he?"

She took her time before shaking her head. "He didn't hurt me."

"Then why don't we sit down and talk this over?" He started to propel her over to the couch, but she remained rooted where she stood. She gripped his arm with a strength that he hadn't known she possessed, and her eyes were wide, surprised.

"Conn, wait. I...I think the baby's coming."

WATER. He knew you were supposed to boil water. First he lit a fire in the fireplace and then, telling himself that this would be a most inconvenient time to get the jitters, Conn went into the kitchen and put a big pot of water on the stove.

"Isn't it too early? I didn't think the baby was supposed to be here for another month," he called to Dana.

"There's some doubt about when I got pregnant. It could have been a whole month earlier than I thought, which means that my due date is coming up soon," she answered, her voice sounding strained.

"Oh," was all Conn could think of to say, because he didn't understand the finer points of such things.

He was still running all possible options through his mind. At the moment, the snow and sleet were beating down too fast for them to leave the cabin, and the wind was howling relentlessly out of the mountains. What if Dana had been by herself when she'd gone into labor? It was too horrible to think about, and he knew that if there was one thing in his life that he wanted to get right, it was this. He hadn't been there for Lindsay when she needed him, and he wanted to be here for Dana now. And his mother's miscarriage all those years ago, when he'd been a little boy, lay heavy on his mind.

"Conn," Dana said, "I think the snow has stopped."

He rushed to the window. Sure enough it had. But for how long?

"Do you want to try to make it to the hospital in Flagstaff? I don't know if the roads will be cleared yet. The snow was heavy along the highway." He wasn't eager to find himself alone in a snowstorm on a deserted road with a woman who was giving birth.

She looked up at him, her eyes huge in her face. She

seemed desperately uncomfortable. A fine sheen of perspiration had broken out on her forehead. "Maybe we'd better."

He let out a breath and rubbed his forehead. "Okay. Do you have a bag packed for the hospital?"

She pointed to two suitcases. "No, but the one on the left will do."

"I'll stow it in the car, then come back for you."

"Toss me my jacket from the closet so I can put it on."

Conn took her the jacket before going into the kitchen and turning off the burner under the water. "I'll be right back," he told her as he slid his arms into his own coat. She nodded, her forehead pleated with worry.

Taking the suitcase, he sprinted through the snow to her car, which was the vehicle he thought they should take in case she needed to get into the back seat and lie down. He opened the trunk preparatory to putting the suitcase in but noticed suddenly that the car's back tires were flat. In fact, further examination showed him that its other two tires were in the same condition. He slammed the trunk and walked over to the hawk wagon. Its tires were also flat.

Damn Philip Grantham! He must have let the air out as his final revenge.

When he went back inside, Dana was sitting on the bed, wearing her jacket and looking forlorn.

"We can't leave here," Conn said, spitting out the words with a bite that he hadn't intended.

She stared blankly. "Why not?"

He shucked his coat and hung it in the closet. "Grantham let the air out of all the tires, both on my truck and your car."

"Oh, no!" For a moment Dana looked as if she were going to cry. He stood there for a second, trying to decide if it would be worthwhile to ask Billy Wayne to come out in his Jeep and get them. He had no idea how icy the roads were between here and town, though, and he didn't know if the kid was a skilled driver or not. He decided against it, mostly because he didn't want to be responsible for putting someone else's life on the line.

Dana was struggling out of her jacket, and he went to help her. "Looks like it's just you and me, babe," he said.

She managed a bleak smile. "Looks that way."

"I'd better call your doctor."

"I'll be in the bathroom," she said. She got up and walked slowly there, leaning slightly backward to compensate for the weight of the baby. His heart went out to her. This couldn't be easy.

When she came out, she asked what the doctor had said.

"I talked to his service, and they said he'd call back. Maybe this is a false alarm," he suggested hopefully.

She sat back down on the bed and propped pillows behind her for support as she explained about her false labor a few days ago. "But I don't think these are Braxton-Hicks contractions," she said, her hands cradling her belly. "It's different this time." Her eyes sought his for reassurance.

"It sure seems real to me," he told her.

"I want to get up," she said. "I want to walk."

This took him by surprise. "Walk where?"

She motioned with her hands. "Around the cabin. Help me."

"I'm not sure this is such a good idea," he said doubtfully when she was on her feet. He kept tight hold of her arm with his other arm around her waist.

"It helps me," she said. "I feel better doing this. Talk to me, Conn, please."

"About what?" he asked, unprepared for this request.

"Anything to keep my mind off this. Your mother, for instance. You said you took care of her when she was pregnant."

He didn't want to talk about his mother's doomed pregnancy. It seemed like a bad omen.

"I was only four. I don't remember much about it." But he did. She had collapsed on the floor of their little house, and he hadn't known what to do. He had tried to wake her up, terrified and crying, and then he had run through the frosty grass to a neighbor's house to summon help. That night his mother had lost the baby, which had been a boy. For a long time he hadn't been able to shake the idea that it was all his fault, although he knew now it couldn't have been. But he still didn't want to tell Dana that the baby had died.

"How is your mother?"

Another thing he didn't like to think about, but at least it was a safer topic. "I went to visit her. The nursing home she's in now is crowded and not even clean. I'm going to switch her to another place as soon as..." He let the sentence trail off, thinking that this wasn't the way to tell Dana that he was planning to return to the *Probe*.

She kept walking. He changed the subject. "I've written an article about the Florida panther. I thought maybe I could sell it to a friend of mine who edits a magazine." He told her about *Nation's Green* and how he had met Jim Menoch years ago at a fundraiser in New York.

"What kind of a fundraiser?"

"An ecology-awareness group. As it happened, I had just come back from canoeing in the Florida Everglades, and I'd talked with a naturalist there who has been tracking panthers for years."

"I don't know anything...anything about panthers," she said with difficulty. He hated the idea of her being in pain, would have said anything to take her mind off it, so he told her about the Florida panther, about its habitat shrinking as more and more newcomers poured into Florida. He didn't know how much she listened, and he wasn't sure it was important if she did. All he knew was that he had to talk, had to keep her mind occupied. He ranged over a whole slew of topics—how he had bought Aliah, the time he had won the county spelling bee when he was a kid, his first job as a bus boy at the Clay Springs Country Club. He even touched briefly on Lindsay, a part of his life that he'd never discussed with anyone.

"So you loved her very much?" Dana asked.

"Yes, I did," he said quietly.

Dana didn't say anything more, but she seemed thoughtful. He continued to talk, finding that it was a catharsis of sorts. He didn't intend to tell Dana about how important it had been to win a Pulitzer at one time, but he found himself telling her, anyway. He told her that he was casting around for new ways to earn money with his writing.

"Have you ever written anything for television?" she asked, proving that she was paying attention.

"It's never occurred to me," he said.

"Maybe you should give it some thought. My friend Tricia produces documentaries. Nature programs."

"It's an idea," he said, considering it.

"Oh," she said, gripping his arm. "That really hurt."

"Is there anything I can do? Anything you need?" He felt frantic at the thought that this was so painful for her.

"I think I want to lie down now. The doctor hasn't called back. Why not? It seems like we're always waiting to hear from a doctor around here, aren't we?" Her smile looked forced.

As if on cue the phone rang.

While Conn was talking to the doctor, Dana lay down on the bed and closed her eyes. She concentrated on enduring the ongoing contractions by picturing the baby. It would be a beautiful child with fluffy reddish-gold hair and gray eyes that would eventually turn cornflower blue. It would look exactly like her and nothing like Philip. It would be intelligent, alert, sweet, and dear, she thought as she gritted her teeth against the waves of the next contraction.

Conn put down the phone and came to stand beside the bed. She thought he looked concerned, but overlying that was an air of calm determination. "I don't think you're going to want to hear this," he said slowly.

She waited until the contraction had passed. "Bad news?" she asked, reminding herself to remain centered.

"This snowstorm's a killer. It's predicted to dump at least a foot of snow in the next several hours, so I don't know when we'll get out of here. The doctor says I can deliver the baby if I have to."

Outside the wind shrieked around the edges of the cabin, rattling the windows and shaking the door. Conn deliver her baby? Not be at the hospital? All along she had planned to leave here before her time came. She couldn't believe it had come down to this.

"I can try to hold off until morning," Dana said desperately.

"No way, Dana. Your pains are only a few minutes apart." All at once she noted how frazzled he appeared, and Dana felt a rush of sympathy for him as she took in his rumpled hair, the knot of concern on his brow, the way he left her side to pace back and forth across the floor. She felt a surge of gratitude that he was there for her, and for once she didn't mind depending on him.

It was in that moment that she admitted to herself that she needed Conn. A few months ago she'd thought she could handle everything about this pregnancy by herself. She'd left her home, her friends, her work—all because she was determined not to want or need anyone after Philip. She had come away scarred and bruised from that relationship, afraid to love or trust or be beholden to anyone. But this man, Conn, had proved that no matter what happened, he would hang in there. How could she have thought that he would hand her over to the *Probe?* In her heart she knew now that he'd been telling the truth when he said that he hadn't told Martin who she was.

She wanted to tell him that she believed him, that she was humbled by his caring for her, but the next contraction hurt so much that it was all she could do not to cry out. She felt a fierce buzzing in her ears before it ended, and when it did, Conn was kneeling beside the bed, clasping both her hands in his.

"You know, it's easier with birds. They just lay eggs

and then they hatch," he said, trying to joke, but she wasn't in the mood for humor.

She felt like such a fool for putting them both in this position. She had mishandled this all along, but overriding her sense of anguish over her own stupidity was her body's imperative. She was going to have this baby, and she was going to have it soon. "Conn, I…I don't think this is going to take long. I feel like I want to push," she said urgently.

"According to what I told the doctor and what he said about it, you can go right ahead."

"Conn, if anything happens—" She clutched his hand.

"Nothing is going to happen. I'm going to take care of you, Dana. Your baby will be fine."

"I didn't expect you to be part of this," she said.

"That's the way it has turned out, my dearest, and if I have to deliver your baby, that's what I'll do."

She turned her head and stared at him, at his eyes filled with concern and caring and something else, too. The only evidence of the strain he was under was the artery beating at his temple. Had he called her his dearest or had she imagined it?

"Push all you want, and when the baby comes I will love it as much as I love you," Conn went on, and she told herself that he was still talking to fill time.

Or was it more than that? He had said he would love the baby. He had said that he loved her. She hadn't mistaken that.

"And then we will get married," he said.

She started to say, "Married?" but the word only ended in a ragged moan. And then she was in no shape to say anything at all because she had to push, had to help her baby be born.

Time was irrelevant, and all she was aware of was the incredible amount of strength that she had to muster to help Conn, she wanted to help him, she wanted to love him, and she did love him, but she couldn't tell him because she had to do this first. Nothing in her life had ever been so painful, and she thought she heard herself scream, but then she was sure she hadn't because she would never do such a thing, not when Conn was working so hard to help her. He kept saying, "Breathe, Dana," and once she snapped at him, "What do you think I'm doing, anyway?" and was immediately ashamed of herself, though she knew she couldn't help yelling at him because the pain was awful.

Then the world retreated into a warm misty haze, and she thought she was walking outside in the snow because everything looked so white. But she couldn't be outside because she was warm, and Conn was there talking about something, she wasn't sure what. She didn't want to know, so she told herself she would sleep, just for a minute, and when the baby's cries woke her, she couldn't figure out why.

"It's a girl, Dana! A beautiful, healthy girl!" Conn sounded exultant, and she wondered how he could be so happy when it had hurt her so much. Then he placed the baby at her breast, and her arms went around it, and with awe she gazed down into Rosemary's face. She had always known what Rosemary would look like, and it was no surprise that she looked exactly the way Dana had imagined her, plump cheeks and all.

"Rosemary," she whispered gratefully, and then Conn was folding his arms around her, holding her, kissing her. She would have laughed in delight if she'd had the strength.

"You're a strong, brave woman, Dana," Conn said close beside her ear.

She looked up at him, and over and above the exhaustion on his face, she saw approval and love radiating from him.

She smiled then, a weary smile but a smile nonetheless. "There was something I meant to tell you before I got so busy with all this," she murmured, gazing directly into his eyes.

"What was that?" he said. Dana was pleased to see that Rosemary had already curved her tiny fingers around his thumb as if she would never let it go.

"I love you, too," Dana told him, and then a veil of sleep descended on her. She swirled down into it, secure in her heart that when she opened her eyes, Conn would be there watching over her, keeping her safe.

AFTER DANA FELL ASLEEP and the baby was settled, Conn dozed in the green chair. He had never been so exhausted in his life. Yet he felt a sense of worthiness, of fulfillment. He couldn't help admiring Dana's fortitude and intense effort as she pushed her baby into the world, and he never could have imagined the mutual trust that they developed during that long, long night. Their emotional interplay had been incredibly moving.

And at the supreme moment, when her baby finally slipped out warm into his hands, when he told her it was a fine, healthy girl, he had felt completely and passionately in tune with Dana. Her eyes, all shining with gratitude, had met his, and he had felt an unexpected rush of joy, of reverence for life and the part they had both played in bringing this new one into being. He would have liked to have been the father of Dana's child. He would probably always regret that he wasn't. But his love for Dana, the intimacy and bonding as he placed the baby at her breast, couldn't have been stronger.

He had sat by the bed, smoothing her hair away from her face, kissing her cheek, her eyelids, her neck, until he couldn't stay awake any longer.

As he slept, he dreamed the dream again, the nightmare about climbing to the hidden caves on the mountainside. Again he was searching for a nest of hawks that he somehow knew was there, but this time when he lost his footing on the treacherous path, he ended up beside a nest in a crevice. Inside were fledglings, and they would make fine birds to train. He reached in and gently removed the birds, handing them back to Dana. He hadn't known she was there, but she was smiling at him and holding out her hands.

And instead of falling backward as he always had in the

dream, he found himself turning to Dana, then setting the birds free to soar away, setting his heart free, too. Wrapping his arms tightly around her, he held her fast, holding her to his heart forever.

DANA SMELLED BACON FRYING. It didn't make her stomach heave. On the heels of these two observations came the knowledge that she wasn't pregnant anymore. She'd had the baby.

Dana opened her eyes and saw Conn at the stove in the kitchen. And then the baby stirred and made a little mewling sound beside her in the bed. Awake now, she murmured, "Rosemary," still unbelieving, still astonished at the turn of events that had kept her here to have her baby.

"You're awake," Conn said, coming out of the kitchen. Poor man, he looked spent. She probably looked worse.

"I smelled bacon."

"I'm cooking our breakfast. How are you feeling?"

She considered this as Rosemary began to cry, her tiny face wrinkling up like a shriveled apple. "I feel all right," she said. She opened the front of her gown and guided Rosemary's mouth to her breast, trusting instinct to tell her what to do, and in that moment she felt a kinship with mothers everywhere and for all time, an eternity of motherhood encompassing her love for this baby. She couldn't imagine loving anyone more than this child—until Conn came over and knelt beside the bed.

"She's a pretty baby, Dana. She looks exactly like you."

"Nothing like Philip," she agreed. "I'm so glad." She'd known that Rosemary would look like her all along. She nursed contentedly until the baby had drunk her fill and went back to sleep.

"I made a little bed for her," Conn said. "It's in a box that was full of baby clothes."

Dana had packed that box in preparation for leaving. "I don't want to put her in it yet. I like having her here on the bed with me," she said. After she settled the baby on the inside of the bed near the wall, she pushed herself to a sitting position, wincing slightly. "I'm so hungry," she said.

"You did a hard night's work," Conn said.

Memories flooded back to her, and she wondered if he had meant all the things he'd said. He'd told her he loved her. He'd said they'd get married. She had told him she loved him, too.

"I can never thank you enough," she said. "For all you did last night, I mean. I know I was hard to get along with. I'm sorry."

"No apology is necessary. What's important is that you and the baby are both fine."

"I bet you never dreamed you'd be delivering a baby," she said with a half smile.

Conn laughed. "Nope, I certainly didn't, but I had a lot of help. Your Dr. Evans was on the phone coaching me through it at the last."

"Are we snowed in?"

"Looks that way." He went into the kitchen and came back with eggs, bacon, toast and steaming hot coffee.

He sat down beside her and dug into the food with relish. "Conn," she said, "I want you to know I won't hold you responsible for anything that was said last night."

He stopped chewing and swallowed.

"Do you mean that?"

She fingered the edge of the sheet. "Of course I do."

He set aside his plate and reached over to grasp her hand. "Well, that isn't acceptable to me. I damn well intend to hold you to what you said."

"Other than screaming a lot and moaning, what was it?" Her look of studied innocence told him that she wasn't serious, so he relaxed.

"You said you love me."

"You told me first. You also said that we were going to get married."

"I remember. I meant it. Since then I've been doing a

lot of serious thinking about how we're going to bring it off.''

"Conn—"

"Hear me through, all right?'' When she nodded, her eyes on his face, he took heart that everything would work out. He plunged ahead before she could tell him to shut up.

"When I came back from L.A. yesterday, I was determined to tell you that I was going to go back to work for the *Probe,*'' he began only to be greeted by a horrified look.

"Oh, Conn, no!''

"Just listen, please.''

She subsided. "All right.''

"I need to get Mom into Catalina-Pacific, the more expensive nursing home. I told you about it, remember?''

Dana nodded, and he continued. "Well, it's going to cost more than I felt comfortable spending, so I intended to go back to the *Probe* where I'd earn a regular salary. But after you went to sleep last night, I did some serious thinking. I've changed my mind.''

"Good,'' Dana said with great finality.

"The panther article won't pay much, but I'll let *Nation's Green* publish it for the two hundred bucks they offered. It's not enough, but that's okay. I have other articles that could be compiled into a book. Jim Menoch said that his publishing company is going under, but there are other publishers. And while my book is making the rounds, I'll be working on a treatment for a documentary about raptor rehabilitation. I'm excited about the idea, and I think I can educate people about the birds, what they're really like.''

"It sounds wonderful, Conn, and I'd love to help you research it. It doesn't sound as though this is going to bring in enough money to put your mother in Catalina-Pacific, though.''

"It won't, but I'll sell my place in Marina Del Rey. I won't ever be going back there, and it will bring in a sizable chunk of money.''

"Are you sure that's what you want to do?''

"I'm positive. What you and I have found together is so good and so right that L.A. holds no appeal for me. My life is here with you, my love."

"Am I really your love? Honestly and truly?" Her eyes searched his face.

"Honestly and truly. You are the only woman in the world for me, and I'm glad we found each other. All these other things—where to live, how we'll make enough money—they're all just fluff. People in love learn how to work around each other, to make compromises. We can do it, Dana. I know we can." He lifted her hands to his lips and gently kissed the fingers, one by one.

Dana forced herself to think. "I'll have to face the music sometime, let people know where I am, tell them I'm retired from the business. I'll need to go back to Chicago, close my apartment," she said. "While I'm there, I can talk to Tricia about your documentary. I think she'll go for it, Conn. She's always saying that she likes doing things that haven't been overdone, and raptor rehab hasn't been, I'm sure of it."

"Then it's settled. We may not have a lot of money, not as much as either of us is accustomed to having, but we'll have each other. What do you say we build a few rooms onto my house? A nursery and a master bedroom?"

"You didn't expect to have a baby to take care of," she said.

He reached across her and caressed Rosemary's cheek. "This baby means that I am doubly blessed," he said, and he meant it with all his heart.

Dana set her plate on the nightstand and slid her arms around his neck. "You've been doing lots of thinking, haven't you?"

"What I'm thinking now is that I want to kiss you."

"I wish you would."

He did, savoring her velvety mouth, tangling his hands in her hair.

"Marry me," he said.

She lifted her face from his neck. "Say again?"

"Marry me. I'll say it as often as I must in order to convince you that it's a good idea."

"It's a wonderful idea, Conn. When?"

"Soon," he murmured, folding his arms even more tightly around her.

"Soon," she agreed.

Epilogue

Three Months Later

"Come to Mommy," Dana crooned as she eased her baby daughter out of Conn's arms. "Did you miss me while I was gone?"

"We both missed you, my dear wife," Conn said. He slid his arm around Dana's shoulders. The three of them had just returned home to Conn's house from the airport, where Dana had disembarked from a flight from Chicago.

"And the hawks? Did they miss me, too?" She glanced playfully up at him, thinking that she would never tire of looking at Conn, of gazing into his dark eyes, of making love with him in the big loft bed.

"My darling, all of Arizona must have noticed you were gone. Billy Wayne says he wants to learn how to make coconut cake and would like to have your recipe. Susie asked me when you and Rosemary and I are going to come into the diner for breakfast. Esther wants you to call her at the library, she has a new book on counted cross-stitch that she thinks you'll like, and—"

"Wait a minute," Dana said with a laugh. "These days I have better things to do with my time."

"And we're going to be doing one of them as soon as you get Rosemary fed, diapered and to bed," Conn said, nuzzling her cheek.

"Don't you want to hear what Tricia said about the idea for your documentary?"

"I'd rather hear how much you love me."

"Stop it, Conn, I'm serious." But she wanted to giggle like a teenager in love for the first time. In fact, that's how she felt around Conn, and they'd been married for almost three months.

"Gaga," Rosemary said, smiling her biggest smile. "Gaga!"

"What does that mean?" Conn said.

"It means that she already knows that Tricia is planning to come for a visit to meet you and the hawks. Tricia wants to see whatever you have as far as a treatment goes. She thinks that if the documentary follows an injured raptor—and Billy Wayne can probably find one, knowing him—if it follows the same bird all through the injured and rehabilitation process, the audience will identify with the bird and be pulling for it. She said a lot more, too, but I can't think when you're kissing the side of my neck."

"Two weeks is a long time to be away from us," he said. "Two weeks were hell without you."

"You had Rosemary. It was a good time for a bit of father-daughter bonding."

"I'm more interested in husband-wife bonding at the moment. Here's Rosemary's bottle. Do you want to give it to her or shall I?"

"I will." The baby patted Dana's face, exploring, and Dana kissed the little hand. She had missed them both terribly, and she never wanted to be away from them again. She wouldn't have to be, either. She had quietly put her Chicago penthouse up for sale.

Conn handed her a warm bottle and she popped the nipple into the baby's mouth. Rosemary sucked, closing her eyes blissfully.

"Anyway, I told Tricia that she can stay in my cabin for a few days while she's here. Raymond might come visit in the summer on his way to Sedona. I can't wait for you to meet them."

"Any news from other quarters?" Conn asked.

"You mean Noelle and Philip?"

"Of course I mean Noelle and Philip."

"Well, Raymond told me that Noelle informed Myrtis that she was a spiteful old hag who ought to mind her own business. They're not speaking. And even though he and Noelle are supposed to be engaged, Philip keeps going for long lunches with the weather girl on one of the local channels' evening news. She's twenty-one, and he's going to be forty-six soon."

"No fool like an old fool, they say. Speaking of friends, I talked with Bentley the other day."

Dana tilted her head as she looked at him. "And?"

"She went to visit my mother at Catalina-Pacific. Mom's comfortable, and the nurses pay a lot of attention to her."

"Good, Conn. I hope we can go visit her ourselves soon."

"We will. And, Dana, Bentley says she can take care of getting out the word that you're no longer going to be in front of any cameras or in any public life again. She was gleeful about her plot—uh, I mean plan."

Rosemary was falling asleep, and Dana set the empty bottle on the table beside the couch before easing her up onto her shoulder and burping her. "I'm going to put our darling daughter in her crib," she said to Conn. "And then you can tell me all about Bentley's plan. But aren't you going to owe her big-time?"

"If Bentley can hide away here in Cougar Creek while she's writing her book, we'll be even, finally, especially if you let her stay in your cabin. And I think I'll let her fill you in on her plan when you call her tomorrow," Conn said mysteriously, and then he laughed.

Later, when they were up under the rafters in bed, Conn caressed Dana's breast and kissed her long and lingeringly.

"No more long separations," he said. "I mean it."

"No more," she sighed, sliding around until she faced him. "I've taken care of all unfinished business. All that remains now is for you to welcome me home. Really welcome me, I mean."

"Like this? And like this? And how about like this?" he said, touching her in the way that she loved to be touched.

"All of those," she murmured, and, full of love for him and full of happiness in the life that they now shared, she urged him to make love to her once and then again.

BENTLEY HOWSER'S final celebrity column in the *National Probe* read:

Well, dear hearts, I was hoping that before I penned my last column for the *Probe,* I'd be able to clear up that mystery about Day Quinlan. You know, the oh-so-popular talk-show host who walked off her show several months ago and disappeared from view? I know, I know—when she first left, I reported that she had eloped with an oil-rich sultan. Blame it on false information from one of my informants, okay? But now here's the straight skinny: Day Quinlan is no more. She has ceased to exist.

Darlings, I don't mean that any harm has come to one golden hair of her neatly coiffed head—far from it. In fact, I talked with Day Quinlan yesterday in what may be her final communication with the rest of the world. Yes, the irony is that the talk-show diva of them all won't be doing much talking from now on. She's joined an order of nuns in a teeny-tiny backward country in Europe. A silent order, no less. Her final words to me were, "Bentley, would I lie to you? I have found true happiness in silence and service. Tell my friends and fans that I wish them all the best." And I'm sure Sister Annunciata's legions of fans wish her well, too.

So this column's a wrap! A new and talented columnist, Ruben Lobos-Sanchez, will be bringing you the scoop in the *Probe* from now on. Sayonara, dear hearts, and buy *lots* of copies of my upcoming book for everyone you know.

Love and hugs to all,
Bentley

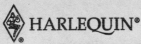

If you enjoyed what you just read,
then we've got an offer you can't resist!

Take 2 bestselling
love stories FREE!

Plus get a FREE surprise gift!

Clip this page and mail it to Harlequin Reader Service®

IN U.S.A.
3010 Walden Ave.
P.O. Box 1867
Buffalo, N.Y. 14240-1867

IN CANADA
P.O. Box 609
Fort Erie, Ontario
L2A 5X3

YES! Please send me 2 free Harlequin American Romance® novels and my free surprise gift. After receiving them, if I don't wish to receive anymore, I can return the shipping statement marked cancel. If I don't cancel, I will receive 4 brand-new novels every month, before they're available in stores! In the U.S.A., bill me at the bargain price of $3.80 plus 25¢ shipping & handling per book and applicable sales tax, if any*. In Canada, bill me at the bargain price of $4.21 plus 25¢ shipping & handling per book and applicable taxes**. That's the complete price and a savings of at least 10% off the cover prices—what a great deal! I understand that accepting the 2 free books and gift places me under no obligation ever to buy any books. I can always return a shipment and cancel at any time. Even if I never buy another book from Harlequin, the 2 free books and gift are mine to keep forever.

154 HEN DC7W
354 HEN DC7X

Name	(PLEASE PRINT)	
Address	Apt.#	
City	State/Prov.	Zip/Postal Code

* Terms and prices subject to change without notice. Sales tax applicable in N.Y.
** Canadian residents will be charged applicable provincial taxes and GST.
  All orders subject to approval. Offer limited to one per household and not valid to
  current Harlequin American Romance® subscribers.
  ® are registered trademarks of Harlequin Enterprises Limited.

AMER01   ©2001 Harlequin Enterprises Limited

Bestselling Harlequin® author

JUDITH ARNOLD

brings readers a brand-new, longer-length novel based on her popular miniseries *The Daddy School*

Somebody's Dad

If any two people should avoid getting romantically involved with each other, it's bachelor—and children-phobic!—Brett Stockton and single mother Sharon Bartell. But neither can resist the sparks...especially once *The Daddy School* is involved.

"Ms. Arnold seasons tender passion with a dusting of humor to keep us turning those pages."
—*Romantic Times Magazine*

Look for Somebody's Dad in February 2002.

HARLEQUIN®
Makes any time special ®

Visit us at www.eHarlequin.com   PHSD

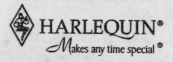